KONNIGER'S
WOMAN

Other books by Terrell L. Bowers:

Crossfire at Broken Spoke
Destiny at Broken Spoke
Feud at Broken Spoke
Judgment at Gold Butte
Noose at Sundown
The Switchback Trail

KONNIGER'S
WOMAN

•

Terrell L. Bowers

AVALON BOOKS
NEW YORK

Published by Avalon Books, an imprint of
Thomas Bouregy & Co., Inc.
160 Madison Avenue, New York, NY 10016

Library of Congress Cataloging-in-Publication Data

Bowers, Terrell L.
   Konniger's woman / Terrell L. Bowers.
      p. cm.
   ISBN 978-0-8034-7700-1 (hardcover : acid-free paper)
   I. Title.
   PS3552.O87324K66 2010
   813'.54—dc22

                              2010018144

PRINTED IN THE UNITED STATES OF AMERICA
ON ACID-FREE PAPER
BY HADDON CRAFTSMEN, BLOOMSBURG, PENNSYLVANIA

To the memory of my dad,
James L. Bowers, and to my mom
and stepfather, Lajetta (Ginger)
and Melvin Hansen

Chapter One

He moved toward the rim of the expansive wash called the Big Gorge by some and the Dry Basin by others. Keith Konniger—most who knew him shortened his name to "Konn"—neck-reined his chestnut-colored mare over near the edge and gazed down at the valley floor. Keeping a vigilant eye for Indian presence was never a waste of time. He had seen fresh signs earlier and, while the Shoshone were friendly to the white man, the same could not be said for many of the Cheyenne, Arapaho, or Sioux.

His survey of the area below caught movement near the middle of the basin, and he focused his attention on the subject. The person was alone, on foot, not much for size, and wearing what appeared to be an ankle-length sleeping gown. As he watched, the small individual staggered, walking uncertainly, as if dizzy or drunk.

"Stand still, Hammerhead," he told his fidgeting horse, giving the reins a yank to demonstrate he was serious. "Let me get a closer look at this."

The horse ceased shifting her weight, but stretched out her neck and ducked her head, trying to get him to loosen the reins. It was a bad habit to allow a horse to munch grass or grab a bite of nearby foliage while being ridden. The animal soon got the idea that it was all right and would attempt to do it all the time. However, Hammerhead had put in a fair day's work, carrying him at a steady clip since before sunup. He figured the mare had earned a bite of grass, so long as she stayed put.

He eased up on the reins, reached back to his saddlebags, and removed the army-issue spyglass he always carried. Putting it to his eye, he focused in on the small figure below.

1

"Sonuvabuck!" Konn moaned, readily identifying a female child. "That little gal ain't but half grown!" He put away the telescope and growled at his bad luck.

"Mixing into other people's affairs causes only grief, Hammerhead. Most humans are a bunch of sheep needing to always be amongst the flock." He spoke to the horse, not because the horse ever paid much attention, but a man who talked to himself was often considered about two blankets short of a bedroll.

Konn had been raised like a lone wolf, taught to rely on himself, and never asked anything from anyone. He enjoyed the solitude of his life, hunting, fishing, and breaking the occasional wild horse, with only nature to share his company. He minded his own business and expected the same from others in return.

Even so, a man didn't ignore a child in need. He quickly swept the area for other signs of life, searching back in the direction from which the youngster had come.

Nothing.

"What are you doing way out here by yourself, little muffin?" he muttered. "Dagnabit! Where are your folks?"

Even as he studied on a course of action, the youngster stumbled and fell. She remained prone on the ground, visibly too weary to get back up. A rest might have been something sorely needed, but a distant movement at the mouth of the basin drew Konn's attention. Where there had been nothing moving a moment ago, a couple of specks appeared in the distance, headed right up the canyon floor. He put a hand up and tipped his hat to shield his eyes against the brightness. There was something there all right— looked to be two riders, possibly a quarter-mile away—clearly following the tracks of the child. He grimaced from an inward apprehension. He couldn't tell much at that distance, and the scope was no good looking into the sun, but he doubted the approaching pair were the tyke's family members.

Konn lamented his moral code, which forced him to act, but he was already examining the cliff's rim, searching for a way down. He sighted a deer or animal trail a short way along the lip of the cliff where the slope became less of a precipice. The descending path wound through some scrub brush, past a hardy pinion here or there and around several outcrops of boulders. Lower down, the terrain gave way to rugged, choppy hills, where it would be easier going.

With no time to waste, Konn nudged his horse with his heels and proceeded over to the path. Leaving the mesa, he made good time by following the faint trail down the steep incline and reached the canyon base in a matter of minutes.

There wasn't time to allow his horse to catch her breath. He started the big mare moving toward the fallen girl, but time had run out. He realized he would be too late to get there ahead of the two riders—riders he now discerned as Indians!

"Whatta'd I tell you, Hammerhead?" he complained. "We're headed for trouble a'plenty."

Konn guided the mare along a shallow gully to remain out of sight of the approaching riders. Picking his way between boulders and brush, he worked quietly along the wash to a point a couple hundred feet from where the girl had fallen. When he stopped, he could hear the two young braves, laughing and taunting their prey.

Konn dismounted, tied off his mount, and pulled his rifle. Using a natural stealth, born of constant living and surviving in hostile territory, he padded along the gully until he found a place where he could soundlessly make his way to higher ground.

Once out of the wash, he circled a small hill and slipped up behind an outcrop of boulders. Poised with his rifle ready, he peeked over the rocks and discovered the two warriors were youngsters, barely into their teens. Konn didn't make war on children, even those who would readily kill him, so he waited until their backs were to him before he made his move.

The little girl was lying on the ground, hiding her face in her hands. The two boys seemed to be arguing about what they should do next. Their preoccupation allowed Konn to move silently to within fifty feet of their position.

"Hold it, boys!" Konn commanded, holding the rifle up near his shoulder to cover the pair.

The two spun to face him, shocked and surprised to find themselves under a white man's gun. They glared back at Konn, but neither made a grab for his weapon. Although young, they were not foolish.

Using his left hand, he motioned for them to get down on the ground. Their expressions remained defiant but they obeyed his command. Konn moved in quickly and bound their hands behind them with strips of rawhide. Once the two were helpless, he knelt down next to the girl. She was not yet half grown, cute as a month-old fawn, with rich brown eyes and a tiny heart-shaped mouth. Her hair was stringy and damp from her extreme exertion in the afternoon heat, and her sleeping dress was torn and soiled.

"You all right, little muffin?" Konn asked, softening his base voice as best he could.

The girl was trembling and frightened, yet she demonstrated a measure of inner strength. She sat up straight, carefully pulled a lock of hair back from her face, and tried to look at him. She shielded her eyes from the brightness of the overhead sun with a dainty hand and looked him up and down. He wondered what thoughts were going through her head. Looking older than his twenty-five years he towered above her, five inches over six feet, in the neighborhood of two hundred and fifty pounds, wearing a buckskin shirt and heavy denim pants. His hat was weathered and misshaped from age, he hadn't trimmed his beard in over a year, and his last bath had been a rinse off at a creek nearly a week past.

However, the youngster displayed a pilgrim's courage. "Who are you?" she asked.

"I'm here to help," he replied stiffly. "What the hel . . . uh"— he knew better than to use profanity in the presence of children or womenfolk—"what are you doing way out here alone?"

Her eyes grew wide, and her expression showed terror at the memory. "We was attacked!" she blurted out the words. "Indians attacked our wagon, and Grandpa told me to run and hide in the brush. The fighting was so loud . . ." She lost her composure and began to cry. "I was afraid. I ran!" She was sobbing now. "I ran until I couldn't run no more."

"What about the rest of your family?"

"I . . . I don't know." The words were almost indistinguishable through her grief. "I think they might all be . . . be dead."

"Not all are dead," the one Indian boy declared in English.

Konn threw a curious look at the one who had spoken. "Where did you learn the white man's tongue, young fellow?"

"I am Small Eagle, son of Two Bears, chief of the Cheyenne."

"Two Bears? The half-white Cheyenne war chief?"

"The mother of my father was a white woman," he confirmed. "She teach me white man's tongue"—he glowered at Konn— "so I can tell them they are to die slow and with much pain."

Konn ignored the threat. "You say your raiding party didn't kill everyone?"

"The woman we take captive. She now belong to tribe." His lips curled back into a sneer. "One day she will become squaw— if any brave want her."

"I don't think that's going to happen, Small Eagle."

"You cannot stop it!" the young man declared. "We have many warriors; you are one man."

"Yes," Konn agreed, "but I also have you, the chief's son." He pulled his skinning knife, knelt down, and grabbed the boy by the hair.

"If you want to die here and now, I'll oblige you," he snarled the words. "You have one chance to live." Jerking the boy's head up, he placed his knife just above his brow. "Do you wish to listen, or do I take your scalp?"

For a moment, he feared Small Eagle might call his bluff. However, the boy was not yet a man. He faltered after a few agonizing seconds.

"I will listen, white man."

He told Small Eagle to translate instructions to his companion. He had picked up enough of the language to understand part of what was being said. Once the non–English speaking Cheyenne youth understood his mission, Konn untied him and sent him riding back to Chief Two Bears.

"My father bring many warriors and kill you," Small Eagle jeered, attempting to reclaim his wounded pride. "You will die before the sun is gone."

"Well, sonny boy, let me be as clear about this as I can be," Konn told the youth candidly. "If I die, you die."

Laura Morrison's legs ached from walking, and it felt as if every step taken was on a bed of hot coals. She figured even her blisters had blisters by this time. Plus, it was awkward walking with her hands tied, being led with a rope around her neck like an animal. She heard hoof beats coming up behind her and quickly ducked her head. A warrior rode up alongside and tossed a handful of sand at her. The tiny particles pelted the side of her face, and the dirt clung to her sweat-matted hair.

"You go!" the Indian snarled.

She wondered if those were the only English words he knew. Staggering, near exhaustion, she panted to draw air into her burning lungs. The pain and fatigue was secondary to the ache in her heart. Married shortly before her seventeenth birthday and blessed with a child that first year, her husband had died from a bout with pneumonia several years earlier. Now she was a captive of the raiding party which had killed her father-in-law. As for her daughter, she had last seen Abby running to hide in the nearby hills. However, the Indian warriors discovered her clothing among their belongings, and the chief sent two young braves to find her. And even if Abby escaped, it was many miles to the nearest ranch or outpost. Her little girl would never make it so far alone. Thinking along those lines, she feared her daughter's fate would be as horrific as her own.

One of the warriors grunted something she didn't understand, and the group stopped. She used the break to attempt to recoup her strength. Bending at the waist, she sucked in mighty gulps of air into her lungs. After a few moments, she looked up to see that they had paused to await the arrival of a single rider. It looked like one of the two boys who had gone after Abby.

Laura straightened upright with trepidation, an unholy terror clawing at her heart. They had caught Abby . . . or worse!

The young brave approached the chief and spoke excitedly in their native tongue. Whatever he said, the words did not please the leader. His face darkened with an immediate anger, and he barked a sharp retort.

The boy ducked his head as if ashamed. Laura could only wonder if that meant they had killed Abby instead of bringing her back alive to be ransomed or enslaved. Her fearful speculation was cut short. The chief pointed at her and growled an order to a couple of his men.

One of the braves dismounted and moved toward her. She flinched when he suddenly reached for her. However, he made no effort to strike her but instead removed the noose from her neck. He let go the rope and pulled his knife, using it to cut loose the rawhide which bound her wrists. Confused at what was going on, the warrior then lifted Laura up onto his horse. She glanced about fleetingly, wondering if the cavalry had been spotted and she was being put on a horse so they could make more speed.

But the chief spoke stridently to his braves and moved over to take up the reins of her horse. He, along with three warriors, took Laura in tow. They started back the way they had come, following the young brave who had just arrived. The pace was hurried, which completely baffled Laura. She had no idea what all of this meant.

Chapter Two

Konn left the boy in the open, tied ankles to wrists, and re-
treated with the little girl. He tethered Hammerhead and the
Cheyenne boy's pony close by, then returned to a small hill and
took up vigilance behind a couple of large boulders. He had selected a position which offered protection, yet allowed him a
field of fire covering most any point on the canyon floor. Once
ready for the wait, he provided the girl with a few sips of water
and gave her a strip of venison jerky to chew on.

"You gonna get my mommy back?" the girl asked after a short
span of time, chewing on a bite of jerky.

Konn didn't want to get her hopes up. There was always a
chance the chief would kill the woman out of anger. She might
have resisted being taken prisoner and had been killed too. Luck
would dictate what happened next.

"We'll sit here a spell and let Two Bears make the next move.
If your ma is alive, he might be willing to trade her for his boy."

Konn heard the girl's movement and discovered her standing
at his side. He cast a curious frown at her, and she lowered her
eyelids to shield her eyes from him.

"I'm scared," she murmured softly.

Konn had never been much good around kids. After the death
of his mother while he was still a youngster, he had been raised
by his trapper father, forced to become a man at an early age.
Having never been a kid himself—to try and communicate with
this tyke, he might as well try catching wind in a bottle.

"When they come, you duck down and stay out of sight," he

instructed her. "I don't want to be worrying about you catching a stray arrow or bullet."

"Yes, sir, mister," she replied submissively. "I'll stay right here."

"Good girl," he praised her good sense.

"I didn't thank you for saving me."

"That's okay."

"No," her tender young voice was adamant, "Mama says to always say 'please' and 'thank you,' 'specially to strangers."

He didn't reply, keeping his attention focused on the mouth of the canyon and watching for the first sign of movement. It wouldn't do to let a couple of Cheyenne warriors sneak up on him.

The girl stood on her toes so she could see over the boulder Konn had chosen for cover. "Can you see them yet?" she asked.

"No," he answered.

"I ran for a long time," the girl told him, fear and worry thick in her voice. "What if the In'jun boy don't come back? What if they hurt my mommy?"

"Let's not fetch the eggs before the chickens lay them," he answered. "We got the chief's son to bargain with. It might take the young brave a bit of time to catch up with Two Bears. He'll be along."

The little girl leaned closer, pressed up against his leg. "You won't let them get me, will you, mister?"

He felt an unfamiliar tug at his heart from the timorous delivery.

"No, I won't let them get you," he avowed.

Her small face still shone with worry. "When they attacked our wagon, there were lots of them," she said. "Maybe you won't be able to keep them from getting me."

"Your people were caught by surprise at your wagon," he explained the difference. "Those Indian warriors come swooping in here after us, and I'll knock a dozen of them off of their horses before they know they're in a fight. Those who are left alive will think twice about trying a second time."

"You must be a really good shot," she said, clearly impressed by his claim.

"Better than most." He told her the truth.

"Are you a hunter or sum'tin?"

"I trap and hunt for a living," he answered, wondering how to politely get the child to be silent.

"Do ya ever hunt buffalo?"

"Sometimes, when I'm doing work for the railroad or when I need a hide and meat."

"We saw some buffalo coming here," she said. "There was a whole lot of them."

"There are a few of them around."

"What else do you hunt?"

"Deer, elk, bear, antelope, sometimes mountain sheep, and I also earn a little money with my trapping."

She uttered a sigh. "Grandpa said he would teach me to shoot a gun."

Konn was beginning to think this kid would never shut up, but forced himself to remain patient with her. "You're a might under-sized to tackle most rifles."

"I turned eight last month," she declared. "But I guess I'm not big enough to shoot one of your guns."

"This here Winchester has some kick to it," he explained. "But it has a side loading port and holds thirteen rimfire cartridges. That's the kind of shooting power you need against a bunch of bloodthirsty Indians."

"You said you were a good shot." She continued to quiz him like some kind of despot schoolmarm. "How good are you?"

Konn hid a sigh of exasperation. "I suppose I could hit a horsefly, if it were to light on our young Indian friend. Might put a nick in his hide doing it though."

"A horsefly!" The girl displayed a wide-eyed awe. "You must be the best shot in the whole world!"

Konn felt a warmth creep up his throat and put his attention back on the basin floor. He had never bragged to a woman before, no matter what her age. Being around the female of the species caused him to perspire and tangle his tongue something fierce. If the gal happened to be courting age, his innards would begin to flounder like a landlocked lake trout and evoke a flush of heat that would rise up along his throat and burn hot about his face. Dang, being embarrassed was near as bad as Indian torture!

"My daddy died when I was real little."

"That's right sad," he said with genuine sympathy.

"Do you have a father?"

"His rifle misfired while trying to finish off a wounded grizzly bear, and he was killed a few years back. I've been on my own since then."

"Did you find the bear?"

"Later that same day," Konn told her. "My gun didn't jam."

"My name's Abby Morrison," she said.

When he didn't respond in kind she tugged on his shirt. He took his eyes away from the canyon to frown at her.

"What's your name, mister?" she asked, undaunted by his hard look.

"Konniger," he replied with a sigh.

"You got lots of friends, Mr. Kon'ger?"

"I ain't exactly sociable."

"You seem like a nice man to me," Abby stated.

"I'd say the same thing to any man who saved my hide."

"And I like your horse," she continued. "He let me pet his nose, while you were tying up the Indian pony."

"Hammerhead is more sociable than I am."

She pulled a face. "That's not a very nice name for a horse."

"Suits her," he replied.

The girl continued to ask questions, chirping and twittering like a magpie. Konn allowed her desire for conversation was partly from the fear of her ordeal. She had witnessed the attack on her family, nearly been taken hostage by Cheyenne, and had no idea if her mother was still alive. Talking was likely the best way to keep from breaking down and crying. He definitely preferred questions to tears.

"Hush now," Konn finally interrupted her inquisition. "Yonder they come."

Abby rose up onto her toes a second time to peer over the edge of the boulder. "Can you see my mama?"

"Too far away to tell yet. You stay low and don't make a

sound." Konn used a firm tone. "We've got to be ready for anything."

Abby hunkered down into a squat, staring up at him with eyes wide with fear, but gritting her teeth against panic. He gave her a tight nod to inspire courage, then lifted his rifle and held it ready for instant use.

As the group approached he was able to see them more clearly, five Cheyenne—four of them armed—the messenger boy . . . and a white woman! His pulse quickened, and he scanned the nearby hills for any movement. It would take some time for an Indian brave to work up the side of the mountain and get above him. As the wash behind him didn't offer concealment in the direction of their approach, it was unlikely any of them would try to sneak up on him that way. He hoped to make this quick, before they had a chance to figure a way to get at him.

The riders moved cautiously, one with a lance and the others each with a shiny, new rifle clutched and ready to use. Upon seeing the boy bound up and lying on the canyon floor, they slowed their advance.

"That's far enough!" Konn shouted, stopping them in their tracks. "Two Bears! You and the woman ride on up to your boy. Any tricks and I'll kill you, then the boy." He let the words hang in the air before adding, "Do it now."

The chief passed his rifle to the man next to him and took up a lance. He grunted to one of his men and the brave shoved the woman off her horse. She was agile enough to land on her hands and knees. Before she could rise, the chief prodded her in the ribs with the tip of his spear. She flinched from the sudden pain and scrambled to her feet. With the lance still at her back, she hurried toward the bound young brave.

Konn kept an eye on the other warriors, while the chief and the woman advanced toward his son. When the chief stopped, Konn leveled his rifle at him.

"It's an even trade, Two Bears," he called out. "The woman for your son."

Two Bears searched the rocks and located Konn's position

from the sound of his voice. Seeing the rifle pointed at him, his face contorted with a mixture of hate and anger.

"Know this, white man," he warned in decent English. "You will die."

Konn ignored the threat and dictated terms. "Before you untie your boy, I want your word that you will let us leave in peace, Two Bears. Give me your word."

The chief continued to glare at him. "You are a white man! No white man keeps his word to Cheyenne."

"I am called Konniger, chief, and I'm a man of my word . . . be it to a white man or an Indian."

Two Bears sneered at Konn. "I know of you, hunter man. You risk much to save this woman." The man lifted his lance and shook it menacingly. "Maybe I say yes now. You give me my son, and I say kill the hunter man. The woman be mine and you die."

"Not the way it's going to be, chief. You let us leave in peace," Konn repeated the condition, "or the boy and you both die here and now!"

In spite of the deadly game being played out, the chief's lips curled upward in a confident smirk. "I will find you again, hunter man."

Konn ignored the ominous vow. "Give me your word we can leave, or I'll drop you where you sit."

Two Bears shifted his icy gaze to the woman. "I will come for you, white woman. You will not escape."

The lady shrank back in fear, lifting her hands to ward off a possible thrust from his spear.

After a brief, scathing look at the woman, the chief glanced around, as if contemplating a plan. However, he visibly relaxed his posture and said, "We kill all whites who cross our land. I warn you of this now."

"This is not your land," Konn argued, "but I will allow you to take your boy and leave. If you try anything I will put a bullet through your lying throat."

The chief's lips curled in leering contempt. "I do not scare . . ." But the blast of Konn's rifle cut his sentence short. The chief ducked quickly, only to discover the tip and six inches of his lance were missing.

"That could have been your head, chief." Konn jacked a fresh round into his rifle and aimed it at him again. "I'm a pretty fair shot and a man of my word."

Two Bears tossed away the damaged lance in disgust. For several seconds, he glowered at Konn with a dark stare. Finally, he straightened to sit perfectly erect. "I not kill you this day, hunter man," he finally allowed, "but when next we meet, I see you die."

"Fair enough," Konn answered back. "Now give me your word that we can leave this basin without any trouble."

With a grim reluctance, the warrior chief bobbed his head a single time. "It is said."

Konn lowered the rifle barrel a few inches, still ready for instant use but no longer aimed at Two Bears. He tipped his head in the direction of the young warrior. "Let the woman come to me and you can untie your boy."

The chief's face remained a mask of hate, but he accepted Konn had won this round. He gave a wave of his hand, signaling to the woman to go. She needed no further coaxing. As the chief slid down from his horse, she staggered a step or two and then broke into a run for Konn's position. She slipped and fell while scaling the embankment, but scrambled up quickly and didn't stop until she had scurried up to where Konn was stationed behind the rocks. Seeing Abby at his side, she uttered a squeal of delight.

"My baby!" she cried, flinging out her arms. "My dear, darling little girl!"

Abby ran to her, and the two of them clung to one another. Konn didn't watch the reunion, keeping Two Bears and the other warriors under his gun. He knew that men of all races, red, white, or any other color, were capable of lies and deception. Once the boy was freed, he might be in for the fight of his life.

The chief, however, wasn't eager to risk his boy's life. He had seen the measure of Konn's accuracy with a rifle. Using a large knife, he cut his son loose. Once freed, he muttered something to the boy before he turned to speak again to Konn.

"Where is the horse of my son?"

"The lady needs something to ride. You took her wagon and team when you killed her kin. I'd say you owe her a lot more than one horse in payment."

One of the braves came forward with the pony the girl had been riding. Small Eagle swung up onto its back and sat there, stonefaced and ashamed. He had been made to look like a fool in his father's eyes. He would never forget this humiliation.

Two Bears mounted his horse, uttered a curse in his native tongue, and cast a final bitter look at Konn. With a lift to his chin, he issued a final threat. "We meet again, hunter man. You die that day."

"Don't expect it to be easy, chief," Konn replied. "I won't die alone."

Two Bears took the lead, and the small band of warriors returned the way they had come. Konn watched until they were almost out of sight, then quickly turned to the business at hand.

The woman had been locked in a consoling hug with Abby. When Konn looked at her she quickly separated herself from the child. She waited for him to speak, her tear-streaked face flushed with emotion and anticipation.

"You all right?" he asked the woman.

"I—I don't . . . I mean, yes, I'm fine." She displayed a sheepish expression. "Just don't ask me to walk too far. I have some nasty blisters on my feet."

"You and your daughter will have to ride the Indian pony bareback. Think you can do that?"

"We'll manage just fine," she assured him, flashing a bright smile.

He hesitated, speechless for the moment. Her hair was tangled, matted with dirt and sweat. Her clothes were blood-stained and tattered. Her face was smeared from dust and tears. Still, Konn was struck by the radiance of her smile.

"Uh, we'd better get moving." He found his voice, yet felt abruptly uncomfortable. "We might not have much time."

The woman nodded her agreement. "How can we ever thank you, Mr. . . . ?"

"Konniger, ma'am. Most folks call me Konn."

"It's Laura Morrison, Mr. Konniger," she responded, still smiling happily. "And whatever you need us to do, you only have to say the word."

Konn was a little taken aback. He had never had a lady look at him in such a way. It was sincere, a mixture of gratitude and faith, as if she trusted him with her life. Of course, it was true of their current situation, but it still sent a quiver down his spine.

"Uh, the horses are over here," he told her awkwardly, leading the way.

"Mr. Kon'ger is the best shot in the whole world, mama," Abby spoke to her mother behind him. "He shoots horseflies!"

"Yes, dear," the woman replied. "I saw how good a shot he was when he made his point with that horrible Indian chief."

"He's got a nice horse too," Abby continued. "But she doesn't have a very nice name. It's Hammerhead." A short but lamented sigh. "Isn't that a terrible name for a nice horse?"

"Perhaps the horse is stubborn or contrary, Abby. She could be a good horse and yet be hard to manage at times."

"Is that how it is, Mr. Kon'ger?" Abby asked. "Is Hammerhead hard to manage?"

"She's a female critter," Konn answered back a bit gruffly. "I 'spect most females have a mind of their own."

Before Abby could ask more questions, Konn reached the horses. He quickly helped the two of them get settled on the back of the Indian pony and then gathered up the reins of Hammerhead and mounted.

"We had best kick up some dust," he told the woman. "The chief might decide a five-minute head start is keeping his word about letting us leave in peace."

"Whatever you say," Laura returned, bobbing her head up and down.

Konn picked an easy route to the basin floor and started a speedy exodus from the basin. They rode along the flat, open ground at a lope and held the pace for about a mile. Once out of the basin, he slowed the animals to a walk and cut away from the main trail. His new route took them into the brush and foothills, where he wound a snaky path up toward a mesa. He wanted to reach the high ground, so he could watch his back trail—a habit he was going to practice for a long time to come.

Once at a point of relative safety, he turned his head and asked the woman, "Where were you folks headed?"

"Lonesome Creek," she replied. "My father-in-law, Ben Morrison, and I entered into a partnership to build and operate a new general store there with a man named Rudy Copton."

"Lonesome Creek," he repeated the name. "My pa and I built a cabin about forty miles south of there. I haven't been back there for a couple years. The town wasn't much more than a desolate mining camp with a cattle ranch or two nearby."

"Yes, but the railroad is scheduled to lay track through the valley, and it is expected to become a regular stop between Denver and Santa Fe."

Konn absorbed her explanation without comment. "We'll pick up a saddle at Tubby's Crossing, over near the Thunder Mountain range. It's a bit out of the way and adds a few miles to Lonesome Creek, but we'd best steer shy of any territory where Two Bears likes to roam. The trail through the basin is the shortest route, but, as you discovered, it's also the most dangerous."

"We were following the directions of Mr. Copton. He sent Ben a map."

"Two Bears hasn't been active around these parts for several months, so he probably figured it was safe," Konn surmised. "That proved not to be the case."

"I can't thank you enough for your help, Mr. Konniger. You will get no argument from me concerning whatever route you choose to Lonesome Creek. And I'm sure Mr. Copton will pay you for your trouble when we arrive."

The idea of payment struck a nerve. "I didn't grab you for no reward."

"Of course you didn't," she said quickly. "I didn't mean to imply you had. It's only that we are completely indebted to you for saving our lives. I would like to repay your kindness in some way."

"No need for that," he said a bit gruffly. "I'd have done the same for anyone."

"I understand," she retaliated with a firm tone to her voice, "but it wasn't just *anyone's* life you saved—it was Abby and me!"

He let the matter drop, but little Abby chose the moment to pipe up. "I need to go behind a bush." She glanced at Konn and flashed a meek little simper. "You know?"

"Can we stop for a minute?" Laura took up her daughter's cause. "Abby needs to answer a nature call."

Konn reined Hammerhead to a stop, climbed down from the saddle, and went over to help Abby down. She quickly trotted over to a tall sage, hurried around to the opposite side, and was out of sight.

Konn sighed inwardly. *It's going to be a long couple days to Lonesome Creek!*

Chapter Three

After several hours of riding and constantly checking his back trail, Konn risked turning across a high plateau and made a direct line for Tubby's Outpost. His precautionary vigilance and alternate route had cost him a lot of daylight, so they would be forced to spend the night on the trail. He resigned himself to a restless night of light dozing while sleeping with one eye open.

Ever vigilant, Konn didn't speak to his two companions except to frequently offer them water from his canteen. That courtesy cost him a nature call every couple hours, as Abby had them stopping and going about as often as a confused jackrabbit.

While traveling, he overheard the mother and daughter speaking softly back and forth. The lady had lost her husband some years back and now she had lost her father-in-law. As for the child, he heard Abby say how she was going to miss her grandpa. He did his best to ignore the occasional weeping, keeping his teeth set firmly and focusing on the chore ahead. His only responsibility was to get the two females to civilization. After that, they were on their own, and he would be free to return to his own life.

As the sun dipped low over the horizon, Konn sought a place to camp for the night. They were fairly high up, but well below the timberline, following a winding trail among stands of scrub brush and a few pinion trees. There had been rain a day or two earlier, so he located a run-off ditch and followed it until they came upon a hollow with a shallow pool of water.

"We'll camp here for the night," he advised the two weary riders. "We can't risk a fire, but there's water for the horses."

"Anyplace we can lie down for the night will do," the woman assured him.

Konn suffered an uneasy sensation, a nervous apprehension, as if he were being watched by several hostile Indians. He doubted that was the case. It was more the problem of, how did a man deal with a couple tenderfeet women in the wild? He had never spent much time around women, not even those who frequented saloons, bumming drinks and doing their best to separate a man from his money. This here was a genteel lady and her incurably curious daughter. He was about as suited to the pair as a naked man trying to break up a fight between two porcupines.

Konn selected a small clearing and dismounted from his horse. He stepped over and lifted Abby down from their animal. He paused for a moment, uncertain as to how to deal with the lady, but Laura reached downward with both hands and placed them on his shoulders. When she leaned his direction, he grabbed her at the waist, swung her around, and set her down. He continued to support her for a moment, until she appeared steady. Then he let go and stepped back quickly, uncomfortable at having been so near the woman.

Konn picketed the horses and stripped the gear off of Hammerhead. As he worked, he was assailed by a host of swirling emotions. Never before had he held a proper woman so close, practically in his arms. It was more than unnerving, it was downright disconcerting.

"I don't have but one pan," he explained, removing a can of beans from his saddlebags. "I'll put your beans in it, but there's only one fork, which I use for turning meat or stirring a pot."

"Please don't concern yourself, Mr. Konniger." He was struck by how extremely polite the woman was when she spoke to him. Plus, her voice was soft and melodic, as soothing and pleasant-sounding to the ear as a mother's lullaby. She smiled demurely and added, "We will manage just fine."

He cursed his brain for wandering around lost in a daze and returned to the chore of preparing the meal. He emptied one of the cans of beans into the pan and added four hard rolls from his stash. For something to drink, he provided his two guests with his canteen.

Mother and daughter sat down side by side, and he passed the lady the pan. They took turns using the fork for the beans and munched the bread in silence.

Konn sat with his back to them and used his knife to fish beans out of the remaining airtight. He wolfed down a hard roll and finished off the beans in about two minutes. It would be enough to last him until morning.

While Laura and Abby were still eating, he spread his ground blanket over a level, rock-free area and then unrolled his thick buffalo coat. Aware of the lady watching as he smoothed out the heavy robe, he immediately felt a glowing heat enter his face. He suddenly wished he had trimmed some of his facial hair and bathed more recently. Realizing what he was thinking caused him to mentally cuss such a silly notion.

What the Sam Hill is wrong with you, Konn? No refined woman would ever want to gaze upon your ugly puss!

"I reckon this will have to do for your bed tonight," he said, once he had finished.

"You shouldn't give up your own bed to us, Mr. Konniger," the lady said, humbly lowering her head. "After all, we owe you our lives. It is we who are thankful and indebted to you."

"I've got another blanket for myself." Konn grunted and retrieved the pan and canteen from the woman. "Besides, you two got to have a place to sleep. It'll be a long day's ride tomorrow and there's nothing but a stick or two of jerky to hold you over until we reach Tubby's place. I don't dare shoot anything, as it might give away our position to the Indians."

"You worry too much about us, Mr. Konniger," she said, displaying a nice set of teeth with a supportive smile. "We'll get by as long as necessary."

He hated the weakness in his knees at her expression. Dadgum, he would have been floating like a cottonwood seed on the wind if the expression actually meant something. He had to keep reminding himself that her endearment was only a thank you for saving their lives.

Once he had wiped the pan and fork clean and put them away, he set about making his own bed for the night. He situated his saddle so he could lean against it with his head and upper shoulders. Next, he spread out the horse blanket to use as a ground sheet and used his poncho for a cover. He didn't intend to remove his boots and would remain fully dressed. If someone came snooping during the night, he had to be ready to react instantly.

About the time he had managed to relax, he heard Abby whisper to her mother that she needed to visit a nearby bush.

They disappeared into the darkness for a few minutes while Konn waited impatiently. The woman and child returned shortly and snuggled beneath his heavy buffalo coat. He knew the robe was a might gamey, having worn it during long weeks of hunting and trapping and often while curing hides or doing other chores. Well, no matter. He had provided them with all he had to offer. It would have to suffice.

Although Laura was exhausted and ached all over from the brutality of her ordeal, she didn't go to sleep right away. She uttered a silent prayer for her father-in-law, wishing they had been able to give Ben a proper burial. She hated the idea of his body lying out in the open, exposed to all manner of scavengers, but there was nothing she could do about it. She then gave thanks for the gallant hunter who had happened along and saved her and Abby from a violent and horrid fate. With a softly whispered "Amen," she rested a hand on her daughter's shoulder and closed her eyes.

Her eyes burned and her body begged for the anesthesia of sleep, yet she could not switch off her brain. Mental images flashed before her mind's eye, brutal and violent, playing over and over in her head. She relived Ben's death, the stark look of horror on his face, the agony of knowing he could not protect her and Abby. His last fleeting thought must have been how he had led them all to their deaths. And there was the terrible memory of being taken hostage, of fearing the very worst would happen to her, the terror that Abby would be hunted down and killed. She winced inwardly, still conscious of the tender places and scrapes on her back and ribs from the constant jab of Indian lances. There remained granules of sand in her hair from the many times dirt had been tossed at her, and she was coated in a layer of dust and sweat and dried blood. She wondered if she would ever feel clean again. Pinching her eyes tightly closed, she tossed her head back and forth, trying to shake off the dreadful recollections. She had to think of the future, of what she and Abby would do next.

With a grim determination, she replaced the hideous sneer of Two Bears with the self-assurance and compassion she had seen on their burly rescuer's face. She pictured Konniger in her mind and took a mental inventory of the hunter. Bigger than most men, he had lifted her to and from her horse as if she were a child. He was muscular in build, though not bulky or awkward in appearance. In truth, it was hard to decipher what the man really looked like under the growth of whiskers and his unkempt hair. His eyes were a cloudy gray, dark, expressive, and often piercing, as if he could look at and through a person. He had a booming and intimidating voice, but had used the tone only when speaking to Two Bears. When he spoke to her or Abby, he mellowed it down until it was more like a husky whisper. Obviously a man who could face a grizzly bear on even terms, he seemed uncertain of himself around her. She wondered how much time, if any, he had spent in the presence of a proper woman or little girl.

Turning to other matters, what did he intend to do about them? He had undoubtedly been going somewhere when he arrived to save the day, but he hadn't said a word about his destination. He indicated he would see them to Lonesome Creek, but that was all she knew of his future plans.

Finally, the burden of loss and swell of emptiness in her chest were overcome by her fatigue. Slumber beckoned and Laura succumbed to the dark void, her final thought being the hope she would be spared the horror of dreams.

Konn was up before first light. He made a careful inspection of the area, backtracking a couple hundred yards, searching for any fresh sign. If anyone was following them, he was very good, as he found no tracks but their own. After a few minutes of scouting and listening to the early morning silence, he returned to camp and quietly tended to the horses. He finished by testing them from their fetlock to the knee for heat—an indicator of muscle strain or injury—and lifted each hoof to inspect for damage or stone bruise. Both animals appeared in good shape for another day's hard ride.

He would have enjoyed a cup of coffee, but he didn't dare start a fire. Two Bears had been humiliated in front of his warriors, something he would not soon forget. After working steadily for two years with the railroad, Konn had intended to run a winter line of traps up in the Sangre de Cristo Mountains. However, he would now return to the cabin he and his father had built and run a few traps for the winter. First off, he needed to pick up a pack animal and supplies before heading up into the mountains. He would do that at Lonesome Creek and get shed of the woman and child at the same time.

Konn returned to camp, ready to bark the order for his guests to wake up and prepare to hit the trail, but the lady was already sitting up and tending to her feet. She glanced up and smiled a good morning, before continuing with her chore. The dazzling beam devastated his resolve, and he felt as if a flock of geese had taken flight within his chest. For a brief moment, he lost all sense of purpose, swept away by a most peculiar sensation.

What the hell is wrong with me? He admonished the giddy sensation. *I'm about as tipsy as if I'd been chewing on loco weed!*

"Uh, are your feet any better this morning?" he asked, immediately cursing the stupidity of such a remark. He should have asked how she was feeling or greeted her like any other normal man!

Laura did not seem to notice his awkwardness. "I do believe I'll walk again," she said lightly, "but not very far for a day or two."

"We can pick you up some clean socks at Tubby's place. That might help."

"I wouldn't want you to spend your money on us, Mr. Konniger. We'll do just fine until we reach Lonesome Creek. I'm sure Mr. Copton will take care of our needs once we arrive."

Copton again! Suggesting the man would take care of her struck him like a wet branch across the face. He had no call to pretend the woman and child were anything more to him than stranded pilgrims, but the idea she would rely on another man. . . .

He resolutely dismissed the sentimentality. "Like I told you last night, we only have a few strips of jerky for breakfast. I was on my way for supplies when I stumbled across your daughter and those Indian boys."

"Don't apologize for not having ready meals for us, Mr. Konniger. You saved our lives. That is something we can never hope to repay."

Again, Konn had no words of reply. He strode over to his pack and retrieved the small package of jerky. Abby was fully awake and putting on her shoes by the time he returned with several of the best strips. She had dirt smudges about her checks—likely from rubbing tears—but still offered up a toothy grin.

"Hiya, Mr. Kon'ger," she chirped sweetly. "Did you sit up and keep watch over us all night?"

"Never gave you two a thought," he teased. "It come as a surprise this morning to find that some mountain lion or hungry coyote hadn't carried you off during the night."

She giggled. "You've got a real comfy coat," she said. Then with a wrinkle of her nose added, "It smells kinda funny, but it's real warm."

He handed the jerky to Laura. "Best not let the daylight catch us sitting in one place too long," he issued the warning. "We need to get a move on."

"We'll be ready, soon as I get my shoes on and we take a short walk."

Konn turned to the chore of packing up and getting the horses ready. He wondered if withholding water would cut down on the number of stops they had to make for Abby. With a grunt, he dismissed the idea. She was a cute little tyke, whether her constant stopping was a bit of a nuisance or not. He would grit his teeth in silence and put up with an extra stop now and again.

Chapter Four

Konniger's party reached Tubby's trading post a little after noon. It was not much more than a large shack with a back room for storage, but Tubby earned enough to keep from starving. He offered travelers homemade liquor—which doubled as horse liniment or rust remover—served up an edible meal, and always had a handful of supplies or groceries to sell at greatly inflated prices. He also carried rope, lamp oil, traps, and a saddle or two.

Konn had known Tubby for several years, but never did much business with the man, as he seldom offered a decent price for a pelt or hide. However, he had company this trip and needed to provide for the two females. He entered ahead of Laura and Abby, keenly aware of the unkempt premises and a year's accumulation of dust.

"Konn!" Tubby exclaimed, recognizing him at once. Tubby was a short man who dressed in buckskin, and the top of his head was bald and protruded like a rock in a patch of short meadow grass. He was probably forty years of age and so thin he could have been made of sticks. As was his habit, he greeted Konn like a lost brother. "Dang my old bones! I ain't seen you in a month of Sundays!"

"Your wife still cooking up winter-kill rodents," Konn joked, "or did you sell her off to the Indians?"

Tubby showed a good-natured smile. "They wouldn't take her, not even when I offered to throw in a couple good horses!"

Konn grinned at his humor. "We'll be needing some grub to eat. Milk or lemonade too, if you've got any."

Spying the two companions with Konn, Tubby's eyes widened.

"Hot dang, Konn!" he exclaimed. "When the heck did you go and get yourself a wife and kid?"

"Mind your tongue," Konn growled a warning. "The tyke don't need to be hearing any bad language. The woman is a lady too."

Tubby bowed shortly before Laura and Abby. "Forgive my manners, ma'am. I ain't used to nothing out here but hunters, renegades, and outlaws. Can't say I've ever had a real lady in my trading post before."

Laura smiled politely to excuse his mild profanities. "I'm sure we must look like two beggars. Do you have some place where we can wash off some of this dust and grime?"

"Maria!" Tubby shouted over his shoulder. "Come in here a minute."

A Mexican woman, short and as round as a flour barrel, entered the room from the back. She raised her eyebrows in surprise, seeing the woman and child.

"*Si*, Meester Jones," she spoke to her husband. "What can I do for thee *señora* and *niña*?"

"They want to wash before they eat. Show them to the watering trough out back and get them a towel."

"*Si*, Meester Jones."

Konn waited until the three had left and put a curious look on Tubby. "You and Maria been together what, a half-dozen years? And she still calls you Mr. Jones."

"What can I say," he shrugged off the question. "My real last name mistakenly got printed on a wanted poster. Some silly thing about embezzling money from a bank. I decided the western wilderness wouldn't notice another Jones, so I told Maria it was my last name. She's never called me anything else. A'course, everybody who knows me at all calls me Tubby."

"Pa always said you had the smarts to be a bookkeeper."

Tubby grinned at the remark before growing serious. "How long has he been gone," he mused, "five . . . six years?" The man grunted. "Never figured there was an animal alive that could best your pa."

"He forgot the first rule of bear hunting—always take along someone you can outrun."

Tubby laughed. "You've got his wit, Konn, you sure have."

"I'll be needing a saddle for the lady's horse, plus supplies for a couple days," Konn said, turning to business.

"Where did you pick up the pair of orphans?"

"Two Bears attacked their wagon, killed the lady's kin, and left them with only the clothes on their backs."

Tubby whistled and gave his head a shake. "There's been talk about that troublesome war chief actively raiding again."

"I'm taking the gal and her child to Lonesome Creek. The woman has some friends there."

"I hear that place is growing like a weed in the garden," Tubby said. "It's one of the few strikes of '59 where anyone actually found gold or silver. Most of the other get-rich seekers left the country years back."

"There are more ghost towns than live ones around, that's a fact," Konn agreed.

Tubby paused to look out the dirty front window of his shack. "Two Bears ain't on your trail, is he? I sure don't want no trouble with him."

"It's me he would be after, and I'm only stopping long enough to eat and get the things we need. If one of his scouts should show up, you point them in our direction. I don't aim to dump any trouble on your doorstep."

A look of admiration entered Tubby's face. Konn was a man who took responsibility for his own actions and expected help from no man. Tubby appreciated that fact and got down to business.

"Let me show you the saddles I have, and we'll get the rest of the stuff put together. Soon as Maria gets you fed, you can be on your way."

"Sounds good to me."

The meal was tacos, cornbread, and refried beans, with a weak ginger beer for Konn and water for Laura and Abby to drink. It was an improvement over what Konn had been providing his guests, but not by much. He finished eating first and handed Laura a couple dollars.

"You two finish eating and pay for the meal," he told her. "I'll get the animals ready to travel."

Laura displayed one of her ready smiles. "We'll be along shortly. I'll see that Abby visits the little house out back first, so we won't have to stop along the trail."

Konn held back a chuckle, knowing it would likely only save them one of many stops. "That will be fine," he said and headed for the door.

Crow spied the cautious rider moving parallel to the main trail and angled ahead of him. When the man drew close enough to recognize, he moved out to block his path and raised a hand in salutation. Walks Tall was the number one warrior for Two Bears.

"You are a long way from home, Walks Tall," Crow said, as the brave stopped his horse.

"I follow the hunter, Konniger. He has the woman and child."

Crow scowled at hearing Konniger's name. He hated to even continue this conversation. "Woman and child," he said warily. "Not the Morrison woman!"

Walks Tall's shoulders drooped. "The hunter capture son of Two Bears. He trade for woman and child."

Crow swore at the news. "You were paid to kill them."

"I follow them for Two Bears. We will do what you paid us to do."

"Where is Two Bears?"

"He take son to camp and get supplies. He will come."

"But you're going to be too late!" Crow wailed. "Konniger will have that woman in Lonesome Creek before you catch up to them."

Walks Tall did not waver from the outburst. "We will find our chance. We will have the woman and the hunter. You have the promise of Two Bears."

There was no use lamenting what had already happened. Crow rotated about and looked down the valley. "Konniger probably went to Tubby's for supplies. Then he'll head up to Lonesome Creek. How far behind you is Two Bears?"

"Half day, no more."

Crow swore again. The Indians had no chance of overtaking Konniger before he got to Lonesome Creek. The plan had failed.

Worse, he had to tell Rudy and his wife. *Rudy was nothing, but that woman he married. . . .* Crow experienced an inward shudder at the idea.

"All right, Walks Tall," he said, trying to formulate an idea. "I'll cut across country, spend the night riding, and I can beat them to Lonesome Creek . . . I hope. You tell Two Bears I still expect full payment for our deal."

"Two Bears will keep his word."

Crow sneered a "yeah, right!" and started his horse moving.

This gruesome chore had seemed easy money. He had contacts with the Indians, being that his mother had been one herself. A man who had done a great deal of swapping and trading with several different tribes over the years, the setup with the new mercantile had been a gift from the heavens. However, the intervention of Konniger had put everything else in jeopardy. He would give the bad news to Rudy and see what they wanted to do.

Damn! Just when I catch a break, Konniger gets in the middle of things and ruins everything!

An hour after stopping at Tubby's trading post, they were back on the trail. The saddle made it easier riding for Laura and Abby, but the terrain was mountainous and fairly hard for traveling. By the time evening arrived, they were riding among the fir and birch trees. Konn knew of a nearby stream and turned in that direction. They threaded through trees and brush until they reached the small waterway. Following its path, he located a small clearing.

"It's about twenty more miles to Lonesome Creek, so we'll set up camp here for the night," he told Laura.

"This is a nice place," she replied. "Being next to the stream, we can clean up properly."

"Might want to soak your feet," Konn suggested. "That should help with the tenderness."

"Yes, I'll do that," she agreed.

"I feel kinda tender all over," Abby piped up. "And I think my bottom went to sleep from riding."

"Better numb than sore," Konn told her, dismounting his horse.

He dropped the reins to Hammerhead and moved over to lift Abby down. She was a bit shaky and began to stiffly walk around. He looked up at Laura. She certainly could have gotten down on her own, but he had set precedent the first time he helped her to dismount. She reached out with both arms so he could assist her. Konn did so quickly, once again taking her at the waist and lowering her to the ground. For the briefest moment he paused. Her hands were still on his shoulders and her eyes locked with his. Peculiarly, he surmised she welcomed the feel of his arms around her, as if she was drawing strength or courage by standing within his embrace. Her breath was close enough it stirred the hair of his beard. Having her body nearly touch his own practically overwhelmed him.

He recovered and took an awkward step back. Laura didn't seem to notice his reaction. She limped away, trying to stretch out some of the stiffness from the long ride.

"I don't think I'll ever walk normal again," she said, flashing a coy look of embarrassment over her shoulder.

He gave an affirmative nod. "I 'spect those blisters will be a problem for a few days yet."

She laughed. "I was referring to sitting a saddle. Until you rescued us, I hadn't spent more than an hour or two at a time on the back of a horse."

"It takes some getting used to all right."

"Can I do something to help with the campsite?" Laura offered.

"I can handle the chores," he replied. "You tend to the muffin and your sore feet."

Konn picketed the horses, stripped the gear, and placed his ground blanket and heavy coat down to use for a bed like before. Laura and Abby had found a convenient place by the creek. He kept busy, but did observe the lady remove her shoes and sit down on a rock, where she could soak her feet in the cold water. Abby stayed at her side and began tossing rocks in the creek to make a splash.

It was unnerving how comfortable it felt having the two of

them around. They had only been together for a couple days and it seemed almost natural.

Sonuvabuck! He scolded himself for both the feeling and thought. *I've got daisies for brains if I think I could ever have a pair like them for a wife and child of my own!*

Feeling a bit more secure at being only a half-day away from Lonesome Creek, Konn arose early the following morning and found himself a short, sturdy branch. He always carried a few feet of line and a hook, and from this he fashioned himself a short fishing pole. Walking along the bank of the stream, he turned over several large rocks. He found a couple worms for bait and then began to search the creek for a likely hole. His fishing expedition took him about thirty minutes and a hundred yards upstream. After catching and cleaning six fish big enough to fry for breakfast, he started back toward camp. He had gone a short way when he heard something moving overhead.

Konn froze, searching the forest of limbs and nearby trees, while he used his free hand to slowly reach for his handgun. When he spotted what had made the noise, he didn't pull the pistol, instead hurrying his step. Certain things in the woods could appear harmless yet be life threatening. This was one of those things!

Moving swiftly, he neared the campsite, when there came a giggle back in the direction of the creek. He bulled a path through a thicket of wild rose and came to an abrupt halt. There at the water's edge were Laura and Abby—the little girl wearing only a pair of bloomers, while Laura was clad in a damp underdress. Being white and wet, it was practically transparent.

"Konn!" Laura gasped, using his abbreviated name for the first time. She hastily grabbed up her dress from the bank and pulled it to her shoulders to cover herself.

"Uh, sorry," Konn stammered, but he dared not look away. "I didn't mean to scare you."

"We're not decent," Laura stated the obvious. "Give us a minute to get dressed."

He remained rooted to the ground. "I can't do that, ma'am," he said quietly. "I need for you both to do exactly as I say."

Laura's face flushed at being caught in such an embarrassing position. She set her teeth and spoke curtly. "You can at least turn your back!"

"I could," Konn replied, his voice carefully void of emotion, "but that old mama bear might decide to make a run at you."

Laura whirled about and spied a huge brown bear standing on the opposite bank, curiously eying the three of them. It chose that moment to growl a warning and shake its head.

Abby squealed and Laura reached for her, ready to run for their lives.

"Stand still!" Konn ordered them both.

Laura did as she was told, but did keep hold of Abby's hand. They remained there, poised fearfully, waiting for him to tell them how to proceed.

"Her baby is up the tree a short ways back of me," Konn explained, "and you don't want to ever get betwixt a mama bear and her cub."

Laura whispered, "Abby! Grab your clothes!" Even as the girl did so, Laura gathered up their shoes.

"Slow and easy," Konn warned. "If you start to run it might excite the old gal. Just walk slowly until you are both in back of me."

The two did as he told them, gingerly picking and weaving their way through the brush until they were behind him.

"Head on back to camp," he said. "If the bear comes at me, I'll toss her the fish. It might allow time for me to make it back to camp and get my rifle."

Without a word and despite her blisters, Laura picked up Abby and carried her away. Konn held his position for a moment, then backed slowly away from the creek, watching the bear and doing his best not to appear as any kind of threat. The bear growled once more and took a couple of menacing steps in his direction. But Konn was no longer between the mother bear and her offspring. He moved off a short way and the bear crossed the stream in three lunging bounds! She wasn't attacking, however, and passed him by to go check on her cub.

Konn uttered a sigh of relief and continued back toward camp. He didn't figure the bear would bother them, but he would keep his rifle handy until they were back on the trail.

He arrived to discover Laura had put her dress on over the damp underclothing and Abby was also dressed. They both appeared shaken by the encounter.

"Nothing to fear now," Konn told them confidently. "That protective she-bear will likely take her young'un and keep her distance from us. The real danger was while she couldn't get to her cub without going right past where you were doing your washing."

"It was a grizzee bear who killed Mr. Kon'ger's daddy," Abby told Laura. "Bet'cha he would have showed that old mama bear if she had tried to get us."

"I only had my pistol," Konn informed the little girl. "A bullet from a handgun will sometimes bounce right off a bear's hard head."

"Your father was killed by a bear?" Laura asked him.

"It only takes one bad cartridge to end a hunter's career," Konn replied. "My pa taught me the proper way to kill a bear, but a misfire cost him his life."

"What's so different about killing a bear over a moose or elk? They can also do a lot of harm."

"A bear won't go down unless you hit him square," Konn replied. "The best kill shot is from in front of him and you aim for his head. If he lifts his head when you fire, the bullet will hit him in the throat and usually tear up his primary vitals inside. If he lowers his head, you hit him in the brain. Either one will usually stop him cold. A shot from behind or from the side, and you can end up with an all-fired angry bear on your hands."

"I apologize for being brusque over your intrusion, Mr. Konniger." Laura was contrite. "I had no idea we were in any danger."

"You called me Konn back at the stream," he reminded her.

"I was momentarily upset," she explained. "I didn't mean to be so familiar."

He chuckled. "You don't mind sharing my camp and bedding

down or sleeping under the same set of stars, but it's too *familiar* to call me by the same name as everyone else who knows me?"

The words caused her to smile, a wonderfully natural simper he enjoyed. There was an honesty to her, as if she shared the same youthful innocence as Abby. He smiled back, and they both laughed.

Chapter Five

Rudy and Elva listened to Crow's report. When he had finished, Rudy took some money from the cash drawer and paid him.

"What a stupid waste of money!" Elva ranted the instant the man had exited the front door. "We could have hired the job done right for what we paid Crow and those incompetent Indians!"

"It sounds as if a wandering hunter caused all the trouble, Elva," Rudy whined a weak defense. "Can't fault Two Bears for him showing up when he did. It was plain bad luck."

"We can sure as heck blame Two Bears for not doing his job right away!" Elva stormed about the room, hands locked at her back, turning over ideas in her mind. "He got greedy and wanted to profit from the same job twice." She continued to seethe. "I'll bet he intended to sell or ransom the woman. He was supposed to have killed her during the raid."

"We can't change what has happened," Rudy told her, not bringing up the fact it was *her* greed that put them in the situation they were in now. He had been willing to own half-interest in the general store, but Elva wanted more. He ran his hand nervously across his brow. "We'll have to let Laura and her child stay here and help run the store."

Elva spun on Rudy, fire burning within her eyes, fists at her sides, and her teeth bared in contempt. "We're not sharing anything with that woman!" she hissed. "I've been in the shadow of the rich all my life, watching women strut about in their fine clothing and being chauffeured in expensive carriages. I grew up living in a dump, while my mother worked as a lowly servant in a big house. I wasn't even allowed to play with their children because I was not worthy to be around them!" She shook one of her balled fists. "I know what I want, Rudy, and I'll damn well have it."

"I'm trying," he squeaked weakly. "I've done everything you asked."

"I came here and married you because you promised me a good life . . . and you're going to keep your promise!"

"The store is already making money." Rudy tried to appease her. "It will easily support the four of us."

"Yes, we can live from hand to mouth for the rest of our days, if we allow Laura and her brat to take half of what we earn." She pointed a long, slender finger at Rudy. "You said we would have it all, the big house and servants. A year or two was what you told me, remember?"

Rudy squirmed under the heat of her fury. "I never made any promise that included having the Morrison family killed. Working with Crow, we can make a pile of money selling guns on the side. I could have hidden that part of the business from Ben until he could afford to buy out our share. It was your idea to take the whole store for ourselves."

"And we'll have it!" Elva vowed.

"You heard what Crow said. The woman and her child are on their way here. Half of the store legally belongs to her. We only have a matter of hours before they arrive. I don't see any way to change the original arrangement."

Elva opened her mouth—likely to shout an obscenity—but then she paused. Her face worked as her mind busily sorted through some options. When an idea came into focus, her lips curled upward at the corners in a sneer.

"There is always a way, Rudy," she said sweetly. "I know just how to handle this little problem."

Ruby had seen that look before, when she had talked him into sending Crow to arrange an ambush. She had been the one to draw a map and mail the letter to the Morrisons. He had resisted the idea, but Elva was a strong-willed woman. She had nuzzled in his ear and rubbed up against him, driving him insane with her feminine wiles. When he had finally agreed, she had been warm and loving, the woman of his dreams. How quickly the ardor had passed once she had what she wanted. He was a sap, a lily-livered milksop, but he couldn't help it. His new wife was dominating and determined. She knew how to get her way . . . and he knew she had an idea for getting her way now.

Elva walked over and picked up her purse. "Lock the door and hang the CLOSED sign." She gave the order as if he was her personal servant. "We've got a little business to attend to."

Rudy sighed inwardly and didn't ask about her plan or where they were going. Ever since he had uttered the words "I do," his foremost words to Elva had been "yes, dear!"

The two most prominent structures in Lonesome Creek were the High Card Saloon and a second two-story building with the name Copton's Mercantile painted over the door. Many of the buildings were little more than shanties, with a number of wagons and tents scattered along the main street. However, four other solid, wooden structures were nearby: a barn at the livery, a small land office/Justice of the Peace, Brown's Pharmaceutical, and a laundry/bath house, which had a sign in both Chinese and English on the front. Lonesome Creek had grown considerably since Konn's last visit. It was on its way to becoming a real town.

An uncomfortable twinge of something—regret?—seeped into Konn's being. He attempted to shrug it off. He was soon to be free from the nuisance of tending and watching over a couple of near-helpless tenderfeet. He ought to be experiencing relief. It was back to normal for him, riding alone, worrying only about himself, with no more than a pack mule and Hammerhead for company. That's the way he wanted it—his own life, solitary, alone, unencumbered.

So why the empty feeling inside?

"There's your store," he said to Laura. "Once you're paired off with your business partner, I figure you'll be just fine." He could not look at her, afraid she might see his weakness and uncertainty. "There's no jail, so I'll stop by the land office first thing and talk to whoever handles the local law. They ought to be warned about anyone taking the route through the Dry Basin country."

"Will we see you again?" Laura asked somewhat timidly. "I

mean, we can't hope to ever repay your kindness, but I hate to say good-bye like this."

"I'll be around town for a day or two. I have to pick up some supplies and a good pack animal. I'll check and see how you're doing before I leave."

"You've been a godsend for us," Laura stated succinctly. "If not for you . . ."

"Don't dwell on the what if's, Mrs. Morrison." He prevented her from humbling herself further. "I was in the right place at the right time to lend a hand. That's the end of it."

"Certainly, Mr. Konniger," she replied. "I will let the matter drop with a heartfelt thank you."

"You're welcome."

They pulled up in front of the store, and Konn quickly dismounted. He let Hammerhead stand while he walked around to lift Abby down to the ground.

"I think I'm gonna walk funny from now on," she complained. "My legs feel kinda crooked."

"Not to worry, little muffin," Konn told her. "Your limbs will straighten out in no time at all."

"You're a nice man, Mr. Kon'ger," Abby said, smiling. "How come you don't cut some of the hair from your face? It makes you look like a big old bear."

"Come winter, a man needs hair to keep his face from freezing."

"It looks like it itches," she continued. "Does it?"

"Not so much."

"Looks like it would," she maintained.

"Well, being a girl, I don't think you'll ever have to worry about it."

She giggled and stepped back. He reached up and placed his hands to either side of Laura's waist, hoisted her out of the saddle, and set her down on the ground. He was quick to let go and step away this time, not wanting her to think he would take advantage of the parting situation and hold her a little too close.

Laura didn't seem to notice and flashed a warm smile. "Don't forget to come by the store later," she said, "once Abby and I have time to get settled."

"You can count on it," he replied.

Laura took Abby's hand, and the two of them turned for the store. Konn again felt an odd barrenness invade his chest, but he grabbed up the reins to his two mounts and started for the land office. Once he spoke to the Justice of the Peace he would head for the livery. Both of his animals needed a rubdown and some food and rest.

Laura noticed an odd expression on Rudy's face when he spied them enter the store.

"Hey there!" The greeting sounded cordial, but there was no warmth in his voice. He purposely looked past her to the door expectantly. "Laura, Abby . . . where's Ben?"

Laura told him briefly about the fatal attack and how they had come to be saved by a man named Konniger. Rudy listened silently. When she finished, he gravely shook his head.

"It's all my fault!" he declared. "If I hadn't entered into this partnership with Ben, he would still be alive."

"It was something we both thought would be worth the effort." Laura accepted her own part of the blame. "My husband's money was being wasted, invested in a farm Ben and I couldn't begin to manage. It was as much my idea as Ben's to sell everything and finance this store."

A woman entered the room, a haughty vixen Laura remembered from Garden City, back in Kansas. There was no warmth in her expression, only a cool disdain.

"Laura?" She raised a single eyebrow. "You look as if you were dragged behind a team and run over by the wagon. Is that a piece of tumbleweed in your hair?"

"They were attacked by Indians, Elva, dear," Rudy told her. "Ben was killed."

The woman gave a not-quite-sincere shake of her head. "I'm so sorry, Laura," she mouthed the words, but the aloofness remained in her icy glare. "Whatever are you going to do now?"

"We're here," Laura replied. "I will do my share to help run the place."

Rudy took a step back and feigned surprise. "You're going to do what?"

Elva snorted indignantly. "We have barely scraped up enough money to open the doors. I'm afraid we can't afford to pay for any help, Laura, hon."

"What do you mean *we*?" Laura demanded to know. "And I'm not offering to be hired help."

"I wrote to you and told you Rudy and I were married last month," Elva reminded her tersely. "Surely you remember that much."

As she attempted to assimilate what their marriage had to do with anything, Rudy moved a step closer.

"I don't understand, Laura," he said, displaying a perplexed expression. "What is it you want from us?"

"What do I want? This is where we belong!"

Elva continued to exhibit a snooty air and her voice was steeped in sarcasm. "You're not working in *our* store," she stated flatly. "There might be a job for you in town; perhaps you could inquire at the saloon. I'm sure it would pay better than working for us . . . even if we could afford to pay wages."

Icy talons, a mixture of ire and dread, dug into Laura's heart. She maintained her composure and put a level gaze on Rudy. "I invested my money in this store too," she stated. "My husband owned far more than half of the farm we sold."

Rudy flicked his eyes away, his facial expression unable to hide his shame. Elva glared at him meaningfully, and he lifted his shoulders in a helpless shrug.

"I'm sorry, Laura," Rudy said, his voice was woeful and apologetic, "but the business partnership was a contract between Ben and I. There was no provision made for you and Abby."

The words were foreign-sounding to Laura. "What contract are you talking about?"

"Before I left Kansas, Ben and I had a lawyer draw up and set forth an agreement on paper. In the event something happened to either of us, there could be no question about the ownership of the store."

"What kind of underhanded scheme are you working here, Rudy?" Laura fumed. "I never saw any contract!"

Rudy refused to make eye contact. "I assure you, Laura, it is straightforward and binding." He took a deep breath, as if the words were difficult to get out. "It was a safeguard for our business venture. If it had been me who died, Ben would have assumed ownership of the store and all of its worth or debts. As your father-in-law was killed, the entire place now belongs to me."

"I don't believe a word you're saying!" Laura bit off the words smartly. "Ben would never have entered into a written agreement without me knowing about it. Where do you get the gall to tell me I don't own half of this business?"

It was Elva who replied. "There is an attorney in town," she literally cooed the words. "He's also Justice of the Peace and the clerk and recorder for Lonesome Creek. We had him review the contract when we bought this parcel of land and began to build the store. He will verify every word of what Rudy is saying."

Rudy bobbed his head up and down. "You can speak to Mr. Dodd if you want, Laura, but I assure you, he read over the contract, and the death of your father has left me as sole proprietor of the store."

Elva went behind the counter and produced a sheet of paper. "We have the contract right here. You can take it over to him and have him read the words to you."

Laura took a step toward her and stared hard at the document. "This is a lie! It's all a lie!"

"I'm sorry you weren't informed," Rudy said. "It was necessary to have a contract for the general partnership."

"And what about us?" she cried. "Do you expect us to live on the streets?"

"This is all very unfortunate, Laura," Rudy said, talking more quickly now. "I can maybe borrow enough money to pay for your return to Denver or back home to Garden City, but I spent every cent of the investment money to build the store. I actually went into debt to purchase much of the inventory."

"But it was my money too!"

"Corporate law is not a handshake agreement that can be

changed with a whim," Elva interjected, taking a firm stance. "Anything Rudy does for you two is out of the goodness of his heart and our own pockets."

"Rudy Copton!" Laura spewed the words vehemently. "I can't believe you would be a part of something so utterly crooked and deceitful!"

"It's not my doing," he whined like a scolded dog. "It's the law. You can ask the Justice of the Peace yourself. I'm willing to lend a hand to help you out, but you have to accept the fact that you have no legal claim to anything in Lonesome Creek."

Laura grabbed Abby by the hand, whirled about, and stormed out of the store. Although tears of anger and frustration blurred her vision, she spied the sign which indicated the clerk and recorder's office. With a purposeful stride, she marched down the street and entered the small building.

A white-haired gentleman was reclined in a chair with his feet atop a cluttered desk. He appeared ready to doze off, hands folded over his paunch while his double-chin rested on his breastbone. Laura slammed the door to get his attention.

"What the . . . ?" he began, before seeing Laura and Abby. He swallowed the profanity upon noticing his guests and removed his feet from the desk. "What's the idea of banging my door so hard? You might have broken the glass window. Do you have any idea how expensive glass is up here, dear lady?"

"Are you the only lawyer in town?"

He bobbed his head up and down. "William Dodd, Attorney at Law. I'm currently the town's Justice of the Peace and the clerk and recorder for this part of the country."

"You are familiar with the venomous snake who calls himself Rudy Copton?" she asked, getting right to the point.

He contrived a measure of shock, but he couldn't mask the glimmer of comprehension, as if he had been expecting her. "I know the Coptons, yes."

"I'm Laura Morrison, and this is my daughter, Abby." Before he could greet either of them properly, she went on. "My father-in-law and I sold our house and everything we owned to finance the building of this town's general store. Well over half of the entire capital used to build that store was provided by the money and property left to me by my late husband. I put my faith and money into this business venture and now that lowlife, sniveling cheat, Rudy Copton, has the nerve to tell me I'm penniless! That I own nothing!"

"And what about your father-in-law?"

"He was killed in an Indian attack."

"Yes, yes," he said, straightening in his chair, "Mr. Konniger was here a few minutes ago with some information about an Indian attack. Most regrettable, most regrettable."

Laura got back to the business at hand. "Those two weasels are trying to steal what rightfully belongs to me!"

Dodd cleared his throat, visibly unhappy about being confronted. "I'm right sorry for your loss, Mrs. Morrison. As for your dealings with Mr. Copton, I would prefer you and he settle any dispute without outside intervention."

"It's no dispute!" Laura cried. "I paid for more than half of that store!"

Dodd remained stolid and unyielding. "Elva and Rudy showed me the written agreement, Mrs. Morrison. It was a customary agreement for a general partnership. I regret, madam, there was no provision for heirs. The company is a singular entity and stands alone, so long as either of the partners survives."

"But it was built with my money!" Laura lamented. "What little we had left for travel and living expense was lost to the Indian attack. I don't have a penny to my name!"

Dodd displayed a sympathetic frown, but there was no give in his stance. "Why don't you give Mr. Copton a couple days and see if you two can't work something out. I'm sure he wants to settle this fairly, Mrs. Morrison. The death of your father-in-law must have come as a complete shock to him. He can't have had time to think how to deal with the situation. In the meantime, I'm sure he will help to provide shelter and food for both of you."

"Food and shelter!" she said, scathing him with her words. "I told you, I invested every cent my husband left me—even my wedding ring! We sacrificed our life's earnings to start a business here, and you're saying I have no claim on the store whatsoever!"

"I've drawn up many a contract for business partnerships, Mrs. Morrison. The agreement I examined appeared to have been signed in good faith. If you wish to challenge the contract in court, the circuit judge comes to Lonesome Creek once or twice a year. He is due to return next spring, five or six months from now."

Laura was crushed by the weight of the news. She had expected to arrive as half-owner of the general store. She would have made a life for herself and Abby, helping to run the store. It would have been difficult to start a new life without Ben, yet she and Abby would have made do. But now . . .

"I have no means to survive until spring," she murmured despondently. "I suppose I could take a job or—"

"There's no work here for a woman," Dodd was quick to inform her, "unless you are willing to wait tables in the saloon." At her sharp glance, he hurried to clarify. "What I mean is we have several Chinese living here. They do the laundry and about any chore the local miners need doing. The few wives here take in sewing or work at the local eateries to make ends meet. With winter coming on, many of the miners will also need to find work to get by. There won't be a decent job to be had until the spring thaw."

"Am I supposed to live on the streets and beg for food?"

Dodd lifted his hands up, palms outward, as if to calm her fears. "Perhaps Mr. Copton can provide you with enough money to help you get back home."

"I don't have a home!" she wailed, trying not to scream the words. "Haven't you been listening? We sold everything we owned in the world. We have nowhere to go!"

Dodd uttered a sigh of regret. "I'm sorry, Mrs. Morrison, but there's really nothing I can do. The contract is completely legal. If you wish to challenge the agreement, it will have to wait until the circuit judge comes back to town. Until then, your only recourse is to try and work this out with the Coptons."

Laura fled the room with Abby and returned to the dusty street. She could not get her brain to function. The idea that Rudy would steal the store had never entered her mind. He had somehow manufactured a phony contract and was using legal jargon to steal her half of the business. The deceitful ploy left her penniless and facing a hopeless situation.

"I'm thirsty, Mommy," Abby finally broke into her gloom.

Laura about snapped at her to be quiet and let her think. Instead, she rallied her composure. As she began looking up and down the street for a place to get a drink of water, Abby added, "I'm kinda hungry too."

Laura fought back tears of helplessness as a thought occurred to her. She had paid for the meal at Tubby's place. The meals there had been four bits each so she had gotten change from the two dollars. She felt around in her pocket and discovered she still had the fifty cents.

"All right, Abby," she said. "Let's find a tavern or café and see what we can afford. We can at least get some water to drink and maybe some soup or bread."

"Where we gonna live now?" Abby asked.

Laura swallowed her dread and bolstered up a show of spirit. It took a mighty effort, but she managed a smile. "I'm not sure yet, but we'll get by. We've got each other, right?"

Abby squinted up at Laura and a crooked smile flashed across her pretty little face. "Right!"

Chapter Six

The important-acting fellow, Dodd—both acting judge and land records man—had told Konn there was a part-time town marshal, and suggested he ought to be notified about the Indian trouble. Naturally, Dodd didn't offer to pass along the information himself, so Konn dropped off his animals at the livery and went down to the High Card Saloon, looking for the random lawman.

Once inside, he paused to adjust his eyes to the dark interior of the room and located a man behind a long counter. The gent was busy using a towel to wipe and clean a row of beer mugs.

"I'm looking for the town marshal, a man named Flynn."

The fellow appeared capable, maybe pushing the long side of thirty, with a hint of grey above his ears. He had a few extra pounds around his middle, but offered up a cordial smile. "I'm Flynn," he answered. "What can I do for you?"

Konn explained about the attack and how Two Bears had threatened to kill any whites he got his hands on.

"I'll get word to the Army," Flynn said, once Konn had finished. "It's about fifty miles to the nearest post, but I'll have the telegrapher send them a report. Doubt we'll see much action, but they might send a few troops to patrol the area."

"Thanks," Konn replied.

Flynn extended his hand. "You probably don't recognize me, but I believe we've been down the same road before . . . Konn, isn't it?" At Konn's nod, the man continued. "I was working for the railroad a couple years back—remember the spur to Coal Canyon, the one so the railroad could have an easy access to their fuel supply?"

47

"I remember," Konn replied, shaking his hand. "That was a winter I'll never forget."

Flynn laughed. "I about froze my cookies on that job . . . and everything else of value to a man!"

"Tough year," Konn remembered. "I came close to losing my scalp to some hungry Cheyenne while trying to get enough meat for you men."

"I learned my lesson. Never catch me driving another spike or hefting one of those steel rails again."

"So you're a barkeep and the law about town?"

Flynn grunted. "You could say that. Folks found out I had been a policeman in Denver for a short while, and I was drafted into the chore. As for anything major, I've never even met the U.S. Marshal. Fortunately, we don't have a lot of trouble here, so what the heck!"

"I imagine the miners get rowdy on occasion," Konn observed. "Being long on drink and short on women usually makes for a good many fights."

"Now and again," he admitted. "The lawman stuff I do is for a cut of the fine or a set fee. Plus, I also help Dodd settle claim disputes or whatever comes along." He waved his hand at the empty room. "This job pays almost nothing, but I do get a room upstairs and earn enough to eat seven days a week."

"Doesn't sound like much of a living."

"What about you?" Flynn countered. "You still hunting meat for the railroad?"

"Usually for them or the Army, but I'm between jobs at the moment. This coming winter, I 'spect I'll hole up back in my old mountain home and do some trapping. There is still a market for the right furs or hides, though it doesn't pay like back in my father's time. When he was my age, a bundle of beaver pelts could earn a man enough to live on for a year."

"About this here woman survivor you brought into town." Flynn showed a renewed interest. "She purty?"

"A cut above most," Konn begrudgingly replied. "And her little girl is cute as a bunny in a basket."

"We can sure use a few more gals up here. Come Saturday

night, most of the miners have to dance with each other. I can tell you, that's not a sight you want to think about when your head hits the pillow."

Konn grinned. "Yeah, I've wintered in a few camps with no women." Getting back to business, he inquired, "What can you tell me about the storekeeper? Can I trust him to look after the lady and her daughter?"

"Copton?" Flynn turned his head to the side and spat downward near his foot. From the sound of the spittoon, he had mastered the knack of spitting tobacco juice. "A short while after he arrived, a lady friend showed up and they tied the matrimonial knot. After that, they supervised the building of the store. That's about all I know."

Konn frowned. "The lady I brought here didn't say anything about her partner getting married. Guess the subject didn't come up."

"Well, Copton's new bride don't allow him to come around here, so I haven't seen much of him. Dodd can maybe set you straight about him, being he performed the marriage."

"Dodd doesn't strike me as the most honest man alive."

"He's a jackleg lawyer whose brother-in-law got him a job as a recorder at the land office. He's not exactly a man I would trust."

"An odd thing to say working with the man like you do."

Flynn stuck out his hand and rubbed his thumb against his first two fingers. "Money binds people together as often as friendship."

"Meaning the fees for your deputy work."

"Yep, Dodd acts as a judge when we have a drunk get out of hand. He levels a fine and he gets half and I take half. If the guy can't pay, he has to work it off cleaning up after the horses or building walkways, whatever."

Konn felt a pricking of the hair along the back of his arms and neck. He often got such a sensation when there was a renegade Indian close by. Why it should come upon him at this moment was curious.

"Thanks for your honesty, Flynn," Konn told the bartender, shaking off the feeling. "I'm obliged for the information."

"Gossip and advice are two things I give freely, Konn. Stop by after dark, and I'll buy you a drink."

"I might take you up on that," Konn said.

Flynn grinned. "Just keep in mind, its *one* drink, my friend, not a whole bottle."

Konn raised a hand in parting and left the saloon. He still had to pick up some supplies, but he would wait until he was ready to leave town to buy what he needed. The horses could use a full day's rest, and he wanted to trade the Indian pony and saddle for a pack animal. It made sense to spend a day or two in town, before he journeyed up into the nearby mountain range.

Glancing skyward, he saw that the afternoon sun would soon set over the horizon, but the sky was still clear. He would get something to eat and then check on his horses. After he ascertained the animals had been properly cared for, he would pick up his bedroll, make a short trek back into the hills, and camp for the night. At least, that was his plan.

"Mr. Konniger!" A familiar female voice stopped him in his tracks. He looked toward the sound and discovered Laura and Abby were on the street. They hurried over to meet up with him.

"I hate to impose on you, but could you do me a very large favor?" Laura asked, as soon as they were at his side.

"What would that be?"

"Could you watch Abby for a few minutes?" Laura pleaded softly. "I need to speak to Rudy again and would prefer that Abby not have to be there. You know how it is—talking business can be so boring for children."

"I was on my way over to look after the stock," Konn replied. "I reckon she can tag along. I'll let her use a curry comb on Hammerhead."

"Oh, thank you, Mr. Konniger," she spurted forth her gratitude. "I shouldn't be but a few minutes," she said, with a subtle shrug of her slender shoulders. "I don't know anyone else in town and I wouldn't want a stranger to look after Abby."

"Shore 'nuff, I understand."

Laura turned to her little girl. "Now you behave, Abby."

"I will, Mama." Abby showed a toothy grin. "Me and Mr. Kon'ger will be good."

Laura smiled at the girl, whirled about, and headed up the street.

"You ever curry a horse before, little muffin?" he asked Abby.

"Nope," she responded candidly. "But I seen grandpa tend to his horse sum'times. He let me feed him sum'times too."

"Sounds like a nice guy, your grandpa."

"I'm gonna miss him a whole lot," Abby said, a renewed sadness in her voice.

Konn gave a nod of his head but said nothing more. He led the way to the stable, with Abby forced to trot at his side to keep up with his long strides.

I should have known better! Konn thought. *Save a body's life and you set yourself up for nothing but a passel of troubles. Now I'm a baby-tender!*

Konn and Abby had long since finished with the animals. He wondered what the devil was keeping Laura. She had said a few minutes. It had been over an hour!

"Let's walk down to the store and see if your mother is about done chewing the fat. It'll be dark soon, and I need to fix me a place to spend the night."

"Okay," Abby chirped, moving over to take hold of his hand.

Konn felt awkward for the first few steps, afraid the slightest pressure of his fingers might crush something so small and delicate. Yet, as they began walking, he was struck by the feeling of kinship, a closeness with the little girl. For the first time in his life, he had an inkling as to how it must feel to be a father. The wondrous sensation filled his chest with an unknown lightness and caused it to expand. Instead of being self-conscious, he walked a little taller, rather proud to have the child at his side.

Before they reached the store, Token Flynn appeared on the street. He waved at Konn and hurried up the street to meet him. As he approached, Konn noticed the man wore a fretful expression.

"Hot dang!" he exclaimed. "I'm glad I found you."

Konn growled. "You want to watch your language around the youngster here? She ain't old enough to be learning no coarse talk."

"Sure, sure," Flynn apologized quickly. "It's just that . . ." His face twisted from a frown to a grimace. "Well, I've had to take custody of a prisoner." Then with a nod at Abby, he said weakly, "The girl's mother is charged with assault!"

"What?" Konn yelped. "Assault? Against who?"

"It seems the lady got into a heated exchange over at the new store. She up and cuffed that owner's new wife right in the mouth. The Copton woman wants to press charges."

Konn groaned. *No wonder the woman hadn't returned. She had gotten into a brawl! What the heck was that all about?*

"Is he talking about Mama?" Abby wanted to know.

"It's nothing to be worried about," Konn assured her gently. Then he asked Flynn, "Can I see her?"

"I have to take her before the judge."

"Meaning Dodd?"

"Yeah," Token replied. "You can talk to her as soon as Dodd makes his ruling."

"You headed there now?"

"Soon as I pick up my prisoner. I had to take the statement from Mr. Copton and his wife, so I put Mrs. Morrison in the saloon storeroom for safekeeping."

"I reckon we'll sit in on the hearing, if it's all right with you?"

"Exactly why I wanted to talk to you, Konn. The lady can probably use someone to stand up for her. Like I told you earlier, this type of charge is usually a pay-the-fine-or-do-the-time-in-jail offense. Anyway, I should be over at Dodd's place in about five minutes. I'll meet you there."

Konn watched him walk away. He tried to think of what might have happened to cause a fight at the store, especially considering that Laura seemed such a mannerly young lady! He might have studied on it more but a tug came to the leg of his trousers.

"What did the man mean, Mommy is charged with salting someone?"

"I 'spect we'll go find out, youngster. This whole thing is clear as mud to me too."

Dodd's office was not much for size: a cabinet, large desk, and four extra chairs. He allowed Konn and Abby to sit in one corner while he perched behind his desk, puffed up like the largest toad in the swamp.

Flynn arrived with Laura shortly. She flashed Konn an I'm-so-sorry look before facing the Justice of the Peace.

"Mrs. Morrison," Dodd began, "you are charged with assaulting Mrs. Copton. Our town peace officer, Token Flynn, has taken statements and witnessed the evidence, namely, the split and swollen lip of your victim. The court finds you guilty of the charge."

"Don't I get to speak on my own behalf?" Laura spoke up.

"It's all in the testimony of the injured party right here." He held up a sheet of paper which contained some scribbling. "It states that, while in a fit of rage, you struck and hit Mrs. Copton in the face."

"She made the disgusting insinuation my child was illegitimate!" Laura shouted at him. "And she's the one who coerced Rudy into stealing my share of the store! They are both dirty crooks! Dastardly thieves! Behind-the-back, double-dealing vermin!"

Dodd raised his hand to quiet her. "When we spoke earlier, I informed you that I had read the contract your father signed. With the death of Ben Morrison, the store belongs to the surviving partner. Everything is perfectly legal."

"My father-in-law didn't sign any contract!" Laura stated flatly. "This is nothing more than a swindle to steal what rightfully belongs to Abby and me."

Dodd gave a negative shake of his head. "I told you earlier, if you wish to challenge the contract in court, you will have to wait until the circuit judge arrives."

"Yes, and you also said he wouldn't be here until spring!"

"Exactly," was Dodd's smug reply. "If you wish to file a challenge over the ownership of the store, you will have to do it in an actual court of law."

Laura fumed. "And how do I and my daughter survive until spring?"

"Our immediate concern is about this assault charge, Mrs. Morrison," Dodd answered back. "You are hereby fined ten dollars or ten days of community service. If you wish to contest my verdict, you can do so in an actual court of law."

Laura glared at him. "Meaning next spring!"

Dodd didn't smile with his lips, but there was a sneer imbedded within the depths of his eyes. "Yes, Mrs. Morrison"—his voice was patronizing—"again you are exactly right."

Laura glanced over at Abby and her defiance melted away. "What about my daughter?" she murmured in defeat. "How am I supposed to care for her if I'm locked away in a storage shed at nights and doing community service all day?"

"If you can't pay the fine, we will find someone to look after the child until your debt to society is paid. I believe one of the miner's wives would be willing to take her in for a short while."

Laura clenched her fists until the knuckles turned white. Her teeth were firmly set in an effort to suppress her rage. She bore into Dodd with hot, smoldering eyes, but her good sense overruled her fury. In her present situation anger did no good. In fact, it was her momentary loss of restraint that had gotten her into this mess.

"I—I can't pay the money," she admitted softly.

"There might be an option available to the lady," Flynn interjected.

Dodd averted his attention to him and waited expectantly.

"Uh, I spoke to Rudy and his wife," Flynn informed Dodd, "after they gave me their statements. They said they might be willing to settle this without causing a lot of trouble."

From his place at the corner of the room, Konn noticed a sedate expression enter Dodd's features. He had been expecting this.

"Did they offer up a suggestion, marshal?" the mock judge asked, keeping a straight face.

"Mr. Copton said he didn't want the lady to be stranded here in Lonesome Creek. He offered to drop the charges if Mrs. Morrison would agree to leave town."

"You don't say," Dodd showed some enthusiasm.

"He also said they would provide the lady and her daughter with enough money to purchase stage fare as far as Denver and kick in a few dollars extra to tide her over until she could settle in with relatives or friends." Flynn's distaste over the situation entered his expression. "Claimed he didn't wish for the lady to have any hard feelings."

Dodd smiled appreciatively. "Well, that sounds like the perfect solution. What do you say, Mrs. Morrison?"

Laura contained her wrath, but there was no give in her posture. "I'd say you're a willing partner in this fraud!" she declared. "Rudy is out to steal my store and you are helping him do it!"

The satisfied look disappeared from Dodd's face. He thrust out his jaw, pointed a pudgy finger at her, and took on a harsh tone. "I suggest you stop accusing everyone of being complicit in a trumped-up conspiracy to steal your store, Mrs. Morrison." He glowered at her. "You had best concern yourself with your present situation. If you refuse Mr. Copton's generous offer, then you must pay the fine. If you don't wish to do either, you will have to work off the debt by doing ten days of community service!"

Konn glanced at Abby. The little girl was close to tears. She didn't understand everything going on, but she was upset at seeing her mother in trouble. He hated the pained expression on her angelic face. Plus, while Laura might have actually hit Mrs. Copton, it seemed obvious the woman had deserved it.

"I'll settle the lady's fine," Konn spoke up, rising to his feet.

A dark frown rushed to cloud Dodd's face. "Mr. Konniger, this is of no concern to you. The matter is—"

"Yeah, I know," Konn silenced his objection abruptly. "You and Copton probably worked real hard on this together so he could steal this lady's store legally. I'm sure you would rather I not interfere."

His accusation caused Dodd's hackles to rise. "I'm acting judge here in Lonesome Creek, Konniger. You can't come in here and accuse me of—"

"*Acting* judge is what you are for now, Dodd," Konn cut him off. "I reckon we'll get to the bottom of your involvement in this here double-cross once the *real* judge comes to town."

Dodd's face colored to sunburn red, and dark, snake-like veins stood out against his forehead. However, he chose not to reply to Konn's accusation. Instead, he remained silent while Konn dug into his pocket and removed several coins. He picked out a gold eagle and tossed it on his desktop.

"There's the ten dollars, Dodd. The lady's debt is square."

Dodd grumbled under his breath and regarded him with a hard stare. "I wouldn't linger about town for any length of time if I were you, Mr. Konniger," he said, issuing a warning. "I dare say a man like you is prone to get into trouble."

"Don't you lose any sleep worrying about it," Konn replied. "I don't aim to put down roots here. Soon as I gather a few supplies, you'll see nothing of me but the tail end of my pack horse." Konn winked. "Be like looking in the mirror for you."

Dodd ground his teeth but again remained silent.

Flynn opened the door for Konn and stepped aside. Abby hurried over to join her mother, and the three of them went out to the street. The sun had dipped below the horizon, leaving only a glimmer of twilight. It would be dark in a matter of minutes.

"Mr. Konniger," Laura whispered contritely, "you shouldn't have . . ." But her voice was blocked by emotion. "I . . . I've made a complete mess of things."

"You trusted the wrong man," he told her. "That could happen to anyone."

"Ben, my father-in-law, was the one who trusted Rudy. My poor judgment was going along with their plan."

Konn sighed. "Yup, and Rudy's map got Ben kilt. Be thankful you and the muffin here came away with your lives."

"You are the one responsible for that," she reminded him. When he said nothing, she added, "And you have once again saved me, this time from a jail sentence. I . . . I don't know how I'll ever repay you for . . ."

"Where are you two going to sleep tonight?" He changed the subject.

Laura looked up and down the street. "I have no idea." Meekly she said, "I must confess we used the change from when you paid for the meal at Tubby's place to buy a bowl of stew and some lemonade. I have exactly three pennies to my name . . . and they belong to you."

"Having a little money wouldn't make much difference," Konn told her, dismissing the few cents she had spent. "There ain't a single room to be had in town."

"We had expected to stay at our store"—a bitterness entered Laura's voice—"except we are not welcome there."

"I 'spect punching one of the pretended owners in the mouth probably wasn't the best way to win an invite," he teased.

In spite of her present dilemma, Laura displayed a good-natured grin. "So you're saying it's my fault that those two under-handed, lowlife maggots haven't got a sense of humor?"

Konn chuckled at her pluck, then grew serious. He had already planned to spend the night under the stars. Now . . .

"I was about to collect my bedroll and find a place to camp."

Laura heaved a sigh at the unspoken invitation. "It seems I'm forever deeper in your debt, Mr. Konniger. I . . ." she floundered for lack of words.

"We can discuss your situation after we're settled in for the night."

The lady smiled her thanks and exhibited a cheerful laugh. "At least it's a clear night so we can sleep in the open. You might make campers of us pilgrims yet."

Chapter Seven

After picking up his stuff, Konn led the way back into the hills. They had walked for a hundred yards or so when he discovered a good spot. It was a sheltered cove, nestled between several trees, next to a steep hill that would block some of the chilly evening breeze. The place had obviously been used a number of times before. There was a circle of rocks marking an old firepit. A short log had been placed a couple of feet away to be used as a seat upon which to sit while cooking or tending to the fire.

Laura laid out the bedding, while Konn scrounged some dead branches and a couple of sagebrush limbs for kindling. Once there was a good fire going, Konn filled and propped the coffeepot so it would perk.

"You should eat something too," Laura remarked. "We had a big bowl of stew."

"Coffee and a couple hard rolls will hold me till breakfast," Konn answered back.

"Don't you ever get lonely?" Laura asked after a time. "I mean, out in the middle of the wilderness or staying in a cabin for weeks or even months at a time. Don't you miss company?"

"Up until my pa died, I wasn't alone. Since then I've wintered with Indians or other hunters on occasion. Can't say it was an improvement over being by myself."

"What about a wife and children?"

He laughed. "Who would want to marry a wandering hunter and trapper like me?"

She bore into him with an icy stare. "Don't you dare belittle the man who saved my life and the life of my child! You have a

58

good heart and"—she wilted enough to relax the hard gaze—
"and you are the most decent and honorable man I ever met." Her
tone became even gentler. "I think you hide behind the long hair
and bushy beard and use the smell of blood on your clothes and
your intimidating size to ward off any interested women."

"Never met one I cared to have an interest in," he said. Then
he added with a crooked smile, "Leastways, not until I met up
with you."

Instead of being offended or even surprised, Laura smiled
back at him. "See? You can be charming too."

He had no reply for that. He poured a cup of coffee and ate his
rolls while Laura took Abby for a nature walk and tucked her in
for the night. She sat next to her daughter for a time, waiting for
her to doze off. Once Abby was asleep, she moved quietly over
to sit down on the short log at Konn's side.

"So what about the contract Copton is flashing around?" Konn
got right to business. "That slick-talking magpie, Dodd, claims
to have seen it."

Laura threw a final glance at Abby—she hadn't stirred—
before answering. "I saw the paper too, but Ben did not sign any
contract, and I can prove it."

"If it's a fake, where did the legal paper come from?"

"I don't think Rudy or his wife have the expertise to write up
such an official-looking document. I'll bet they paid Dodd to
draw it up for them."

"Hard to believe such an upstanding sort as Dodd could be
mixed up with your partner." Konn grunted sarcastically. "Coyotes
do tend to run in packs."

"Yes, they do, and Elva Pratt is the leader of their pack."

"I reckon you can't trust a woman," Konn spoke automatically.
He immediately cursed himself, pinned under Laura's harsh
gaze.

"I happen to be a woman!" she said sharply.

Konn felt a rush of heat climb up into his face. Damn but he
hated the discomfort of being embarrassed!

"I didn't mean to mix you in with the herd, ma'am," he said,
attempting to squirm out from under her smoldering glare. "Truth

be told, I haven't known all that many women in my life, not regular women, at least."

The explanation didn't appease Laura. "For not knowing many of us regular women, that was a pretty sweeping statement."

Konn fought to regain his self-assurance, but his backbone had all the stiffness of warm butter. Holy Hanna! What kind of weakling was he to allow a wisp of a woman to cow and belittle him? He squirmed uncomfortably and cleared his throat, attempting to regain a minute fragment of self-assurance.

"Most women I've come across have a cruel nature to their ways," he explained. "They snicker and whisper to their friends when I'm around. Ain't a man I can't face head-on, but a woman?" He gave a lift and fall of his broad shoulders. "A woman can make me feel more worthless than a stray dog in about two seconds."

Laura simmered a few degrees. "I suppose I understand, but it's your fault too."

"My fault?"

"You should make a point of wearing clean clothes whenever you are going to visit a town. A shave would also make you more presentable."

"Man's face can freeze out in the mountains," he argued. "A beard is for warmth and protection."

"It gives you a wild man look, and that naturally puts off most women."

Konn didn't care for the direction of this conversation. "We were talking about you and your problems," he reminded her curtly. "What are you going to do now?"

The bluntness of his question caused Laura to lower her eyes. The feisty attitude she had displayed vanished. She had a world of confidence in a verbal exchange with him, but was insecure and without direction concerning her own predicament.

"I don't know," she admitted quietly.

"You could take Copton up on his offer to send you as far as Denver," Konn suggested. "Come spring, you could return and have your say in court."

"How would I know when the circuit judge was going to arrive so he could hear my case?" she asked. "And if I filed a claim in

Denver, it would be necessary for an official to serve papers concerning the case. I'm sure any judge would not be too happy about having to send a deputy all the way to Lonesome Creek to serve notice to the Coptons. And that's if I could get a judge to even look at the case. After all, women aren't allowed to own property in a good many states. Without Ben, I would be representing myself and might encounter other legal problems." She gave her head a negative shake. "No, I have to do it here, right here, so the judge will consider nothing but the facts of ownership."

"How are you going to make it through the winter?" he asked. "There are no decent jobs to be had. You don't even have a place to stay."

Laura shrugged. "I don't know. I've got to be strong." She sighed deeply. "I have to get back some of my investment, or Abby and I won't be able to live. The store was to be our future."

Konn remained in silence, staring at the burning chips of wood in the fire. He could compare his life to a piece of tender within the flames. His youth had been devoured like the outer bark, and the heat now burned near the core, consuming the precious years of his adulthood. Once his youthful energy was gone, only the charred residue of growing old would remain. His life was without purpose or fulfillment.

He reputed that thought at once. He had saved a woman and her child from probable enslavement or death. However, it would be a bitter victory if Laura lost everything that rightfully belonged to her.

"I'd be obliged if you'd allow me to help you through the winter," he commented on impulse.

Laura started from his unexpected suggestion. "Do what?"

A jolt of reality penetrated Konn's witless declaration and an inner voice screamed, *Hey, meathead! This is your common sense speaking! What the hell is your big mouth doing, tossing out an idea like that without checking with me first!*

He discovered Laura staring at him with wide-eyed astonishment. He, meanwhile, sought desperately to recover a trace of rationale from his complete lack of forethought.

"Uh, I . . ."—he paused to clear his throat—"that is . . ."

Laura lowered her head demurely and said something. Konn gaped in complete puzzlement, unable to muster enough willpower to hear her softly spoken words. A dense fog encased his mind, clouding all lucid thoughts within a nebulous cloud. He focused on Laura's mouth, trying hard to pick up what she was saying.

Dad-gum! It sure was a lovely formed mouth. It seemed that, with each word she uttered, her lips parted and closed to form the slightest hint of a pucker. He gawked uncontrollably as she paused to trace her pert tongue along her lips to moisten them.

Konn felt lightheaded, his gut twisted about like a stepped-on snake and his senses assailed by a furtive craving he had never before experienced. His mind's eye conjured up the image of Laura at the stream, the wet clothing clinging to and outlining her petite figure, poised like a fabulous work of art. Sitting beside him was the most desirable woman he had ever known. He clenched his fists at his sides, fearful the intense yearning would cause him to reach out, grab the woman, and yank her into his arms.

Konn grit his teeth and commanded his faculties to work. It took a supreme effort, but he managed to finally understand what Laura was saying.

"You're a very sweet man, Mr. Konniger," she said, purring the words warmly, "but I don't think we could . . ."

She stopped speaking and the smile faded. Konn swung his head about, thinking there must be an intruder or wild animal nearby. He saw nothing. Whirling back to look at Laura, he discovered the prowler was not a person or animal, but an idea, a sneaky, backdoor kind of culprit that had entered Laura's mind.

"There might be a way . . ." She baited the word like a fish-hook.

Not recognizing danger, because it had beautiful brown eyes that sparkled brightly in the firelight, Konn uttered a wholly gullible response.

"What way?"

Laura looked directly at him. Konn met her gaze and suddenly understood what a deer must feel when it glanced up to discover that it was locked in a hunter's sights. This was a different woman than the one he had saved from Two Bears. That gal had been frightened and tearful, worried about her daughter, mourning the loss of her father-in-law. This woman was filled with doggedness and purpose . . . a durned scary combination.

Konn held his breath, anxious yet hesitant, to learn what was coming. Laura explained her idea, and it did nothing to ease his dread.

"You want us to do what?" he asked, confident he had not heard correctly.

She summed it up in one short sentence. "We would have to be careful, but it could work."

The words rattled about in his head like so many loose rocks in a coffeepot. He waited for her to laugh at the absurdity of the notion, ready to join in with a hearty guffaw of his own. Laura certainly had a keen sense of humor.

When she continued to maintain complete sincerity, he displayed a wolfish grin. "Yeah, right, you, Abby, and me, holed up like bandits on the run."

"It would be necessary to keep it a secret for the plan to work," she said, continuing with the proposition. "Come spring, once the court settles the charge against Rudy, it won't matter if someone finds out where we spent the winter."

Konn was no longer grinning. "Danged if you don't sound serious!" he wailed. "That's the most loco scheme I ever heard!"

Laura leaned away from him as if the sting of his words hurt her physically. Her head moved from side to side incomprehensively.

"You offered to help."

"Help, yes!" he shot back. "But I was thinking of loaning you some money or something. I didn't offer to be hobbled and tethered with a pair of females in a one-room cabin for the entire winter."

She bridled. "I don't see that it would be such a big problem. We've got along well enough during our time together, and Abby really likes you."

"Well, I ain't saying—"

"Haven't you ever thought about living with . . . being married and having children?"

Konn was trapped. "I guess so, maybe a squaw some day, but I've never thought about living under the same roof with a proper lady."

"Did you or did you not offer to help?"

He felt a sudden empathy with a muskrat caught in a trap. "Well, kind of," he squirmed, but was unable to free himself from the tangled web. "But I didn't . . ."

"And you are a man of your word, are you not?"

"Sure I am, but . . ."

"Don't you see?" She cut him off a second time. "It's the perfect solution. I can cook and keep house for you. I can also help with your furs and hides. When spring comes and the judge makes his visit, we can present my argument in court. Once I win back my store, I'll pay you for your trouble and we will be out of your life. You'll be free to continue with your hunting or trapping, whatever you want to do."

Konn had heard stories about how women had a peculiar way of thinking. This idea had all the earmarks of female logic, and it was mighty unsettling. Worst of all, the more Laura talked, the more it seemed to make sense.

"Dodd and Copton might be crooks, but they ain't complete fools." Konn tried to slow her runaway team. "They will sure enough know the reason why you didn't leave the country."

"That's why we have to keep our staying with you a secret."

Konn had been surrounded by unfriendly Indians a time or two, but never had he felt more in peril. His offer to help a lady and her waif had transformed into an invite where he would have them for the entire winter. And then what? She claimed it was only until she got her store, but what if she didn't win her case? How could he continue a wandering nomad life and also care for a mother and child?

Even as those thoughts were circling the wagon of his brain, there was an equally important fact about which he had a genuine concern. Sitting next to Laura—she was the most beautiful and desirable female he had ever been this close to—it took all of his willpower to control the impulse to reach out, draw her into his arms and kiss her inviting lips. How could he be around

such an extraordinary woman for several months and not want to
do more than just look at her?

Laura's enthusiasm was daunted by his uncertainty. She
reached over and placed her hand on Konn's arm.

"I'm sorry," she murmured, an apologetic smile curling her
lips. Her eyes met his, twin pools which shimmered in the flicker
of the dying campfire. A man could drown his every care or
worry in such deep and inviting pools. "I didn't intend to get so
carried away. I suppose it was a silly idea."

Konn knew he should say something, but what? A word of en-
couragement would be like putting a noose around his own neck.
He wanted to help the lady and her little girl, but spend an entire
winter with them? It would drive him mad.

The silence of the moment saved them both. Konn's keenly at-
tuned sense of hearing detected the sound of a soft step crushing
a dry leaf underfoot. With the swipe of the back of his arm, he hit
Laura across her chest, knocking her off the log. She squealed
with surprise when she hit the ground, while he sprang up and
dove for his nearby rifle.

An arrow thudded into the dirt inches from his chest and a second swished past his head. Laura started to right herself, shocked
by the sudden and unexpected swat, until she saw three Cheyenne
Indians come racing out from the trees.

"Konn!" she gasped, ducking down behind the log. "Look out!"

The warning was both too late and wholly unnecessary. Konn
had hold of his rifle but didn't have time to lever a bullet into the
chamber. He leapt to his feet to meet the charge of the Cheyenne
Indians, propelling the rifle in an arc. The front attacking Indian
fighter threw up his arms for protection, but the barrel got past
his efforts and struck him a glancing blow on the top of his head.
It was a lucky swing for Konn, as the clout not only stopped the
brave dead in his tracks, but caused him to stumble blindly into
the path of the second Indian Warrior. The two of them went
down in a tangle of arms and legs.

Before either man could recover, Konn used the butt of his gun
to ram the second one in the temple. He spun about and landed
on the ground, temporarily out of the fight. Konn backed away to

gain an instant of time as the third Cheyenne Indian flew at him. Two Bears! The Cheyenne chief had his killing knife at shoulder level. A snarl was on his lips and his face was contorted into a mask of hate. Konn swung his rifle barrel at him, and he had to apply the brakes or get a mouthful of iron.

Fortunately, the three attackers had not wanted to alert anyone in town, so the idea had been to kill Konn silently. Had they come in shooting, Konn would already be dead. Two Bears batted away the rifle barrel with his left hand and lunged with his knife hand, trying to take out Konn's eye.

Konn whipped the rifle back smartly, blocked the blade with the stock of his gun, and drove forward, slamming his shoulder against the chief's chest. The force knocked the chief off balance and sent him reeling backward.

The other two braves shook off being struck with his rifle and were back on their feet. They moved in quickly for the kill, knowing Konn didn't yet have a round in the chamber. Konn was a large, powerful man, but he was no match for three Indian warriors at one time. Laura knew her life depended upon his staying alive too. She came up from behind the log and jumped on the back of the warrior Konn had hit on top of the head. She wrapped her legs around him and hooked an arm under his jaw, attempting to throttle him.

Her attack was distraction enough that it caused the other warrior to look in Laura's direction. The minute pause allowed Konn to wield his rifle butt around, horizontal to the ground, and club him squarely alongside his head. He dropped like a felled hog.

"You die!" Two Bears snarled, cursing at Konn, coming forward with his knife ready again.

The third brave batted blindly at Laura and managed to shake her loose. As she landed on the ground, Konn took a precious half-second to jack a round into the chamber of his rifle. The action cost him dearly in reaction time. Before he could bring the rifle up for a shot, Two Bears drew back and threw his knife.

Konn felt a sudden, penetrating stab to his left side. He set his teeth against the incredible pain, kept his feet planted firmly, and fired his gun.

The bullet hit Two Bears in the chest. He took a backward step, slapped a hand over the entrance wound, and sank down to his knees. The malevolent expression on his face twisted into a mixture of surprise and loathing. He managed a final glare, uttered a snarl of defiance, then pitched forward and landed facedown on the ground.

The knife sticking deep into the left side of his chest made it difficult to work the lever on the rifle, but Konn managed to cock it a second time. He knew the shock and pain would soon make it impossible to focus, so he had to act quickly. The brave still on his feet would be on him in an instant.

To Konn's surprise, that brave ignored him and turned toward Laura. He yanked his knife free, lifted it for a death strike, and rushed at her.

With a swift rotation of his body, Konn leveled the barrel of his weapon and fired a second time. The shock waves ignited a blinding agony from the kick of the rifle, but the bullet carried with it a quick trip for one to the Happy Hunting Grounds. The brave staggered from the slug's impact, still three feet from Laura. He stubbornly managed one more step before he collapsed. A groan escaped his lips as he lay facedown, knife still clutched in his hand.

From her bed, Abby was screaming for her mother. Laura picked herself up from the ground, dazed, but able to crawl over to her daughter's side. The final warrior was still groggy from the vicious clout from Konn's rifle butt. He came to his knees and started to reach for his knife.

Konn jacked a third round into the chamber and trained the rifle on the warrior's chest. The young brave immediately moved his hands out to his side, showing he lacked both a weapon and hostile intent.

Battling the intense pain that spread throughout his chest and a swirling blackness that threatened to block his vision, Konn kept the rifle steady.

"What's it going to be?" he asked the last man. "Make your choice."

"Walks Tall say no more fight," the Indian brave said in English. "Hunter man have victory this day, you bet."

"And what about tomorrow or the next day?"

Walks Tall held up a hand and gave a signal. Another warrior came out from the darkness. He carried a rifle in one hand, but it was not ready for use, as he was leading four horses.

"No more fight," Walks Tall repeated. "I take Two Bears home."

"How do I know you won't come back?" Konn asked.

The brave shook his head. "No more fight. Two Bears say kill hunter man and white woman. Two Bears dead. No more listen to his words."

Konn's vision blurred and he knew he couldn't stay on his feet much longer. He had a gut feeling Walks Tall was telling the truth and lowered the barrel of the gun a few inches.

"Go then, Walks Tall," he ordered. "Take your chief home and don't come back."

"I go," the Indian said decisively. "We fight no more, hunter man."

Konn remained upright, his strength drained, hardly able to keep from dropping his rifle. He willed his body to stand and watch while Walks Tall and the other brave loaded the dead men on the backs of their mounts. Without another word or even a look in his direction, the Cheyenne Indians swung up onto their ponies and were quickly lost to the darkness.

Laura had remained with Abby to quiet and comfort her. She didn't approach Konn until the warriors were out of sight. When she came up to him she gasped, seeing a knife sticking in the flesh a couple inches below his shoulder, and her eyes grew wide.

"Konn!" Laura cried. "You're hurt!"

He wished for the vigor to smile at her and say something clever, like "Really? I hadn't noticed," but he had exhausted the last bit of his strength. He took a final glance at the darkness to confirm the Indian warriors were gone and then allowed the black void to sweep over him. Reason and awareness dimmed, his knees folded, and he went down. Through the fog he heard the shouts of several men from town.

"The shooting came from over this-a-way!" one called. "I see the campfire!"

"Bob said he seen them going through the trees!" a second man shouted. "Several Injuns riding for hell and gone just now!"

"Keep your guns handy, boys!" another voice warned. "Might be more of them red devils around."

The voices grew distant and faint. The last words to echo in his head were Laura's calling out. "Here! We're over here!"

Chapter Eight

Konn struggled from within a tar-black abyss, haunted by bits of dreams and an urgency to awaken his fog-encased brain. The lids of his eyes felt rusted shut, like an iron gate too-long closed, but he battled and persevered until he managed to force them open. He was greeted by a piercing light, forced to blink against the tears which immediately flooded his eyes. It took a few moments before he began to focus.

He discovered a ceiling overhead, thick crossbeams and wide wooden planks, which had been slathered with a coat of stain, probably an attempt to brighten the room. A single window provided daylight, and he was prone in someone's bed. He made an effort to sit up, and a stab of pain shot through his entire left side. The jolt convinced him that sitting was not a good idea, and he immediately relaxed.

"It sounded as if a bear was stirring from hibernation in here," a familiar voice spoke up.

Konn looked to the doorway and saw Flynn standing there. He had a bowl in one hand and a mug of beer in the other. A half-grin was etched into his face.

"How do you like my bed?" he asked. "Bet it's been a spell since you slept on a mattress of anything other than pine boughs."

"Mattress, is it?" Konn replied. "I wondered why my back hurt worse than the ache from the knife wound."

Flynn chuckled. "You go bad-mouthing my bunk, I'll sit down and eat the chili con carne and drink the beer I brought up here for you."

"Like I said," Konn made a contrite reversal, "most comfortable bed I've ever slept on."

"You don't lie worth a damn but I suspect you earned a meal. The lady said you killed Two Bears."

"Don't suppose you have a quarter of venison or side of beef to go along with the chili?" Konn queried. "I feel hungry enough to eat a half-grown bull elk."

"If I can work it into my schedule, I'll see if I can find a cow or sick old nag to butcher for your next meal," Flynn quipped as he crossed over to the bed. He set the items down on the night-stand and helped lift Konn enough to prop a couple of pillows behind him. Once Konn was upright, Flynn handed him the bowl.

"How did I get here?" Konn asked. "Last thing I remember was watching Walks Tall leave our camp."

"Tall chore, killing Two Bears and another of his braves, then running off another two Indians."

"The lady helped," Konn said between bites. "She jumped on the back of one of the warriors so I could get my rifle into play."

"I saw the bruise on the side of her face where she got hit."

Konn paused from his eating. "She all right?"

"Shook it off like a trouper," Flynn replied. "That little lady has some grit."

"Bounced back from the attack that killed her father-in-law in a matter of hours too," Konn told him. "Makes me feel weak as a newborn lamb for passing out from a little pinprick."

"That pinprick went in about three inches deep, fella. A skosh more to the right and you would have been planted in the local bone yard, instead of being all comfy and cozy here in my room."

"What about Mrs. Morrison and her little girl? Where are they at?"

"The men from two rooms down the hall were nice enough to double up so she could have a room for a couple days. Your two pilgrim orphans won't be out on the street until you're up and around to see to their disposition." He grinned. "See? There are still a few gentlemen here in town."

"I'm obliged to you and to them."

"And what about when you are back on your feet?" Flynn asked. "What's going to happen to the lady and her kid?"

"She's a smart gal," Konn said. "I expect she'll find a way to get by."

Flynn pulled a chair over to the bed and sat down. Konn could tell the man had something on his mind.

"What is it?" he queried between mouthfuls.

"No less than six men have approached your lady friend." He lifted his shoulder in a shrug. "I kind of done the same."

"You done what?" Konn demanded harshly. "What the devil are you talking about?"

"The lady is a widow," Flynn stated. "The guys and I were"—he displayed a sheepish look—"well, we were trying to get a feel for what her frame of mind was, you know?"

"No, I ain't got a clue. What about her frame of mind?"

"Whether or not she is available!" he blurted out. "We were curious if she might be open to a courtship, that sort of thing."

Konn did not respond, but it suddenly felt as if he had swallowed a dust devil and it was hell-bent on escaping right through the walls of his chest.

Flynn hurried to continue. "Thing is, she said she wasn't interested because she already had a man lined up back in Kansas. He is waiting for her to contact him once she gets things squared away here." He sighed. "Broke a few hearts with them words, she sure enough did."

The memory of his last conversation with the woman came flooding back. It exploded in his brain like a flash of lightning in a bottle. She had suggested living with him till spring! But why would she propose something like that if she had some dandy waiting for her back home?

"Did she say anything about her betrothed to you?" Flynn asked.

"Uh, well," he muttered, taking another spoonful of chili, "if she did, I wasn't paying attention. That woman could talk the ear off a cornstalk."

Flynn showed a perplexed expression. "I'm just saying, if she has a guy, why not return to him instead of coming here or fighting over the store?"

"How the hell do I know, Flynn?" Konn snapped at him. "I ain't a newspaper man trying to get her life story. I took her away from Two Bears. That's my only investment in her and the tyke."

The man held out both hands, palms forward, to ward off Konn's defensive outburst. "Hold your temper, Konn, I didn't mean nuthen," he said quickly. "You saved the lady's life and spent a couple days with her. I figured she might have told you her plans. That's all I was thinking." With a trace of ire himself, he continued, "Plus, you did pay her fine for hitting Mrs. Copton. It seems the woman sure owes you something, even if it's only an explanation."

"You've got a point, Flynn," Konn admitted. "I didn't mean to skin your hide."

"No offense taken," the man said, back to smiling again. "And I passed the word around town about her being spoken-for so other would-be Romeos won't come around and bother her."

Konn gave a nod of approval and shoveled in another spoon of chili. It was not very filling, but it helped to be doing something besides talking. Dagnabit, he hated foolish chit-chat, especially talk that set off a raging inferno inside of his chest. He couldn't define the feeling—it was a burning fury he had never felt before—yet he knew the cause. Laura Morrison!

"The lady has been asking after you," Flynn remarked. "I promised to let her know as soon as you were awake."

Konn scooped out the last bite of chili and downed the beer in about four swallows. He passed the empty containers to Flynn and wiped his mouth with the back of his hand.

"I'm obliged to you for the hospitality, Flynn. If I can pay you something for your trouble?"

Flynn shook his head. "Two Bears was going to keep on killing people until he was stopped. You done stopped him, that's thanks enough."

"I'll be up to moving out by tomorrow," Konn promised. "One more night's sleep ought to have me as fit as a new saddle."

"If you manage to get on your feet tomorrow with the help of me and three other strong men, I'll be surprised."

Konn grunted. "It's not that I don't appreciate it, Flynn. I'm just not in the habit of lying around and doing nothing."

"Maybe so, but I'll wager you won't want to be arm wrestling any grizzly bears for a spell either."

"Probably not."

"I'll tell the lady you are awake."

"Hand me my pants first."

Flynn frowned. "You're not getting dressed. You've got the blanket covering you."

"I only want my pants, okay?"

Flynn passed him his bundle of clothes. "Those things need washing something fierce. I've had two skunks come snooping about, thinking one of their females was in season and hiding in my room."

Konn grinned. "Maybe they come to visit because you left your boots by the door, and they figured one of their litter had been left behind at one time or another."

Flynn grunted. "You're getting better by the minute, Konn. I'll tell the lady she can visit."

"Thanks, Flynn . . . for everything."

Not five minutes later there came a soft tap at the door followed by, "Mr. Konniger, are you awake?"

"Come ahead," he said.

Laura peeked inside before she entered the room. It was the first time Konn had seen her with her hair brushed out and loose about her shoulders. It appeared she had used a bit of rouge to hide the bruise on one cheek, and her dress, though tattered and patched, was clean and neat.

"I suspected you were a pretty woman," Konn spoke without thinking, "but you're more like a vision from heaven."

The flattery took Laura by surprise. It caused an immediate flush to color her cheeks, but she met his gaze and smiled.

"Mr. Flynn provided us with a bath and one of the women who . . ."—she hesitated, searching for the right word—"who works downstairs—her name is Alice. She was kind enough to lend us a hair brush. I believe I lost enough hair to stuff a pillow from the tangles, and Abby about cried from all the tugging and pulling."

"Tough being a refined lady, that's a fact."

Laura continued to smile. "And you look better than I had expected. When the men from town carried you away from our camp, there was no color to your skin. I . . . I thought you might die."

"Take more than a little poke with a knife to kill me."

She moved closer until she was next to the bed. "I saw the size of that Indian's knife," she said. "You're lucky to be alive."

"Flynn said some of the guys have been making a nuisance of themselves," he said, watching for her reaction.

"Nothing serious," she dismissed his concern. "Like most mining communities, there are a lot of lonely, unmarried men in town."

"I don't remember us having anything settled before Two Bears showed up," he said. "Have you decided on a plan?"

Laura ducked her head as if ashamed. "I . . . I don't know," she murmured softly. "I mean, unless you are willing to go along with my idea about us staying with you through the winter."

"I can't say I feel all that comfortable with the idea."

"It was a silly suggestion," she said quietly. "I was desperate when I—"

"However," Konn interrupted her, "there are a few things we need to sort out."

Laura lifted her head in anticipation. "I'm listening."

Her beguiling eyes were quicksand for his heart. He had no idea as to when he had become such a complete fool, but if Laura asked him to give up an arm for her, his only question would be "which one?" Masking his gaze before she could read his sappy weakness, he turned his attention to the plan.

"If you want to get away with this scheme, Mrs. Morrison, you're going to have to go back to Copton's store and take the traveling money they offered."

"I couldn't do that!"

Konn gave her a hard look. "You have to make them believe you've left town on your own or else the rest of your plan is wasted effort. How are you going to travel with no money? They will know you are up to something."

"I—I . . ."

"It's the only way, ma'am," he avowed. "If they find out you intend to winter with me, they will know you are sticking around to fight for your store. It could give them time to hire some joker to back their story. One paid liar saying they witnessed the agreement between your father-in-law and the Copton fellow, and it won't matter how much evidence you have on your side."

Laura squirmed under his gaze. "Yes, I understand what you're saying."

He reached into the pocket of his pants, removed his supply money and separated several bills.

"Here," he said, "once you have whatever money Copton gives you, take it and this here cash and buy whatever you require for the time being. Remember, it has to look as if you are buying what you need and are going to catch the stage at the nearest way station. Everything else you buy is for the cabin, so you be sure to let people know you are buying supplies for me."

"But I can't—"

He cut her off again. "Buy yourself and the muffin new clothes, coats and shoes, plus whatever personal type dainties a woman and little girl need—hair brush, unmentionables, toiletries, and such. It won't be suspicious to anyone 'cause you're starting out with nothing. Any frills or such you two need you'll have to buy here, because there isn't a blessed thing of value at the cabin." He gave a tip of his head. "I'm not altogether sure the place will still be standing. Like I told you before, I haven't been back there for a couple years."

"What if Rudy won't give us any money?" she asked. "It seems terribly wrong to use any of your funds, Mr. Konniger, after all you've done for us."

Konn reached out with his right hand and caught hold of Laura's wrist. He pulled her close enough so, with limited use of his injured side, he was able to stick the money in her hand. For a moment she stood there, saying nothing. Then her eyes misted and she blinked against a rush of tears.

"I—I don't know what to say."

"I would be buying supplies even if you were actually leaving," he said. "Once this affair is settled and you get your store returned by the circuit judge, you can pay me back whatever you spend for yourself. That ought to be fair enough."

Konn figured Laura to be the heartiest white woman he had ever known, yet she broke down and began to cry!

What did I do now? he wondered. *I thought my going along with her plan would make her happy!*

Laura sank down on her knees and placed her head on his chest. The flood of emotion totally confounded Konn. He was helpless to console her because he didn't know what he had done wrong. In a futile gesture of compassion and comfort, he patted her on the back. The act made him feel even more stupid and inadequate. He might as well have been patting Hammerhead after a hard ride. How the devil did a man deal with a weeping woman?

Thankfully, Laura gathered her aplomb after a short time. She lifted her head and used the backs of her knuckles to wipe away the tears that had wet her cheeks.

"I'm sorry," she whispered hoarsely. "I don't know where that came from."

"You've been through quite an ordeal," Konn said, to excuse her emotional eruption. "I'm more than a little amazed at the way you've handled yourself these past few days."

"I relied on my husband until he died," she explained timorously. "Next I turned to Ben and was able to use his strength for comfort and support. Now he is dead too."

"Like I said, you've had a tough time of it lately."

"Yes, but don't you see?" she said, gazing into his eyes, mesmerizing him with twin tranquil pools of untapped delight. "I attached myself to you like a lost puppy, trying to maintain my self-control through your goodness and strength. I've never really faced adversity on my own."

Konn wasn't sure what he was supposed to say but gave it a shot. "That there 'adverse city' thing can sure enough scramble your brain," he agreed.

"But it means I'm using you!" she declared. "Doesn't that bother you?"

"It's not using someone when he up and volunteers, Mrs. Morrison, and everyone needs someone they can rely on."

"What about you?"

Konn was caught with his brain asleep. "Me?"

"We are relying on you, but who do you rely on?"

"Up until he passed, I suppose my pa was the one I looked to for advice and help. Living the lonely life of a hunter, I tend to count more on myself than most. It ain't the same thing with civilized folks."

"I wouldn't want you to think that I . . ."

"Whoa!" Konn didn't let her finish. He put forth a serious expression. "I don't figure you've got a genuine dishonest bone in your whole body, ma'am. I know you want to take care of yourself and Abby, but I don't for a minute think you would do me dirt to accomplish your goal. If staying with me for the winter is the only solution to the problem, I reckon I can tolerate the company."

Laura rose up from her kneeling position and leaned over the bed, her face inches from his own. She hesitated for the briefest moment then kissed Konn lightly on the lips. She pulled back at once and smiled.

"It would have been more proper to kiss you on the cheek, but you've too many whiskers."

Konn was both shocked and pleased at the warm touch of her lips. He summoned forth a smile and teased, "It's about time this here beard come in handy for something besides the cold."

Either his words or her bold action caused a pink hue to again enter her cheeks. "Yes, well"—she diverted her gaze demurely—"I wouldn't want you to think I was trying to coerce you with my wiles."

"You go ahead and curse all you want."

Laura laughed and took a breath that lifted her carriage nicely. Konn had to kick himself squarely in the self-control to keep his eyes on the woman's face.

"I wonder if Mr. Flynn would be my liaison."

"Your what?"

She showed him a sheepish grin. "I believe I'll ask him if he would kindly collect whatever money Rudy and Elva are willing to part with. I wouldn't want to lose my temper again and do something . . . unladylike."

Konn grinned. "Yeah, be best if you didn't punch one of them in the mouth a second time. You might earn yourself a bad reputation."

"I also have to send a letter off to Kansas. I wonder how I can manage to keep the reply confidential."

Konn felt a lead weight settle in his stomach. There *was* a man in her life. She probably wanted to let him know her plan. The idea caused a trace of ire. What kind of man let his sweetheart wander off several hundred miles and nearly get herself and her daughter killed? And now, when she really needed someone, he would sit and wait for her to send word about when he should come to be with her?

He dismissed the train of thought, but he could not keep a sharpness from entering his tone of voice. "I reckon I can handle your secret letter."

Laura didn't seem to notice the change. "Really?"

"I've had more than one postmaster hold mail for me. Never knew when I would be around again, you know?"

"How will that help?"

"You have your reply letter sent with my name on it instead of your own. I can pick it up for you and no one will be the wiser."

"That's a good idea."

"And I can talk to Flynn about visiting the store if you want."

Laura was back to her old self, steadfast, confident, and in control. Her lips lifted at the corners to allow another of her bewitching smiles, and her voice was that of a mother. "No, I'll speak to him. You stay right here in bed and get rested up." She sighed. "I don't wish to impose on the charity of the men who gave up their room for Abby and I any longer than necessary. You need to get enough rest to mend your wound, Mr. Konniger."

Not knowing what else to say, he merely nodded his head.

Laura pivoted about and left the room to find Flynn. When the door closed, Konn felt a vast emptiness invade the walls of his chest. He had never been in love, but he had heard stories about how it could raise a man's spirit to the clouds or crush him like being buried in an avalanche. He feared his experience with love would be the latter.

Chapter Nine

Crow was about to enter Copton's store when he spied Flynn at the counter. He and Rudy appeared to be having a heated but hushed argument. Crow took a step to the side and kept watch through the window.

Shortly, Rudy opened his cash drawer and dug out a wad of bills. He reluctantly passed the money to Flynn and the bartender stuck it in his pocket.

"I'll tell the lady you gave as much as you could," he heard Flynn say, as he turned for the exit. "The little extra will help her get by until she can find work and a place to live."

"Yeah," Rudy grumbled. "Give her my best."

As Crow hurried around the corner of the building he overheard Elva's shrill voice. "Rudy! You idiot! You completely cleaned out the cash drawer! What were you thinking?"

Rudy started to reply, but she cut him off at the knees. "How much did you give him?" she cried. "We decided fifteen dollars was enough to get her as far as Denver! We had twice that in the drawer. How much more did you give him?"

Flynn was smiling as he walked down the street. Crow could not help but laugh too. He heard a saying once about how to tell when a man was henpecked—he had to wash his own aprons! Rudy was likely doing that already, and he and Elva were still on their honeymoon!

Crow waited in the alleyway until Flynn was well down the street. No need having anyone thinking he had a relationship with Rudy. It was better if he appeared to be an ordinary customer. Fewer questions that way.

Elva had stopped her raving by the time Crow entered the store through the front door. He paused to look around. Elva looked in his direction, gave him a distasteful glance, and stuck her nose in the air. He deliberately smiled his amusement at her swollen lip—the action causing an immediate scowl. He was impressed; the Morrison woman packed a pretty good punch.

Crow spied Rudy. He had moved to the back of the store and was working next to the storage room. His head was hanging like a scolded pup, but he looked up as Crow approached.

"What's the word on the hunter?" Crow asked the storekeeper. "I only got back in town a few minutes ago. Saw Flynn leaving your store, so I waited for him to leave before I came in."

"Flynn was picking up traveling money for Mrs. Morrison."

"Hey, that's good news!"

"And it sounds as if the hunter will recover," Rudy continued. "Skinny Bob and Spanish stopped by this morning. They had a drink or two at the saloon and overheard Flynn telling a customer the trapper was already wanting to get out of bed."

"I figured him to be a tough hombre. Man takes on four Indians at one time?" He snorted. "Don't remember hearing about anyone doing that before . . . not living to tell about it, anyway."

"Konniger never was a part of our plan. He about ruined everything for us. If you hadn't gotten word to me ahead of time that the woman was coming, we could have had a real problem on our hands."

Crow showed a smirk. "From Elva's puffed-up lip, it appears the Morrison woman didn't approve of your get-rich-quick scheme."

"Without your warning, she would have taken over half the store!" He lowered his voice. "Elva would have made my life unbearable."

"She's a beautiful woman, but does seem a little headstrong," Crow said.

"General Grant's Army would still be fighting against the Confederacy if my wife had taken up a gun for the South," Rudy responded.

Crow grinned at his candid humor, then turned to other business matters. "It took me all night to catch up with Walks Tall. He said that with Two Bears dead, there would be no more help from the Indians concerning Konniger or the woman. He claimed our former deal was with Two Bears, not the tribe itself."

"Seems like everyone has the scruples of a politician anymore," Rudy complained. "No mention of a refund for not doing the job we paid them to do, I suppose?"

"They did kill Ben Morrison," Crow pointed out. "And Two Bears died trying to complete the chore. Walks Tall figures his death was payment enough, and it ended the arrangement."

Rudy heaved a sigh. "The Indian attack did accomplish enough to put the store in my hands. I believe that will suffice."

"So we're done with Konniger and the woman?"

Rudy threw a look at Elva, but she was occupied at the counter accepting payment from a customer. Rudy spoke in a hushed voice. "We have managed to get a deed to the store. That will have to do."

Crow smiled his relief. "Then Mrs. Morrison is going to accept the contract between you and old Ben as binding?"

Rudy lifted one shoulder in a careless shrug. "It doesn't matter if she does or not. With Dodd on our side the store is legally ours. She accepted the money we offered so she could leave town. Flynn told me the hunter was going to take her as far as Dover Flats to catch the stage to Denver. Once she and her brat are gone, we can all breathe easy."

"That's it, then."

"Yes, even if Laura somehow manages to show up when the judge arrives, Dodd assured me the contract will hold up in court. She has no way of proving her father-in-law didn't sign the paper. The woman has no recourse but to give up and go home . . . or to wherever she has friends or relatives. The fight for ownership is as good as over."

"Well, I'll tell you the truth, Copton," Crow said solemnly. "I'll feel a whole lot better when she and Konniger leave town. And I don't care where they go."

"You still have a job to do," Rudy replied. "Walks Tall told you our arrangement was complete because Two Bears was dead, but what about down the line? Can we count on any business from him in the future?"

"The tribe will have to sort out a new war chief first, Copton. But I have a few other contacts who will likely be interested in what we have to offer. You just get the merchandise here, and I'll move it at a premium price."

Rudy displayed a grim smile. "It's already on order."

Konn made the decision to get up the next day, but he suffered considerable discomfort whenever he used his left arm. Each time any of the muscles would flex on his left side he nearly doubled in the middle. Pulling on his trousers and boots took the better part of an hour, doing all of the work with his right hand. When he finally managed to get himself dressed, he sat back down, too exhausted to leave the room. Changing his mind about going out just yet, he kicked off his boots and reclined back on top of the bed.

A short time later, Laura and Abby came to visit and show him their new store-bought clothes and other items they had purchased. The little girl did a pirouette so he could see her new outfit. When she smiled, her bright eyes shone like polished jewels.

"Do ya like my new dress, Mr. Kon'ger?" she asked.

"Durned if you ain't the prettiest gal I ever did see," he told her truthfully.

"I picked it out all by myself," she said proudly. Then with an exaggerated sigh she added, "They only had two what fit me."

"Not a lot of demand for dresses hereabouts," Laura affirmed. "I also had two choices and both were the same style, just different colors."

"Well, it's a real improvement over what you were wearing when we arrived."

Laura displayed a smile of agreement, but Konn still had a sore spot no simper could wipe away. Try as he might, he could not get Laura's mystery man out of his head. The all-important letter and what she had told Flynn about having a man waiting for her was like a drill bit boring a hole in his gut. However, he didn't wish to speak of such an intimate subject with Abby in the room. Before he could think of a way to approach the topic from a subtle angle, Laura was back to business.

"Now that Abby and I have taken care of ourselves, we should make a list of the supplies we're going to need," Laura said. "When you described the cabin, you said it was not much more than a shack. I packed your things from the campsite, and we're going to need a kettle for cooking and a pan for baking bread. Besides the supplies, we need more serving plates and utensils, plus bedding and a washtub."

"I commence to think one pack horse won't be enough," Konn commented dryly.

Laura laughed and a bright excitement shone in her eyes. "I made a point of checking, and they have most everything we need at Brown's Pharmaceutical. Before Rudy arrived it served as an all-purpose store. I also saw an early reader for Abby. It looked to be a used book, so I think we could buy it for a few cents. That way Abby could practice her reading, and I will work with her on her numbers. She must continue her schooling."

"Remember to pay separately for anything you buy for the muffin or yourself, because it must look as if it's for the two of you and your trip back home."

"I'm ready to make a list," Laura said. "How about you tell me what you think we'll need, and I'll add anything else I think of. I doubt anyone will think twice about my trying to help you gather supplies after your near brush with death."

"I shouldn't think so," he concurred.

"So what items are there at your cabin—pots, pans, and the like?" she asked. "We don't want to buy anything we don't absolutely have to."

"My father and I built that old shack some years back. Like I told you first off, I haven't been there for a couple seasons. I'm not even sure the place will still be standing. And even if it is, the cabin was little more than four walls and a fireplace. There's one fair-sized room, the floor is dirt and the roof is cut-notched planks and tree poles covered with shingles we cut from billets. Even so, when there was a hard rain or the snow began to melt, the roof often dripped in a good many places. The last winter I spent up there I shoved fresh mortar into the cracks between the slabs of pine used for walls, but the cold still seeps through. The only water has to be carried from a nearby stream and the cooking and heat come from the single fireplace. It's going to be rugged going for you two."

"We'll fashion a bed of straw so we don't have to sleep on the dirt floor," Laura replied. "We can cover the walls with pasteboard to keep in the heat and prevent the wind from blowing through the cracks, and I'll carry the water we need from the stream for washing and bathing. There's nothing we can't endure for a single winter."

Konn grunted. "You're becoming more of a pilgrim all the time."

Laura began to calculate in her head as she scribbled on the paper. "We'll need candles, matches, some tins of milk, and as many oranges, onions, lemons, and limes as we can find. Its common knowledge about how people deprived of those things develop a number of illnesses." She frowned in thought. "We may be forced to shop at Copton's for a few items."

"You get whatever you can from Brown, then make a list of the other stuff we'll be needing. I'll go by and pick those things up."

"I'd sooner grab a skunk by the tail than give them a dime's worth of business, but we don't have a lot of options."

"It comes down to necessity," he said, "and it is supposed to look like the supplies are for me. I won't have a choice but to buy some of the stuff from Copton."

"Well, I'll make sure we patronize them as little as possible."

In spite of his concerns over the upcoming arrangement, Konn smiled. "You are a practical woman, Mrs. Morrison."

"You did say this cabin was a long way from civilization, didn't you?"

"Forty miles from here, and there are no neighbors. Even the occasional miner has shut down and cleared out up that direction."

"So we can't very well run to the store every time we need something. We'll have to make do with whatever we have thought to take along."

Konn grinned. "That's a fact."

Instead of smiling back, Laura grew serious. "I need to write that letter I mentioned and send it off to Garden City, Kansas," she said. "It is something of great importance. You said to have the mail returned with your name on it?"

"Write your letter and drop it off along with one or two I will write so it won't draw any special attention. Just make sure to explain in your letter that the reply has to be addressed with my name on it. That way no one will be the wiser that you are still around."

"And Mr. Brown—he handles the post here in town—will hold the mail for you?"

Konn gave an affirmative nod. "I often contact the railroad or a couple of road and bridge builders I know to arrange for hunting jobs. As I am going to winter up at the old homestead, won't anyone think twice about my having the mail delivered here."

"I understand. In a few weeks or whenever you make the trip back here, you can pick up fresh supplies and the mail."

"Sounds like a plan."

"How will we know when the judge arrives?"

"When I talk to Flynn, I'll ask him to contact me soon as he learns the date," Konn offered. "I'll say I promised to be here in case you decided to come back and dispute the contract, something like that."

"He can't tell anyone I'm coming," Laura pointed out. "If it gets back to Rudy that I am going to be here for the court hearing, he might do like you said and hire someone to lie about witnessing the contract."

Konn gave a subtle tip of his head at Abby and met Laura's inquisitive gaze with a meaningful look.

Laura understood and placed her hand on her daughter's shoulder. "Uh, Abby, I left our new hairbrush on the table in our room. Would you go fetch it?"

"Sure, Mama," Abby replied.

Once she had scampered out of the room, Konn grew serious. "It strikes me as no small coincidence that your crooked partner sent you a map outlining the route through Dry Basin. I think he expected Two Bears would be waiting."

Laura's features hardened. "The thought occurred to me too. I would not have thought Rudy capable of such treachery, but Elva is certainly cold-blooded enough to want us all killed."

"And you remember the last attack?" he asked, an obvious question. "Well, that second warrior might have killed me, but he went for you instead." He watched for her change of expression, but her brows only inched together slightly. "Two Bears swore to kill me because I had humiliated him in front of his son and the other warriors. However, it sure looked as if you were the main target of the other brave."

Laura swallowed something, perhaps a dawning of the truth, before responding.

"I remember the bloodlust in the eyes of that Indian," she said quietly. As he watched, Laura shuddered at the memory. "He had a most murderous look. I . . . I thought for certain I was about to die."

"It was a close call all right."

"So you saved my life again," she said. "I have never been so indebted to anyone in my life."

The fires of embarrassment began to burn and the heat would soon surface. Konn desperately tried to stave off the hated emotion by changing the subject.

"I should have questioned Walks Tall before he left."

"It's nothing short of a miracle you were standing up long enough to force him to leave!" Laura retorted. "You had a knife sticking out of your chest, imbedded not an inch from your heart and lungs! I won't have you blaming yourself for not acting the part of a detective too!"

Konn dropped the issue, thankful to feel the heat receding from his face. It allowed him to relax a bit.

"Back to our plan, Mrs. Morrison. I believe we can trust Flynn to send word to us when the judge is to arrive. Even so, we won't tell him you're staying with me."

"He seems an honest man," she agreed. "He was most apologetic when he arrested me. I almost felt sorry for him."

Konn grunted. "He was likely concerned for his own sake, knowing he had to face me with the news."

She smiled at that. "You have been more protective of me than, well, more than any man I've ever known."

Uh-oh. The heat began to rise a second time. Konn immediately sought to head it off. "We still have a long road ahead, Mrs. Morrison. Being in the right concerning your store might not be enough. Guess time will tell if we are wasting our efforts with this plan of yours."

"I hate having those men give up their room to us," Laura said. "How long do you think it will be until you can ride?"

"I can sit a horse tomorrow."

She showed an immediate frown. "I mean, how long do you think it will be until you can ride and not reopen the wound and have it maybe kill you?"

"With a tight bandage in place, I see no reason we can't get started. We might have to keep a slower pace, but it's a two-day ride to the cabin. I'll heal as we travel."

"I can buy the supplies," she said, ceasing further debate. "But what about the pack animals you mentioned?"

"I spotted a couple at the livery. I'll get up that way and buy what we need."

Laura appeared uneasy. "Do you have enough money for all this?"

"Don't worry about the money," he told her abruptly. "I've got enough to take care of everything."

"Mr. Flynn got me twenty-eight dollars from Rudy, so I can pay for some of what we need too."

"It isn't necessary."

"I'd like to not go further in debt to you."

"You can pay me back once you get control of the store."

"Yes, but what if I don't get my store back?" she asked. "What if Rudy figures out a way to buy or fool the circuit judge?"

"An actual judge ain't going to be as easy to put in his pocket as Dodd," Konn assured her. "You stop thinking about everything that can go wrong and concentrate on buying what we're going to need. This afternoon, I'll talk to Flynn and pick us out some pack animals over at the livery. With any luck, we can be ready to move out first thing in the morning."

Laura moved closer and lowered her voice. "Do you think Rudy might have someone follow us as far as the way station?"

Konn hid the flood of emotion her nearness caused and battled to keep his voice normal. "I'll watch our back trail. If we have a shadow, we will continue as far as Dover Flats and make it appear you are taking the stage to Denver. We'll do whatever we have to in order to sell the idea that you've gone back to your beau in Kansas."

Laura blinked in surprise. "You heard about that?"

"About broke Flynn's heart," he said, masking his own bitter disappointment.

"I didn't think he would say anything to—"

"I need to get on my feet." Konn didn't wait to hear about the man in her life. He put a hand on the head rail of the bed and, battling against the rush of pain that shot through his entire left side, swung his feet over the edge of the bed.

"I'd be obliged if you would help me with my boots. I had them on once, but decided to wait and talk to you first."

"It's too soon," she said, worry etched into her comely features. "You should remain in bed for another week."

"This ain't the first time I've been shot or stabbed. I'll mend in a few days regardless of whether I'm in bed or on the back of Hammerhead."

Laura lowered her head as if ashamed. "Abby and I have been so much trouble to you. And now this. I hate taking further advantage of you."

Konn ignored her comment. "Once I've gotten the extra animals lined out, we can write our letters, and I'll take them to Mr. Brown. I'll explain things to him and the mail will be taken care of."

When she looked at him, there were tears in her eyes. "Mr. Konniger, I . . ."

He winked at her. "Don't you fret none, Mrs. Morrison, we'll pull this off without a single person being the wiser." *And once you win back the store, you can send for your worthless, no good man to join you!*

Laura finished helping him get his boots on as Abby appeared at the door. "Why do we need the brush, Mama?" she asked. "We gonna get our hair all mussed?"

Laura blinked away the moistness in her eyes as she took the brush and began to touch up Abby's hair. "We need to look our best," she told her firmly. "We've got some more shopping to do today. Don't want to look like street beggars, do we?"

"Nope," Abby replied, showing her toothy grin. "Grandpa always said we got to look 'spectable."

Laura laughed. "Yes, we must do our best to appear respectable."

Chapter Ten

Crow kept an eye on Konn. The big hunter was stove-up, moving gingerly from his recent knife wound. He had some dealings concerning animals at the livery and gave the hostler instructions before returning to his room. As for the woman and child, they carried around a list and appeared to be buying Konn's supplies for him. Crow considered that small enough payment for him saving their lives.

Crow met up with Skinny Bob when the man was heading to the saloon for his first beer of the day. It was strange how he stayed as thin as a pencil, because he certainly enjoyed his beer.

"Looks like me and Spanish will have to find more honest work," Bob said. "No more paydays from Copton for a spell."

"That will change when we get another delivery of goods."

Bob frowned. "Selling guns to the Indians ain't the most healthy thing a man can do for a living."

"Earn a month's pay for a day or two's work," Crow reminded him. "Not so bad when you look at it like that, huh?"

"Getting our necks stretched by a hangman's noose is what would be bad."

Crow frowned. "You want out? I can find a couple more men to replace you and Spanish."

Bob threw up his hands. "No! Hell no!" he exclaimed. "I was just talking, that's all."

Crow pinned the man with a rapier-like stare, eyes hard and cold. "You want to be real careful when it comes to *talking* too much, Skinny. One wrong word might just get you killed."

Bob backed up a step, and his face blanched with fright. "I'd never do that, Crow. You know me. I keep my mouth shut about business. Always have, always will."

Crow allowed the man to escape his deadly peruse. "Knowing that is a comfort to me, Skinny."

The thin man glowered defensively. "You are one scary son, Crow," he said. "I sometimes wonder why your ma didn't stuff you in a sack and toss your hide into the nearest river."

"By the time she figured me out, I was too quick for her to catch."

Skinny Bob laughed, and the tension was broken. "If you need us, me and Spanish will be around town for a few more days. Come next week, we hired on to ride shotgun on a couple wagons of ore."

Crow chuckled. "What better men for the job than a couple sidewinders like you two?"

"Exactly," Skinny replied. "Guess they figure it's better to pay us to protect the shipment than take a chance we would steal it instead."

"Easier money for you boys too," Crow said. "You don't have to try and find a crooked owner at a smelter to take the ore off your hands."

"You got that right, Crow. Just so long as those Indians don't start thinking they can trade ore for guns. That could pose a problem for us."

"Don't worry on that count. The Indians we deal with know we only take refined gold, jewelry, and cash money."

"I heard that the Morrison woman and her kid are leaving in a day or so."

"Looks like it."

Skinny grunted. "After the way she busted the Copton woman in the mouth, I thought she was more of a fighter than a quitter."

"Common sense," Crow suggested. "With a written contract and Dodd's testimony, the lady wouldn't have a prayer in court." He grinned. "Not even with an honest judge."

"Can't say I wouldn't have liked to have the gal stick around. She's quite a looker."

"Pretty don't always mean good. You've seen how Copton's wife treats him!"

Skinny snorted his accord. "Enough said, Crow. Pretty woman or no, I ain't of a mind to have a gal digging her spurs into my ribs and telling me which way to jump for the rest of my life."

Crow chuckled. "Tell that to someone who hasn't seen Alice bleed you dry a half-dozen times."

Skinny grinned, thinking of the saloon hostess. "Funny how she knows whether a man is packing gold or has empty pockets. If I were ever charged with a crime and had to stand trial, I sure wouldn't want her to be on the jury!"

"I'd wager that woman has siphoned more gold from you and the other miners up here than the total amount of gold shipped to the smelter."

"And she don't give nothing back," Skinny said with a sigh. "Never goes beyond a little squeeze when you're dancing with her. She'll drink, dance, and laugh with you, but you get fresh and it's so long."

"That's why they have Molly. She'll let a guy kiss her when the mood strikes."

Skinny chuckled his agreement. "Yeah, good ol' Molly. Never met a man she didn't like . . . so long as he's got money."

"So why spend your time on Alice?" Crow asked. "It's like leading a saddled horse around the corral and never taking a ride."

"It probably sounds dumb, but I favor being around a woman who acts more like a lady, you know?"

"No," Crow replied. "I don't. But it's you who is wasting your time and money, not me."

"Maybe one day," Skinny said wistfully. "Maybe one day she will take a liking to a man enough to want to do more than dance with him." He rolled his eyes. "Though I'm betting the guy will have to marry her and be rich to boot!"

Crow grinned at the silly comment. "Speaking of money, are you and Spanish still nesting in the tent behind Dodd's place?"

"Yep," Bob answered. "Not so noisy as when we camped next to the saloon."

"What are you going to do for the winter?"

"We joined together a couple old wagon beds and cut down the middle rails. With added canvas, we made a good roof and we have two bench-type beds. You ought to come by and see the fancy place we've made for ourselves. The tent keeps off the rain and snow and we are up off the cold ground at night. We've even got room for another man or two, should the need come up."

Crow considered the news. "You thinking of renting out part of your tent setup?"

"We've got the room, and we would only ask a couple bucks a week and chipping in on the food," Bob replied. "Ain't a bad setup for the price. You know what they are asking at the saloon for one of them rooms upstairs?" He grunted in disgust. "Twenty bucks a week! Twenty bucks to share a room or thirty-five for one to yourself!" He snorted at the notion. "And other than those few rooms, there ain't another place to sleep in the whole damn town. We are offering a real bargain."

"Tell you what. I'll pay you and Spanish five dollars a week, and you boys supply the food," Crow offered. "With my being gone a great deal of the time, that ought to be more than fair."

Bob didn't hide his surprise. "You want to move in with us?"

"I'm one of the suckers paying twenty bucks a week, and the guy sharing the room with me snores like a freight train climbing a steep grade. Besides which, he's always getting the room to himself because I'm not there more than a night or two a week!"

"Well, sure, Crow!" Bob said eagerly. "We'd be glad to have your company."

"I'll drop off my belongings before I head out."

"That's great, Crow. I'll get hold of Spanish, and we'll put in a third bed."

Crow didn't reply to that. He lifted a hand in farewell and started for the livery. He had some contacts to make and figured he had wasted enough time on Konn and the Morrison woman. Copton figured she had given up and tomorrow she would be gone. Crow's chore of watching them was finished. After he got his horse, he would clear the things out of his room and drop them off at Bob's tent. Then he would be on the trail, heading out to do the business that earned him the most money.

Up before daylight, Konn was stiff and tender. He managed to dress without crying out aloud or fainting from the pain, so he decided that was worth a pat on the back. However, he was sweating from the effort and in the process of buckling on his gun when a soft tap came at his door. He sucked in a deep breath to summon forth his strength and pulled it open. Laura stood in the hallway, dressed for riding, wearing a woolen jacket and a wide-brimmed hat to protect her from the sun.

"I wasn't sure you would be up," was her greeting. "But you did say you wanted to leave at sunup."

"Are you both ready?" Konn asked. "It's going to be a hard ride."

"More for you than for us, Mr. Konniger." Laura displayed a concerned frown. "What if you suffer a dizzy spell and fall from your horse? We could never get you back on, and you might lie there and bleed to death!"

He dismissed her fears. "Hammerhead has a natural feel for the trail. If she stumbles more than once, I'll put a knot between her ears."

"I would feel better if we waited another day or two."

"The longer we stick around town, the more chance someone will get the idea you don't intend to leave the country. Flynn told me the stage is scheduled to arrive at Dover Flats this afternoon. There won't be another one for four days. We can't wait."

Laura gave a slight nod. "If you're sure you will be all right."

"You got everything packed?"

"We only need to bring the horses over from the livery. Mr. Flynn helped us carry our belongings to the porch." She displayed a sheepish grin. "Poor man, he was trying to sleep on a couple chairs he had put together downstairs."

"I owe him for his courtesy. He gave me his room and looked after me and my animals. I wish I knew of a way to repay him."

"A real man doesn't require payment for doing what is right and lending a helping hand," Laura pointed out. "Look how much you have done for Abby and me, without asking for so much as a thank you."

"All the same, I will return the favor should he ever need it."

"That's all anyone should ask," she said.

Abby came up the hallway, still rubbing sleep from her eyes. She displayed her ready smile when she spied Konn.

"Hi'ya, Mr. Kon'ger," she greeted him. "You sure do get up early."

"We've got a long way to ride today," he told her. "You ready to sit a saddle all day?"

"My legs is just beginning to feeling straight again," she said, showing a worried expression. "Hope I don't end up with crooked or bowlegs from riding."

"I'm sure you don't have to worry about it. We'll stop every few hours to get down and stretch. That ought to help."

"Okay," she chirped. "I'm ready."

"Let me grab my hat," he said. Konn turned and picked up his coat and hat. His rifle and most of his other things were at the livery, so he only had to ready the pack animals and they would be on their way.

"How far do you think we will have to go before it's safe to turn for your cabin?" Laura asked.

"We'll start out of town in the direction of Dover Flats. We can make a wide circle just past the creek crossing. There is an old trail through the hills that bypasses Lonesome Creek. I would guess it's a mile or so down the road. That should be ample time for me to make sure we are not being followed."

Konn closed the door to Flynn's room, and the three of them started down the hall. As he walked along with Laura and Abby, he felt concern for the future. Five or six months with these two females, sharing the small cabin, being confined day after day during severe storms—it was going to be a long, hard winter.

Yup, I offered up an olive branch and the whole damn tree fell on me!

Konn was beat by the time the sun set. He was relieved to spot a familiar cove a short distance from the creek. Being a full day's

ride from Lonesome Creek, there was little chance of anyone using the seldom-traveled trail.

"We'll stop here for the night," he informed Laura and Abby.
"I've used this camp a number of times before. We're well over
halfway to the cabin."

"You find a place to sit down and rest," Laura ordered. "I'll
tend to the camp tonight."

Konn hated to let her do everything. There were the horses and
pack animal to unload and tether. They also had to be watered
and staked out where they would have enough feed for the night.
Then they needed wood for the campfire, the beds had to be
placed, and the meal had to be cooked. Lifting his eyes to look
through the trees, he saw a few clouds overhead. There might be
rain before morning.

"I really ought to construct a lean-to," he told her.

Laura was already off her mount and helping Abby down. "We
can get by," she said. "We'll use your poncho to cover the bed if
it starts to rain."

Konn would have argued, but that required strength he didn't
possess. He used his good arm, holding onto the pommel of the
saddle, and gingerly eased his right leg over the back of Hammerhead. Then, careful not to use his left arm, he lowered himself to the ground.

"You can hardly stand." Laura's tone was that of a concerned
mother. It was the second time she had talked to him that way.
"We should have stopped hours ago."

Before he had a chance to defend his decision to reach the
camping spot, she took hold of his right wrist, lifted it up, and
slipped in under his arm. She offered support and tipped her head
in the direction of an old fallen tree.

"Over there," she directed. "You can tell me what to do if I
can't figure something out or need help."

Konn was less steady than he would have liked, having to lean
on Laura after the first couple steps. The long ride had taken
more out of him than he had anticipated. Then again, the feel of
the woman so close, while offering him aid, probably added to
his feebleness.

Laura eased out from under his arm once they reached the log. "You sit down here and regain your strength," she instructed him. "Abby and I can take care of everything for the night."

"Whatever you say, Mrs. Morrison."

His acceptance brought a slender smile to her lips. "I like the sound of that, much more than the other way around. We've been such a burden to you, it helps to think we are giving something back."

It took little guidance and advice to finish off the chores, as Laura and Abby were regular troopers. They managed to have the animals watered and picketed, a fire going, and a large bed in place before full dark. Konn watched as Laura began to heat up a pan of beans and salt pork, while Abby rounded up sticks for the fire. They were a pretty good team.

Once the meal was out of the way, Laura walked over to the nearby stream and washed the pans. Abby took a final walk into the bushes for the evening, and they were soon ready for bed.

The bedding had been laid out a few feet from the log, wide enough for all three of them. Laura indicated Abby would sleep in the middle, both for her warmth and protection. Konn had never slept next to anyone and worried he might turn over and crush the little tyke, but kept it to himself. With his injured left side, he would undoubtedly wake up if he attempted to change position.

Konn waited until they were in bed before he eased carefully under the covers. He usually removed his foot gear, a precaution for allowing his feet to breathe and the leather boots to air out, but this was a unique situation. He kept on everything but his hat and coat.

Once asleep, the night passed quickly. It seemed Konn had no more than shut his eyes when he was awakened by the twitter of a magpie—camp robbers, some called them. They would scavenge anything they could find and even pick the crumbs right out of a man's beard if he was a sound sleeper. He started to raise his head to look around the campsite and suddenly froze, fearful of moving the slightest muscle.

A small arm was draped over his chest!

Rotating his head ever so slowly, he discovered Abby had snuggled up to him like her favorite pillow. He figured the slightest movement might wake her, so he lay back and remained completely still.

Pinned like a man beneath a ton of sand, Konn experienced the most bizarre feeling he had ever imagined. His heart pounded like a war drum, and he felt the blood heat in his veins. Each breath was drawn slowly and deliberately, as if he dared not allow his chest to expand too quickly.

What the hell's the matter with you, Konn?

It was only Abby, a child he could lift with one hand and as pretty and delicate as the pedals on a flower. He suffered a surge of humility and a twinge of satisfaction at the same time. In an instant, he knew how a father must feel, gazing upon or holding his child for the first time. It was a difficult situation to be in, both weird and wonderful at the same time.

He lay as still as a stone for what seemed an eternity. His body began cramping, and his good arm was numb from the awkward position. Nevertheless, he didn't wish to break the spell of having someone as precious as Abby to hold and keep in his care.

Daylight had been upon the land for several minutes and a crispness was in the early fall air before Laura began to stir. She lifted her head to look around and then sat up. When she noticed Konn was awake, she summoned a smile of greeting.

"I thought you would be rousting us from our bed well before dawn."

"It's only about six hours to the cabin, depending upon the trail," he said, offering justification. "I needed the extra rest."

Taking note of the way Abby had draped herself all over Konn, Laura made a face. "Yes, I can see how you would need to sleep late this morning."

"She's plumb wore out from the ride yesterday," Konn said, excusing the child for still being asleep. "Reckon a few extra winks won't hurt her none."

"You'd best watch out for Abby's little finger, Mr. Konniger," Laura warned.

He didn't understand. "Do what?"

"You are in danger of finding yourself wrapped around it," she concluded.

Konn had nothing to say to that remark.

"Wake up, little sleepyhead," Laura coaxed her daughter, lightly touching her shoulder. "I need you to get some firewood so I can start breakfast."

When there was no response, Laura slipped her hand down to the child's ribs and playfully tickled her. The action brought forth an immediate giggle. Abby had been faking still being asleep.

Once Abby removed herself from Konn's side, he loosened up his good arm and pushed himself up to a sitting position. That little bit of movement caused his left shoulder to throb, and he realized it was going to take a few more days to mend.

"I'll check the horses and make sure they are ready to ride," he suggested.

"All right," Laura replied, "but you wait until I am there to help you load and saddle them. We don't want you to open your wound."

"Yes, ma'am," he quipped. "You're the boss."

A smile settled on her face. "See?" she teased. "You needn't worry about us staying the winter. With you displaying such a sensible attitude, we'll get along famously."

In spite of the discomfort from his shoulder, Konn had to grin. This lady was something special.

It was mid-morning and Crow was miles from the nearest settlement when he spotted a rider and pack animal passing through the trees. He moved to intercept the man and discovered the fellow had a shiny new prospector's pickax and shovel tied to the side of his heavily laden mule. The gear looked sorely out of place because the man was dressed like a dude. Even his head covering was expensive looking—a flat-crowned hat adorned with a wide silver band. An Indian warrior could have seen this guy coming from a mile off.

"Hey there, partner!" Crow called to him, continuing forward to block his path.

The man stopped and immediately offered a wide grin. "Hello, good sir!" he replied. "I didn't expect to see anyone up this way."

Crow took a quick survey of the area. "You do know there are some unfriendly Indians in this part of the country, don't you, friend?"

A stark horror flashed on the man's face. "Indians?"

"Cheyenne war party attacked a wagon just the other day, not ten miles from here."

The man's head swiveled back and forth, wide eyes searching. "Indians? Attack?"

"I believe it's safe enough for the moment," Crow said, to put the man's worries to bed. "I ride these hills all the time and keep track of most hunting parties moving around."

"I never even gave it a thought."

"Where you from?"

"Ohio," the guy answered. "I traveled by rail and coach to Denver and bought everything there I needed to strike it rich."

Crow hid a smile at the brainless assumption. "A good many of the gold and silver mines played out after the strike of '59," he told him. "Lonesome Creek is one of the few towns left with any working digs."

The man reached for his pocket but hesitated. "I don't think you told me your name."

"Everyone calls me Crow," he replied. "My real name is too long and cumbersome for anyone in a hurry."

The words caused the man to laugh. "Yes, I can sympathize with that. My name is Jerome Winfield Fentworthy." Another grin. "My friends call me JW."

Crow chuckled. "With a highfalutin name like that, you should be rich already."

"The family was well-tailored back in England when I was a child. My grandfather had a small fleet of ships and a thriving business, until they caught him transporting slaves. The family lost most of their holdings and fled to America to seek new fortunes."

"And prospecting is how you intend to make your fortune?"

He waved a dismissive hand. "Not at all. I have a rather lofty position with my uncle's business, but I wanted to try and go it on my own, as it were. I realize striking a bonanza is more of a dream than likelihood, but I wanted to give it a go."

"Most of these hills have been scoured by hundreds of other prospectors, except for a few of the most rugged mountains. I don't know how much luck you'll have."

"You seem an honest man, Crow."

"When it comes to digging in the ground, you can trust me not to want any part of your business. I'm not cut out for that kind of physical labor."

JW pulled out a piece of wrinkled paper, yellow and tattered from age and wear. "I've got a map," he said excitedly. "I'm having trouble with the landmarks, but I believe I'm on the right trail."

He passed the paper over to Crow so he could look at it.

"Yep, you are about here." Crow pointed to a couple lines near the middle of the page. "I'd guess this here item on the sketch is a rock formation known as Skull Cap. It's about two miles yonder to the east. And this stream is the one that gave Lonesome Creek its name—winds about to hell and gone before it empties into the Colorado River." He studied it a moment longer. Obviously a phony, the treasure map appeared to run all the way to New Mexico Territory.

"These lines appear to be much longer than they should be," Crow said, deciding to save this pilgrim a ten-day ride only to end up lost in a private purgatory. "Sometimes when a man draws a map their memory makes the journey seem longer than it really was—you know, the scale isn't quite right."

"You mean the map is no good?"

Crow didn't want to have this guy die from following a stupid fake map, so he pointed to a range of mountains. "These circles probably indicate the beaver ponds yonder above the timber line. If so, this map is going to lead you up past several old mines." He pointed. "There beneath that shellface cliff. Do you see it?"

"Yes, I do."

"That would be my best guess," Crow told him. "But you

won't have a lot of time to search. The first snow could come at most any time."

"It's only the middle of October," JW countered. "I should have a couple weeks to look around."

"If we have a normal winter you're right, but this is Colorado. We sometimes get snow in September right up until June. You can't depend on much of anything."

"How long do you think it will take me to reach those high ridges?"

Crow gazed up at the location. It didn't look far, maybe ten miles, but the getting there would mean going up and down hills, winding around through a maze of canyons and steep ravines. Travel in the hard country took many times as long as the flatlands.

"If you don't get trapped by one of the dead-end canyons, you might make it in a couple days."

JW rubbed the stubble on his chin and frowned. "It looks so close."

"If you had wings, you would be there in an hour or two," Crow told him. "Up here, crossing that rugged terrain, it's going to take you a full two days."

The pilgrim accepted his word and changed the subject. "So the nearest settlement would be this Lonesome Creek you mentioned?"

"That's right. Once you reach those shellfaced cliffs, it's about fifty miles due north. You hug the creek when you come to it, and it'll lead you right to town."

"You've been a big help, Crow," JW said. "I'm certainly glad we crossed trails."

"Good luck with your prospecting," Crow replied. "Most of these old she-mountains are real stingy about sharing their wealth. You keep an eye skyward for dark clouds and if you feel a cool nip to the breeze, a storm is likely coming. If you get snowed in up in the high country, you might have to survive weeks or even months before you get out again."

"I'll remember."

Crow gave a nod of his head. "If you do happen to strike it rich, stop by Lonesome Creek and buy me a drink."

"Nothing would please me more!"

Crow turned his horse and headed back toward the trail. He had done his good deed for the day. JW would have ridden until both his rations and animals gave out following the fake map. At least the guy had a chance for survival now.

Chapter Eleven

The cabin looked worse than Konn remembered. The single shutter for the lone window was hanging by one corner. As they approached the shack, a bird flew out of the window and another varmint scampered through the brush near the rear, concealed by the bushes as it made a hasty getaway.

He stopped the small caravan and cringed at the awkward silence. This had been a horrible idea. A respectable raccoon wouldn't have chosen such a hovel for a winter home. How could he expect a lady and her little girl to survive with not a single amenity?

"It'll take some fixing before the snow comes," he said, stating the obvious. "First off, I'll patch the window and repair the door. The roof and fireplace look intact, but the walls are going to need a lot of work."

Laura cleared her throat, as if she was having trouble forming her words. "It is a little smaller than I had imagined. When you said you and your father stayed here, I . . ."

"Not to worry." Konn tried a positive approach. "Soon as I'm fit, I'll knock out the side wall and add a second room. It shouldn't take me more than a few days, once I can use my left arm again."

"I hope we don't get an early storm," Laura replied. "I can't imagine you being able to do much work for another couple weeks."

Konn scoffed at her assessment. "Come tomorrow I'll start cutting some smaller poles and trimming off the limbs. We can stir up some mortar for the cracks and start filling them in. You

106

don't fret about it none, you and the muffin. We'll have this place near airtight before the first snow."

Laura regarded him with something akin to admiration, then mustered forth her charming smile. "Yes, I'm sure we'll do just fine, Mr. Konniger"—she switched her attention to Abby—"won't we, dear?"

"Uh-huh, but where is the little hut at?" Abby asked, searching the area. "You know, Mommy, like the one behind Grandpa's house?"

Konn swallowed a lump of embarrassment and gave a negative toss of his head. "Some big old bear probably used it for a scratching pole and knocked it flat. I'll sure enough dig a pit and make one first off."

"Well, you're not going to do all the work yourself," Laura told him. "Abby and I will pitch in and help too. After all, we are imposing on your hospitality, not the other way around. Between the three of us, we'll have this place looking like a store-bought doll house before the snow flies."

Her optimism caused the corners of Konn's mouth to lift upward, but he stuck to the business at hand. "I reckon we can tether the animals on a picket line until I get some poles together and mend the old corral. I'll also have to throw up a lean-to for shelter so the animals can get out of the weather. It appears the old pen has suffered from as much neglect as the house."

Konn eased down from his horse and was relieved when there was only a dull ache throughout his left side. He was on the mend, but he knew he would have to work carefully for the next couple weeks. Laura and Abby dismounted and joined him at the door to the cabin. The door had been the finest workmanship he and his father had done, because it had to withstand being constantly opened and closed, yet still had to fit snug enough to keep out the snow and cold. Remarkably, it was intact and needed only a couple new pegs for the upper hinge.

Konn pulled the door open by lifting on the front corner. The musky odor of a long-closed-up room was mixed with the natural smell of decay from old wood and two seasons of dust. Leaves had blown in through the open window and a bird had nested in a corner between the roof and makeshift cupboards. The counter for the wash pan and fixing meals was still standing, mostly rough-hewn boards except for the smoothly sanded countertop.

Laura walked directly over to the fireplace. "Oh, good!" she exclaimed. "You have an iron crane for the cooking pot." Then hunkering down, sitting on her heels, she peered up the chimney. "And there is a damper to contain the heat."

She whirled about and smiled at Konn. "That's wonderful. The fireplace will hold in the heat, and the crane will work fine for hanging pots for meals or heating water for laundry and baths."

"My father knew how to construct a fireplace and chimney," Konn told her. "He did some blacksmithing as a young man, before the trapping fever caused him to head for the wild and unknown. We never did have a cabin with a real stove, so he used his knowledge of forges and the like to get the most out of a fireplace. He also taught me how to make some simple furniture."

"I'm all set then," she replied. "I have a long-handled hopper and a kettle and pot for cooking. All I need is a couple pieces of iron or rock to make a base for baking bread."

"The table is still standing," Konn observed, looking to the corner he had used as his kitchen. "Only two stools, but I can fashion a third one in the next day or two."

"We have but one lamp and a couple gallons of oil," Laura said. "We'll have to use candles and the fireplace for most of our light. During the day, we can leave the window open, whenever the weather is good, to save on our supplies."

Konn nodded his agreement. "I'll unload the animals and take them to the creek for water. It's a short walk to the stream, and it pretty much freezes along the edges in the middle of winter. However, I will keep a good rock near the edge for busting the ice."

"If you want to tend to the animals, we'll start cleaning the house," Laura told him. "I'd like to get the dust and leaves brushed out before we try and move anything into the cabin." She exhaled a sigh. "I should have bought something for sweeping the floor."

"I recall there are some yellow birch in the next valley," Konn told her. "Soon as I tend to the livestock, I'll slip over the hill and find a suitable sapling to make into a broom."

That dazzling smile appeared again. "You continue to remind me of how handy it is to have a man around, Mr. Konniger."

Konn felt the warmth flood upward toward his face and turned for the animals. "I'll get going while you start with the cleaning. Being that the place is so small, I reckon the chore won't take very long."

She showed a resolute determination. "No, not long at all."

Minding to use mostly his good arm, Konn offloaded the horses at the front of the cabin. Then he took the string of animals to the stream so they could drink their fill. The corral behind the cabin had been constructed for two horses, and many of the poles were broken or lying on the ground rotting, while the shelter had mostly fallen to ruin.

He still had some misgivings about this bizarre arrangement, but he had seen the light of fortitude in Laura's eyes. The woman had a will of iron. Come the devil on the wind or the raging fires of Armageddon, she would see this through.

Crow returned to Lonesome Creek after several hard days of riding. He put up his horse and went to the shelter he now shared with Spanish and Skinny Bob. It was a little cramped with three beds, but none of them had much in the way of possessions. This particular night the other two men were playing Casino on one of the bunks.

"Hey, Crow!" Bob greeted him. "Didn't know when to expect you back."

"I'm beat," he told the two men. "Hope you don't intend to sit up and play cards all night."

"We're only killing time, Crow. Both of us are leaving in the morning to ride guard for the ore shipment from the Peterson Mine."

"Hard to believe Peterson and his two sons are still finding color."

"They sure enough have the best dig around," Spanish said. "I sometimes think I ought to work in the mine for the three dollars a day they're paying."

Crow grunted. "I wouldn't dig rock down in a hole for ten times that."

"Nor me either," Bob agreed. "I like to look up and see the sky, feel the wind on my face, and breathe fresh air. I was down inside once, and it was like being buried alive."

"I was just saying the money sounded good," Spanish replied.

Crow shrugged out of his jacket and sat down to pull off his boots. He shivered and pulled his coat back on.

"Damn! It's colder than an ice house in here."

"We're going to have to think about getting something for heat," Bob said. "The makeshift stove we used last year didn't work worth shucks."

"I was looking in the catalog at Brown's store," Spanish spoke up. "They have a small iron-box style combination cooking and heating stove for a good price."

"I'm broke," Bob reminded him. "If I remember right, you don't have two nickels to rub together either."

"Well, we need to do something," he complained. "We near froze to death using that barrel with holes in it last year, plus it was a royal pain leaving the flap open to keep from dying from all of the smoke."

"What do you think, Crow?" Bob asked.

"I think we ought to get off our back pockets and build us a cabin."

Spanish groaned at the idea. "You know how much work is involved in that? Cut down the trees—when all of the good nearby timber has been taken—then cut and saw for endless hours and put it all together. I tell you, it would take the three of us two months to build a decent size outhouse!"

"Unless we got together enough money to buy the lumber and have it shipped from the nearest sawmill," Crow suggested.

"You're talking money we don't have," Spanish argued.

"A couple of gun sales, and we'll be able to buy what we need."

"The Army is sending more troops westward all the time, Crow. It won't be long until every tribe has been defeated and moved to a reservation. I got to wonder how long there will be a demand for rifles."

Crow paused to think. "You might be right, Bob. We need to figure a way to make a living on our own."

"Doing what?"

"If we could get together a fair chunk of money, we could start our own freight outfit. The three of us could make a good living with something like that."

"There's plenty of money to be made hauling ore and freight," Bob agreed.

"Yeah, but we would need several hundred dollars to start with," Spanish contributed. "Two or three wagons, a dozen draft horses, and twice that many mules, plus enough cash to hold us over until we had money coming in."

Bob grunted. "Take some kind of special job to earn that kind of loot."

"Especially without getting our faces on a wanted poster," Crow added. "We've been doing pretty well because no one can point a finger at us. We need a job where the reward is big but the risk is small."

They all sat in silence for a few moments, each absorbed with their own thoughts. Finally Spanish uttered a sigh.

"We can only take things a day at a time, you know?"

Bob tossed down his cards in disgust. "And freeze another winter like we did last year."

"No, we buy the stove and take it from there," Crow said. "However, if I pay for it myself, you two can forget my paying any more rent."

"That's sure fair enough," Spanish said.

"Until we starve from lack of work," Skinny complained.

"Something will come up," Crow offered some hope. "You boys keep your eyes open for anything out of the ordinary. It might mean something."

"I did see something a bit unusual," Spanish spoke up. "It might be nothing, but it did make me a little curious."

"Give," Crow encouraged him.

"It was that big hunter, Konniger," Spanish explained, "the day before he left town. I was working at the saloon, removing empty beer barrels from the storeroom—they send them back to the brewery for refilling—when I saw Konniger talking to Flynn. Didn't think much about it, except Konniger was drawing something on a piece of paper. A few minutes later, I stopped for a mug of suds while I was waiting to get paid. Flynn had left his apron on the counter and was out back talking to the teamster who picked up the load of barrels. The paper was sticking out of the apron pocket, so I took a quick look at it."

"And?" Crow prodded him.

"It looked like a map to Konniger's cabin."

Crow felt a spark of interest. "You're sure about this?"

"It had directions scribbled on the bottom, and Konniger had drawn a line that appeared to run well past those vacant mines up the canyon. I recognized the beaver ponds from a time when I went off hunting and wound up to hell and gone. I'd guess Konniger's place is thirty-five or forty miles back in the hills."

"So what?" Bob scoffed. "So he showed Flynn where he would be hanging his hat for the winter. I don't see anything curious about that."

"Why would Flynn need a map?" Crow asked.

"You think it means something?"

Crow did some quick thinking. "If Flynn wanted to know where Konniger's cabin was located, the man only had to point and give him a rough idea. Taking the time to draw a map means he expects Flynn to come visit him."

"Why would Flynn want to go all the way up in the mountains to see Konniger?" Spanish wanted to know. "That would be a two-day trip each way."

A smile crossed Crow's face. "I know why." At the two men's puzzled looks, he chuckled. "So the hunter can be in town when Mrs. Morrison comes to fight for her store!"

Bob scowled. "The lady took the money Rudy offered and left town. Me and Spanish watched her go!"

"Yes, but the circuit judge isn't due to arrive until next spring, five or six months from now. I'll bet you a dime to a dollar Flynn is supposed to contact Konniger so he can be here for the lady's day in court."

"That makes sense," Spanish said. "The guy did save her life and look after her and the *niña*."

"And he personally took her to Dover Flats to catch the stage. I'll bet he promised the lady he would come to the court hearing. With him around, Rudy and Dodd aren't going to try and stop her from having her say."

Bob shrugged. "So what good does that do us?"

"Yeah." Spanish did not comprehend Crow's line of thought either. "A promise from the hunter don't mean nothing. I thought we were looking for a way to make some big money."

Crow laughed at their stupidity. "Think, you two! If the woman intends to return to challenge Copton, she must have a pretty good idea she can win the case!"

A dim light flickered in Bob's eyes. "Oh, I get it," he said. "Rudy isn't going to want that woman to challenge his owner-ship in court."

"And I'm betting he'll pay plenty to keep her from doing just that."

"What about Konniger?" Spanish asked.

Bob's face grew serious. "Yeah, Crow, I don't aim to tackle him unless it means a whole lot of money."

"He's not the problem for Copton," Crow pointed out. "It doesn't matter if the hunter shows up. What difference to the judge or anyone else so long as the woman isn't here to present her argu-ment?"

Spanish grinned, now that he was thinking along the same lines. "I get it now, no woman, no hearing. It's that simple."

"It's something we can keep in mind."

"You really think he'd pay big money?" Bob asked. "After all, Rudy has a signed contract. And even if the Morrison woman was to win the case, the judge would only give her half the store."

Crow shook his head. "You're not thinking this through. If Rudy loses the case, the judge would award Mrs. Morrison the entire store and everything that goes with it."

"Why should he do that?"

"Because, not only did Rudy steal the place from her, he is responsible for her father being killed. She only has to say how Rudy sent a map for them to follow, and it led them right into an ambush! Any judge with a speck of sense is going to know that was no coincidence."

"I see what you're talking about now!" Spanish declared.

Bob also climbed on the same wagon. "Yeah, me too! We can make them pay big this time around. To prevent that Morrison woman from coming up here and testifying at the hearing, Rudy will likely fork over everything he has!"

"Only if Copton thinks he will lose," Spanish cautioned. "He still has a contract, remember. Plus there's only the woman's say-so that Rudy sent a map knowing Two Bears would be waiting. There's a good chance Rudy will think he can win the case. He might not pay a dime."

"If the woman can find one single witness about the map, or if she can prove the contract is a fake, it would be the end for Copton," Crow said. "And we made the deal with Two Bears and delivered the rifles."

"We can't threaten him with that," Bob said. "He would go to jail, but we would all be hanged too!"

"He won't take that chance, and we won't have to threaten him. Konniger let Walks Tall leave without killing him, and Walks Tall knows about our deal. Konniger is the one Rudy should be afraid of."

"You think Walks Tall told the hunter about the deal and that's why the gal thinks she can win in court?"

"It's a possibility."

"Yeah, but what Konn thinks or knows doesn't matter one bit so long as the woman doesn't show," Spanish deduced. "Isn't that so?"

"Yes, but it's something we don't have to worry about for the time being," Crow summarized for the two men. "When spring comes around, we'll present a case to Rudy and his charming bride. We'll convince him the truth might come out, and I'm betting he won't risk losing his store, his wife, and his freedom. I figure he'll pay dearly to keep Mrs. Morrison out of court."

"Before we start looking to buy those freight wagons, we better think this through," Bob said. "Konniger probably told Flynn to contact him far enough in advance that he can meet Mrs. Morrison at Dover Flats. Who better to make sure she gets up here safely?"

"And he's proven that he's a tough man to kill," Spanish granted.

"I told you, we don't have to concern ourselves about Konniger," Crow clarified. "We only have to see to it the woman never catches the stage from Denver. I'll track her down, and we'll make sure she suffers a few delays. By the time she gets here the judge will already be gone."

"I like it much better when you say it like that," Spanish said.

Crow clapped his hands together. "Yes sir, this could be our golden goose, a pathway to our own freight outfit."

"What's a gold-colored goose got to do with anything?" Spanish wanted to know.

Crow laughed. "I'll tell you the story sometime."

Bob also laughed. "Yeah, next time you are snug in your bed and want a bedtime story."

Spanish didn't say another word but continued to regard his two friends with a mystified frown.

Chapter Twelve

Konn smoothed and skinned the relatively straight pole to begin the chore. It had been some years since his father showed him how to fashion a broom from a birch sapling. Short one stool, Konn had taken his meals while sitting on the dirt floor. As Laura and Abby cleaned the few dishes from supper, he began to meticulously slice one-inch strips. Starting from the base of the branch, he peeled several slivers back about twelve inches.

Laura and Abby went to bed, so Konn used a single candle to work by. It was not that hard to see, as he often worked hides or made things from wood in near-dark conditions.

Once the end of the pole was suitably splintered, he worked downward from a spot about thirty inches up the handle. Cutting one-inch strips from mid-pole toward the base, he left a core of a couple inches in diameter. Next he folded the top strands over the notch, matching the second set of bristles with the strips on the bottom. He held them in place between his knees and secured both sets with a small band of rawhide. When tied off, the numerous splints meshed together to make nearly two dozen sturdy strands for the broom.

Sitting in the nearly dark room, he shaved the excess wood from the strands and trimmed the ends to make them even. Satisfied he had done a passable job, he placed the finished handiwork against the wall and crawled over to the bedroll the three of them were forced to share. The aged framework of the old cot had been eaten away by time and clawed and chewed on by some varmint. It would have to be replaced before it would serve as a decent bed again.

Konn eased carefully under the edge of the top blanket and slowly stretched out. Abby stirred and he held his breath, not wanting to disturb her sleep. When a hand came over to rest on his arm, he froze. Then he realized it was an adult hand, not Abby's, and he about leapt out of bed!

"Thank you again, Mr. Konniger," Laura whispered. "I know this must be a terrible imposition for you."

"No, I'm in an okay position," he replied, trying to muffle his base voice.

"I mean, we are a burden to you, and it is causing you to do a lot more work."

"Not so much," he said. "I was going to work on the place this winter anyway. Be a sight less lonely with you and Abby here."

"It's sweet of you to say so . . . even if you are only trying to make me feel better."

Konn didn't know what else to say, so he kept his mouth shut. After a few seconds, Laura gave his arm a slight squeeze and removed her hand. Konn enjoyed the gesture of endearment. It was something a man and woman might have shared before going to sleep each night.

A kiss would be nice too, he thought. Be real pleasant to end each day with a kiss and start the next morning the same way. A guy could sure enough get used to that.

He immediately scolded himself for thinking along those lines. Laura had a guy in Kansas somewhere. She had probably written him and asked him to wait until she got her store before coming to join her. Maybe he had a job he couldn't leave until she had the store up and running. He might have been caring for his parents or grandparents, something he had to do until such time as they could all move to Lonesome Creek. Or he could have had a job where he couldn't leave until it was finished. There were a thousand reasons why he hadn't made the journey with Laura and Abby.

Konn uttered a silent grunt. There was nothing in this world he would have put ahead of the safety of those two. He didn't know the reason the guy hadn't come along with them, but it was not good enough!

JW inspected the leg of his pack animal and knew the horse was done. The old nag had been limping for the better part of the day, and now he refused to put any weight on the leg at all. Worse, for their intended route, the terrain was rocky and steep, with only the faintest of animal trails. He had a good idea of where the beaver ponds were located, but the landmarks on the map no longer looked familiar.

"JW," he cussed himself aloud, "you are a greenhorn pilgrim on a fool's errand. This ridiculous map isn't worth the paper it's written on."

However, he had seen a number of abandoned digs in the area. Dozens of miners had combed these slopes and valleys in search of gold or silver. And the fact that Lonesome Creek still had a working mine gave evidence there was ore in these mountains. His chance of finding some color was remote, but even a blind dog would find a bone on occasion. He wasn't going to give up until he had dug a few dozen holes and panned a creek or stream. Dreams didn't materialize into reality without hard work and a bit of luck. He was willing to do the work and hope Lady Luck smiled down on him.

Pausing to wipe beads of sweat from his brow, he thought about the man he had met on the trail some days back. He wondered if Crow had recognized the map as being a fake and simply pointed out a decent place to search. JW shielded his eyes from the sun and searched the landscape ahead. There was a cleft between two jagged walls and a shallow bowl near the base of an even higher range of mountains. He remembered the stream Crow had mentioned was a mile or two off to his left, and he had caught sight of the beaver ponds from atop a nearby peak. If he stuck to this ridge, he would eventually reach that small basin and he would begin his search. There should be water nearby and he would use pick and shovel for digging his samples. Without his pack animal, he would not be able to haul all of his supplies, but he could still gather a number of samples to transport to the nearest assay office.

Heaving a reluctant sigh, he began to offload the pack animal. He would turn the horse loose to fend for itself and take only what he needed from this point forward. Once he reached the search area he could construct a temporary shelter. He was determined to see his dream through even if he had to carry the supplies on his own back!

As time passed Konn grew stronger. He fashioned a stool, so there were three places to sit at the table, but decided that wasn't good enough. He worked to build a chair with longer legs than the two stools. Using rawhide for binding the pegs and elk hide for a seat cover, he made a chair for Abby. When placed at the table, she was raised to a height even with him and Laura. The reward was instantaneous, as Abby was delighted with her own special chair.

Of course, one of his first chores had been to dig a pit, then split a few smaller trees and cut the halves into proper lengths for constructing a small hut for the convenience of his house guests. He used a piece of burlap over a bough frame for the door, and a square piece of canvas covered the lattice roof. The location was a short way back into the trees, but only about a dozen steps from the cabin.

At the end of most days he felt the weariness in his bones and a dull ache in his left shoulder. However, the work was not without rewards, as each night he was treated to the sweet smell of baked bread or beans and rabbit or venison for supper. Laura set a fine table offering a welcome selection of stews, soups, and fried or baked foods.

Of the supplies he had brought along there was extra salt and alum for the tanning of hides. He began soaking a deer hide from his very first day of hunting. When it had been thoroughly worked with the tanning solution—five or six days was usually plenty for a mule deer—he rinsed it in the creek and then hung it to dry. Once it was cleaned, scraped, and ready, he smoked it Indian fashion to cure the buckskin so it would remain soft and eliminate the animal scent. The hide, when stretched and secured with a bough railing, sufficed as a substitute mattress for Laura. A smaller hide was used for a hammock for Abby. With those two taken care of it meant only he had to sleep on the ground, something he was used to.

As the days passed, he managed to make time for a little hunting and also put out some traps. He rebuilt the corral, with a shelter at one corner offering protection from the wind and storms. He next added a lean-to for their wood supply and removed and expanded one wall to add ten feet of space to their dwelling. Laura and Abby were great help in that they trimmed branches and helped to carry or drag lumber and firewood from the nearby woods. With their doing much of the legwork, he was able to concentrate his efforts primarily on the actual building projects.

Konn had hoped for a late winter, but the rains came to halt their progress. Within two days it had grown cold and the rain turned to snow. It was wet and heavy, blanketing the mountains with several inches by the third day.

"Glad we got the extra room finished before doing some of those other chores," he remarked the morning after the storm had moved on. He cracked open the window to feel the immediate bite of a bitter cold wind, which was blowing through the hills. "We only needed a few more days to be in good shape for a major snowfall."

"Can't do anything about the weather," Laura replied, from over at the table. "The mortar seems to be holding in the cracks and the roof only leaks in a place or two. That's much more than I had hoped when we first arrived."

"Keeping the snow removed from the roof should keep the leaks from getting any worse."

Laura and Abby had been working some bread and cookie dough on the smooth plank tabletop. Laura stopped the chore and came over to stand at Konn's side.

"You have done more work in the past few weeks than three ordinary men," she told him quietly, "and all with one bad shoulder."

"It's pretty much healed up now," he said, dismissing her concern. "I hardly ever notice it anymore."

"It won't hurt to rest for a little while."

"I still need to make mattresses for you and Abby," he said.

"We each have our own bed," she replied. "It will do us fine for the time being."

"I'm going to bundle up and check my traps," Konn said, changing the subject.

"Bur-r-r," she rubbed her arms with her hand, "it feels too cold for traipsing about."

"Might be something in one of the traps," he told her. "I ain't one to let an animal suffer . . . especially if I'm the reason he's in a bad way."

"A compassionate trapper," Laura said with a slight upturn of her mouth. "You are a rare man, Mr. Konniger."

He didn't know what to say to that, so he kept his mouth shut.

"Some fish for supper would be a nice change," she said after a few awkward moments of silence. "But only if the wind lets up."

"I'll take along some line and have a try below the beaver ponds."

Laura flashed one of her smiles. "Well, don't be late. If the weather is bad or the fish aren't biting, we can have bread and beans tonight."

"Yes, ma'am." He returned a grin. "It used to be I seldom worried about my next meal, but since you've been doing the cooking, I look forward to supper every night. You're one fine cook."

"I only worry we didn't bring enough supplies."

"This is a spring storm," he told her. "I 'spect we'll have another good spell before the serious snow flies. You and I can sit down and make a list. Once we get a break in the weather, I'll ride to Lonesome Creek and bring back whatever we need."

"Won't that look a little suspicious?"

"I'll blame it on being wounded and not doing my own buying. I doubt anyone will think twice about it."

"I've never tried to buy supplies for such a long period of time before," Laura said. "I'm afraid I wasn't much help."

"Tough to figure what all to pack, what with there being three of us and neither of us knowing much about the other. When I'm up before daylight, I often take along a couple pieces of jerky or a crust of bread and don't worry about a meal till dark. You two, on the other hand, are probably used to eating two or three times a day on a regular basis."

"Yes, we're spoiled that way."

Konn chuckled at her teasing delivery. "I'll take both pack animals when I go. That way I can bring back a couple bales of straw to make you a decent mattress."

"I don't mind the travois-style bed."

"Come winter, the cold will seep up from the floor. You need something between you and the ground."

"What about Abby's hammock?"

"I'll layer the bottom of her bunk with several rabbit hides and it should insulate her from the cold. Plus, she is up higher and the cabin holds the heat more at roof level than floor level."

"Yes, cold air settles closer to the ground while heat rises."

He drew his brows together at her statement. "You read that somewhere, did you?"

She laughed. "No, I was raised in a small house and my room was in the attic. I about roasted in the summer, but I was warmer than everyone come the cold season."

Konn enjoyed hearing her laugh. It was different from the women he had been around. His mother seldom showed a humorous side—not that he could remember anyway—and women in saloons had a harsh or blaringly loud tone when they would cackle or howl with mirth. And he also knew well the sound of laughter or ridicule between a couple of females. This was something different, an enjoyable sound, like the song of a bird on an early spring day.

"You've an odd look on your face," Laura observed. "What are you thinking about?"

Konn started and abruptly cleared his throat. "Uh, nuthen."

"Want me to fix you something to take with you to eat?"

"We had breakfast," he replied simply, "and I'll find my way back before dark." With not even a twinge from the shoulder wound, he shrugged into his heavy buffalo robe and donned his hat, which he pulled down to cover his ears.

"Aren'cha gonna wait till my cookies are baked, Mr. Kon'ger?" Abby asked, having noticed him bundling up.

"I'll be looking forward to a couple of those when I get back," he promised. "I bet they are going to be the best cookies I ever ate."

She displayed a worried look. "We had a real stove last time I made them. I don't know about trying to bake cookies in a fireplace."

"It works well enough for the bread," Laura chipped in. "I'm sure they will bake up all right."

Konn picked up his rifle and smiled at Abby. "See you in a little while."

"Bye!"

The wind was cold, but it was not much below freezing. If the sun managed to break through the overcast sky, the wet snow would begin to melt at a rapid rate. It was a little early for a prolonged cold spell, although Colorado could have some bitter winters. Konn hoped this wasn't one of them.

Crow cursed his luck. The man at the Dover Flats station did not remember a woman and child boarding the stage, but he said sometimes a passenger would board between stops. If so, only the driver would know and that much was a dead end. The driver who had worked the past few months had moved on to another job. No one knew anything about Mrs. Morrison and her daughter.

Jonas Brown, who handled the post in Lonesome Creek, had also given him no details about the letters Laura and Konn had mailed. He had not pressed him on the subject, only mentioned her plight in passing and hinted he would like information. Mr. Brown, however, took his job very seriously and never said to whom or where the letters were addressed. Now Crow wished he had been a little more insistent.

He thought about riding to the next stop or two along the stage route to see if someone might remember the woman and child. But there was little chance anyone would have known their destination, even if they recalled the two passengers.

Either Konn put them on the stage and the man running the way station didn't pay them any mind, or they missed the stage and he took them down the line where they could catch a connecting route from another town. It seemed the only possible scenarios.

Crow didn't want to spend a week searching for the woman. It was feasible she had gone to Denver and would try to winter there. He could always make a trip in that direction later, after he had made contact with some of the neighboring tribes. The warriors would soon be returning to peaceful camps for the winter and the market would be lost until spring.

He grunted at the peculiar paradox concerning the Indian hostilities. Black Kettle and his Cheyenne had been labeled as friendly Indians, but the Sand Creek attack had left over two hundred of his people dead. The aftermath had cost a great many lives of settlers and soldiers alike, while the assault had been bitterly condemned by the newspapers and politicians from the east. They stated the raid had been a massacre, although the fighting had lasted eight hours and a number of soldiers were killed or wounded.

For people like Crow, who understood both the white man and the Cheyenne, he recognized the problem as being complicated to sort out from either side. Among the Cheyenne there were braves known as "dog soldiers," and they accepted no ordinary chieftain as their ruler. They were free to leave camp and do their raiding, then return and blend in among the rest of the tribe. It was not Black Kettle's fault that he could not control their marauding and killing ways, because dog soldiers did not recognize his authority over them. When the Army insisted Black Kettle turn over the guilty parties, he naturally refused to surrender any of his people to be imprisoned or hanged for their crimes.

On the white man's side, they knew the men doing these raids had come from Black Kettle's camp. They were furious how the braves would raise hell all during the summer, and then return to the safety of the camp for the winter. An additional affront for the soldiers—the tribe was given supplies and blankets, comforting and feeding the very people who had been harassing and killing white settlers! With the enlistment of the Colorado Volunteers coming to an end, they had decided to act. The result was the battle at Sand Creek and the ensuing months of reprisals from most every Indian tribe for a hundred miles around.

At this time, some of those had made their peace; others were being relocated to reservations, and a few still roamed free like Two Bears. Crow needed to contact the warring tribes while there was still time to trade rifles for gold. Once the heavy snows came, those warriors would be holed up for the winter months and would not be dealing for weapons.

"Mrs. Morrison," he said aloud, "you and your little nit can wait." With a tug on the reins, he turned his horse toward the hills.

The weather cleared and most of the snow melted quickly, except for a few pockets back in the deepest shadows. The hunting and trapping was not great, but Konn put in a fair supply of meat and kept Laura busy tanning hides. With Thanksgiving only two weeks away, he decided he had better make the trip to Lonesome Creek and pick up the supplies he would need to get them through till spring.

It was clear and cool the morning he saddled his horse and readied the two pack animals. Laura came out to stand near him and waited for him to give her his attention.

"Four days?" she asked, her arms crossed, hugging herself against the chilly morning air and appearing a little uncertain.

"If it don't come on to snow I 'spect that's about right. I'll check with Mr. Brown and see if any mail has come in for you yet."

Laura lowered her lids to shield her eyes from him. He wondered what had caused her to suddenly seem so . . . apprehensive. Perhaps she feared her fiancé would ask her to return or be furious she was living alone with some rough-edged, unsociable hunter. She had been like a rock these past few weeks, shouldering more than her share of the work, tending and teaching Abby, seeing to the meals and keeping the house and laundry in order. He hated to allow the thought to enter his head, but he had really grown used to having the two of them around.

"Something troubling you?" he asked, half afraid she would bring up her betrothed.

"I . . . it's just having you gone for four days. I . . . I worry about . . ."

"Flynn knows where the cabin is," he assured her. "If something should happen to me, I told him how to find the place. It might be a few weeks before he came up here, but you could get by with the supplies you have, considering I wouldn't be eating up the largest share of our store."

"That's not it," she murmured softly.

Konn stood awkwardly silent, but Laura did not offer to continue. He wondered if she expected him to guess at whatever was stuck in her craw. In an effort to move things along, he turned back to Hammerhead.

"Oh," he said, digging into the saddlebag and removing his spare pistol. He rotated back around and held it out for her. "Here you go. You had better keep this handy, in case you have to chase off a wild animal or something. It's loaded, so don't leave it where the muffin can get hold of it."

She took the gun but gave him a sharp look. "Mr. Konniger"— her words carried a crispness he had not heard in her voice before—"I was trying to say that we are going to miss you!"

He was taken aback by her statement. "Uh, yeah . . . I mean, I guess I know what you mean."

"You guess?"

"Well, I 'spect I'm not the most outgoing gent, and I don't wash as often as I should, and I've usually got some blood on my clothes from—"

"Oh, forget it!" she snapped, sounding even more irate. "Get going and hurry back." She whirled about and stormed off to the cabin.

"Uh, all right," he muttered after her, unable to think of anything better to say.

After the cabin door slammed shut, he looked over at Hammerhead. "You got any idea what that was about?"

The horse must have had an itch, as she shook her head and mane.

"Yeah, that's about what I figured."

Chapter Thirteen

JW couldn't believe it. He'd only been gone a few minutes, to scout a rock ledge a short way from the trail, but now his horse was missing! In a moment of irrational panic, he clumsily drew his gun and scrambled behind a rock. His heart thundered in his chest and he gripped the pistol, holding it out in front of him, his hands trembling with fear.

It had to be Indians!

Straining his ears, JW suffered a petrifying cold, the chill encasing his body, while a flush of fever engulfed him from the neck up at the same time. His stomach burned with a release of acid, and it felt as if there was no air in his lungs. It took a few seconds to realize he had stopped breathing!

JW released a stagnant exhale and gulped down a swallow of fresh air. He saw nothing and heard no approaching footsteps. The only thing audible was a slight rustle of leaves from the wind. He risked a glance from his place of concealment, lifting his head like a ground squirrel peeking from its burrow.

Still nothing.

After five full minutes of hiding between the boulders, JW crawled from his hole and looked down the canyon trail. Keeping his pistol ready for instant use, the rocky terrain prevented him a good view, but he was reasonably certain he was alone.

Feeling a little more confident now, JW slowly made his way down toward where he had tied off his mount. He was two steps away from the spot when he heard the rattle.

The sudden warning caused him to jump back as if he had stepped on a giant spring. He pointed his gun at a coiled snake. It was staring right back at him, shaking the rattles on its tail, its head lifted a few inches, tongue darting out and back, poised to strike.

JW fired . . . a second time . . . and again!

The snake obviously didn't care to share the hillside with a human. With something akin to disgust, it leisurely slithered off through the rocks and vanished from sight. JW looked down at the useless gun in his hand and cursed. Six feet away and he had missed with all three shots! Still, he rationalized, he *had* managed to drive the snake away from the trail. That was a small consolation.

Standing there like a wooden statue, the sun rose on his faculties and he realized what had happened. The snake must have frightened his horse; the animal had broken loose and sped back down the trail. Keeping his gun at the ready, he pointed it at the place where the rattlesnake had disappeared and then hurried past, going a few steps along the trail before taking a long, hard look. He expected to see the horse a short way down the hill, but there was no sign of him anywhere.

Picking up the pace, JW hurried to catch up. *All right, so the horse had been frightened by a snake, so he had pulled his reins loose from the sagebrush branch. How far would he go? Surely it wouldn't be very far down the trail.*

Hours later, as the night sky began to grow dark, JW stopped in his tracks. He was tired, hungry, and thirsty for a drink of water. He had found a couple of patches of old snow, but it had barely wet his lips. He sighed dejectedly. *Where had that stupid horse gone?* He had been tracking him for miles and miles. Common sense dictated if the animal had been going to stop, JW would have caught up with him by now. Even as the thought occurred to him, he recalled the words of the hostler at the livery. "Make sure you tie and hobble Cyclone at nights or you'll find yourself afoot. More'n once he's come home without his rider." It had been a warning he had heeded, always securing both his pack horse and his riding mare at night. Once the pack animal had come up lame, he had been even more careful with Cyclone. But he hadn't thought about the miserable critter breaking loose while he was only a few hundred feet away, not after riding him for several weeks!

JW tried to swallow but his mouth was too dry. It was time to face facts. The horse was gone and he was not going to catch up with him. He was on foot, possibly a hundred miles from the nearest town. He had not even seen a farm or ranch house in the past few weeks. No tent, no food, and nothing more than the tiny bits of snow and a puddle or two of water remaining from the recent storm to quench his thirst. He would need fresh water and food to survive. He did have a gun, but he had missed the snake from two steps away! Not much chance of surviving on rabbits or pine hens—unless he could stun them by throwing rocks!

Thinking hard, he remembered the beaver ponds he had seen from a nearby peak. He might figure a way to catch a fish or frog—*frogs were edible, weren't they?* He had no matches—they had been on the stupid horse—but he knew there were people who ate raw fish. He could survive by catching and eating fish while he followed the stream to the town Crow had mentioned. *What was it? Lonesome Creek!*

Starting up the canyon, he began to walk with purpose. It would be dark soon, but he would continue for as long as he was able. He would keep watch for a pine tree where the earth had been protected from the storm. He might be able to burrow in and cover himself with the fallen needles for a makeshift blanket. He was wearing a warm jacket and the temperature was not so low at nights that he would freeze to death.

"Maybe not," he grumbled under his breath, "but it's going to be damn cold sleeping at night!"

Konn rode until dark, was up before daylight and pushed hard, arriving at Lonesome Creek around midday. It had begun to drizzle an hour or so before he reached town and, with dark clouds forming over the mountains, it appeared he had waited too long to make the trip. He left his stock at the livery and gave orders to feed and water the animals before making his way to a canteen to get something to eat.

Flynn had not yet gone to work at the saloon and was in the

middle of making a bowl of stew disappear. He spied Konn, rose to his feet, and waved him over to his table.

"Well, I'll be the son of a suck-egg mule!" His face broke out in a wide smile of greeting as he reached out to shake Konn's hand. "Didn't expect to see you until spring!"

Konn pulled up a chair, and they both sat down. "I didn't do a very good job of stocking up on supplies, and it looks to be a hard winter coming this year."

"If this storm sticks around you might be treading a foot of snow on your way back," Flynn warned.

Konn ordered himself a bowl of stew and half a loaf of bread. Once the order was given, he leaned across the table, keeping his voice low.

"You hear anything I ought to know about?"

Flynn surveyed those men around him, but most were busy talking or eating. None appeared to take any special interest in him or Konn.

"There's a man named Crow around town—you heard of him?"

"Recall sharing a fire and a meal with a fellow by that name one time. Not the most talkative man I ever sheltered with for the night, but he was good company for being in hostile territory." Konn gave Flynn a curious look. "Why do you ask?"

"I was only a Denver policeman for a year—believe I told you that—but the training sticks with a man." Flynn once more swept the room with his eyes, as if making certain no one was paying them any particular attention. "There's something I was going to mention to you, but forgot all about until after you had left town."

"What's that?"

"After I visited Copton's store to get Mrs. Morrison's money, I caught sight of Crow. He'd been watching me. He scooted down an alley, but soon as he thought I had gone on about my business, he made his way into the store."

"You think he was trying to hide from you, or didn't want you to know he was going to the general store?" Konn asked.

"I'm not sure."

Konn made a face at the absurdity. "Everyone goes to the store. Why should he not want you to see him?"

"Exactly what I'm saying, Konn. Had he entered and said howdy as we passed, I wouldn't have given it a second thought. That's the training I was talking about from back when I was a policeman. It's being curious when something strikes you out of the ordinary."

"And you figure he was up to no good?"

"Everyone knows Crow is half-Cheyenne," Flynn pointed out. "He might still have contacts with some blood relatives, if you know what I mean."

"Meaning he could have been doing business with Two Bears."

Flynn gave a nod. "And I recall you mentioned how Two Bears and his war party were carrying new rifles, not the old single-shot carbines from the war."

Konn climbed aboard the same train of thought now. "I don't suppose you know if the new general store brought in a shipment of guns?"

"They rented a wagon and used a couple of undesirables from here in town to transport goods from Faro Junction. Two guys, Spanish and Skinny Bob. I wouldn't trust either of them to watch my dog . . . providing I had a dog."

"If Copton set a plan in motion to kill the Morrison family, I'd sure like to find the proof. Ain't no vermin lower than those who would order the killing of a woman and child."

"Don't know how we would prove it, Konn, not unless one of those Indians confessed to being hired by Crow and Rudy Copton himself."

"We could maybe track the guns from the other end?"

"I recall Rudy mentioning to me how he had lost the invoices from his early shipments, something about burning the wrong trash one day. I didn't think anything of it at the time, but it has a bad smell to it now."

"No records of his shipments," Konn deduced.

"And we only have Crow acting a little suspicious to start with. He might have had his own reasons for wanting to go into the store unseen."

"The timing seems convenient," Konn said, "what with you

stopping by to pick up the money for Mrs. Morrison. Where's Crow now?"

"He left town a while back. He often disappears for several days at a time. He also moved his things out of the saloon and is sharing a tent with Spanish and Skinny Bob."

Konn's food arrived, and he began to eat. There was little about the meal to equal what he had grown used to in the past weeks, but he ate out of necessity.

"Hate to think of Copton being behind the Indian attack and not make him pay," Flynn said after a bit. "But I don't see any way to prove he is guilty, not without a witness."

Konn tried to stay impartial. "He might only be guilty of trying to steal Mrs. Morrison's store. The Indian attack could have been a random thing."

"Weren't you the one who mentioned something strange about the attack the night you hit town—how the one Indian went after the lady instead of you?"

"Yes, it struck me an odd thing to do," Konn agreed.

"Maybe he thought you were done for, standing there with a knife sticking out of your chest?"

"I had just shot and killed Two Bears," Konn recalled. "He might not have seen the chief go down, as he was a bit behind him. Even so, an Indian warrior doesn't attempt to kill a relatively helpless woman before taking out a man with a gun."

"Sure makes a man wonder."

"My guess? Two Bears gave the order to make certain the woman was killed. The brave was following orders."

"You think so?"

"Walks Tall called off the attack once the chief was down. He said the fight was over because Two Bears was dead. I think the chief made the deal—whether a deal was made with Crow or whoever—and he intended to keep his end of the bargain. It made no sense for him to come all this way just to kill me."

Flynn looked out the window. "Starting to snow, my friend. Where did you say you were spending the night?"

"The animals need a night's rest," Konn informed him. "I figure the livery man will let me toss down a blanket in the loft."

"You're welcome to make your bed on the floor of my room," Flynn offered. "I don't get to bed until after midnight and I don't snore louder than a passing freight train. Also, I haven't done any sleepwalking since I was caught in the same bedroom as a mayor's wife."

"Must have done some fair *sleeptalking* too, considering you're still walking around a free man."

Flynn laughed. "It was more her fault than mine. I didn't know the gal was married until he showed up."

"Funny how those little things come up sometimes."

The man showed his good-natured grin. "And I'll expect you to not be bringing any female companions up to my room. I've got a reputation for being a gentleman here in town."

"Not too tough when you figure there aren't but a couple decent women who ever come into town. And none who frequent the saloon."

"So you want to share the room?"

"It's mighty accommodating of you, Flynn," Konn said. Then he frowned in thought. "Fact is, you've done a number of things for me and never asked so much as a thanks. Were I the suspicious sort, I might think you had a motive for your kindness. I don't suppose you have any idea of how I can pay you back?"

Flynn's smile vanished, and he grew somber at once. "Their name is Jacobs," he said quietly. "Heath, Luke, and Barney. The miners call them the Bad News Brothers."

Konn wondered if he was kidding him, but the man appeared deadly serious. "Bad News Brothers, huh?"

"They aren't the biggest men around, but all three share the temper of a scalded badger," Flynn replied. "I got the best of Heath a couple weeks back, and I'm dead certain those boys will be looking to get even."

"I 'spect you started this tale in the middle, Flynn. What is between you and these Jacobs characters?"

Flynn took a deep breath and let it out slowly. "The brothers cast tall shadows hereabouts and everyone pretty much gives them a wide berth. They have acted as if they owned the whole town since they arrived a couple months back. They are kin to one of the mine owners so they all landed good jobs. Most of the miners resent the hell out of them, but if they step up to complain about one or more of those boys, it could mean their jobs. And you know how it is this time of year—tough enough to make it through the winter even working when you can. Lose your job and a fellow could die of cold or starvation.

"Anyway, the Jacobs boys began to push people around right off, and they've beat up more than one or two who tried to stand up to them. Two weeks back, I locked horns with Heath, the eldest. Barney and Luke had gone off with a couple of friends when Heath decided he was going to bust up the place. Before he could do much damage, I corralled him." Flynn shrugged his shoulders. "By the time his brothers knew he was missing, I had herded him over to Dodd and he was fined twenty-five dollars—mostly to pay for damages. His brothers showed up, and I thought we were in for it, but I had my shotgun with me. They finally paid the fine and left Dodd's office. Heath swore he would get me the next time they hit town. They didn't come round last week, but today is Saturday."

Konn hadn't kept track of days. "It's Saturday?"

"I figure they'll all three come calling tonight at the saloon, and nary a soul has offered to stand with me. I'm no coward, but I know my limits. I'm no match for three of them at the same time."

Konn certainly didn't want to involve himself in a feud, but he owed Flynn a debt. The man had given up his bed while Konn recovered from his wound. He was also the only man he could trust to get word to him about the circuit judge. When thinking about it, he was as close to a friend as Konn had.

"Maybe I can help you work this through," Konn suggested. "Once they see you're not alone, it could make a difference."

"I don't like asking you to fight any battles for me," Flynn said quickly. "It's just that, well, hell's bells, Konn, I know I can't whip all three of them."

"When do you expect them to come around?"

"It's usually sometime after dark. They keep drinking till they decide to either leave or tear the place apart."

Konn finished the last of the stew and sat back in his chair. He never went looking for trouble, but Flynn had been there for him. A debt called in was an obligation, one he intended to honor.

"I'll get my supplies lined out and be around."

Flynn's look of relief was thanks enough for Konn, and the man's mood was instantly more cheerful and happy.

"Oh," he said, as if it had previously slipped his mind, "Brown mentioned you got a reply to one of the letters you sent, said it was from Kansas. You thinking about a job over that way come spring?"

Konn felt as if someone had set a huge rock on his chest. *Laura's fiancé!* He had tried not to think about the woman as anything more than a guest in his house—Abby too—but it was impossible. His brain could not control his heart. He knew it was a stupid thing to do, but he had grown very fond of them both. Though he battled against it with all his might, he suffered daydreams about how Laura would feel in his arms and how wonderful it would be to have Abby call him "daddy."

"Uh, Konn?" Flynn asked after a short time. "Did you hear me, about the letter I mean?"

"Yeah, I . . . I guess my mind kind of took a hike down a side trail for a minute there. I'm obliged to you for looking out for my interests. I'll pick up the letter when I buy supplies."

"Anything I can do for you?"

"Not unless something happens to me. I'd hate to let Mrs. Morrison down and not inform her about when the circuit judge was due to arrive."

"Not to worry." Flynn gave him a positive nod. "Nothing is going to happen, and I'll sure enough get word to you when the judge is due to arrive. I'll see to it you have plenty of time to notify or fetch the lady for the hearing."

Konn put enough coins on the table to pay for the meal, and a little extra, before he rose to his feet. "I'd best see about those supplies." He winked at Flynn. "Hate to say it, but I'll likely have to buy some of it at Copton's store."

Flynn chuckled. "Good thing Mrs. Morrison isn't here. She'd shred your hide for being a traitor!"

Konn bid Flynn farewell and went out into the storm. The falling snow was wet, not yet a severe winter snow with cold temperatures and ice. So far, it was melting instead of laying as it hit the ground. He glanced upward, but the nebulous haze from the dark, gray sky was all he could see. It was impossible to know if this was a passing fall storm or a major blizzard that would dump a foot of snow on the ground. If the weather was too severe, it might be impossible to return home tomorrow. He sighed, knowing it did no good to worry about something over which he had no control.

As expected, Brown's Pharmaceutical didn't have everything he needed. He bought what he could and picked up the letter, which he tucked into his inside coat pocket. Before leaving, he paused to browse at a couple items. He didn't dare buy them outright, as it might start someone to thinking. Nonetheless, he pondered on a way to make a purchase without anyone knowing he was the buyer.

The snow increased and soon covered the ground with a wet, heavy layer. Konn made his way back to the saloon and took the supplies up to Flynn's room. He would have been excited about his notion to buy something special from Brown's store, but carrying the letter around caused him to suffer a depression.

He returned to the street and walked to Copton's Mercantile. After taking a moment to kick the worst of the snow and mud from his boots, he entered the store. It was getting late, but there were several customers, being that Saturday was a shopping day for many in the area. A small group were at the counter, obviously from a nearby ranch: one elderly white-haired woman, two younger motherly sorts, and five kids aged four to twelve or so. They were busy sorting out the different groceries and placing them into boxes for travel in a wagon, while a couple of the kids were petitioning for hard candy or sugar sticks. Konn gave them some space, while waiting to place his order.

As he watched the transactions he took stock of the Coptons. Rudy was polite and professional, whereas his wife was aloof, as if she was doing the people a favor by selling them merchandise. He wondered how long it would be before the woman demanded

Rudy sell the store and give her a better life, one where she didn't have to work.

The group finally had everything organized for travel, including candy all around, so they bundled up and paraded out the front door. A team and wagon were outside awaiting the supplies and passengers. Konn sauntered over to the counter and placed a sheet of paper on the counter. Having scratched out everything he had been able to buy from Brown, it still left several items he needed.

Rudy glanced at the list before looking up at Konn. Recognition dawned in his glance, yet he made no mention of the fact Konn had done much of his shopping at Brown's Pharmaceutical.

"Didn't expect to see you until spring," he said, displaying an impersonal smile.

"I wasn't up to doing my own buying when I left town," Konn explained. "Can you fill everything on the order?"

Copton stared over the list more carefully this time. "I don't see any problem. I'll need to fill a jar of honey from the barrel, bring the flour from the storeroom, and the like. How soon do you need these things?"

"I'd like to have them ready when you first open your door tomorrow, if you can manage it."

"I'm sorry, but we don't work on Sunday. Day of rest, you know."

Konn paused in thought. He didn't want to stay an extra day, but a second glance out the window told him the storm was growing worse. If it continued the trail would be slippery and hard on his horses. To insist Copton put together the order right away might cause suspicion. After all, he was living alone. Why would he be in a big hurry to get back to his cabin?

"Right," he said, "I don't keep track of time much. Didn't realize what day of the week it was."

The man looked up at the clock on the wall. "We close in a few minutes, but I can stay late and put this together tonight if you are set on leaving tomorrow morning."

The offer was innocent enough, but there was an inquisitive glint in Rudy's gaze.

"No, it's too late to beat the storm now," Konn told him. "And it's hard on the animals traveling over fresh snow. I'll stick around town an extra day and hope it clears up some by Monday."

The man relaxed, as if totally unconcerned one way or the other.

"I do hope Mrs. Morrison caught the stage all right," Rudy said, changing the subject.

"She's shore 'nuff gone," he replied simply. "Tough on her and her tyke, losing everything they had."

"Yes, we were very sorry about Ben. He was a good friend."

Konn about mentioned how he would still be alive if not for Rudy sending him a map that led him right to Two Bears but refrained. As far as anyone in town was concerned, Laura had left the country and he had moved into his hunting lodge until spring. He knew it was best to keep his mouth shut.

"All right, Mr. Konniger," Rudy said, once he had decided Konn was not going to offer anything more about Laura. "I'll have this order ready and waiting for you when we open the doors Monday morning. That would be at seven sharp."

Konn gave a nod of his head. "Add a dozen sugar sticks to the order," he said. "Watching those ranchers reminded me that I sometimes get a hankering for something sweet."

"I know what you mean," Rudy agreed, showing a smile. "I often steal a stick of candy for myself."

"I'll be here when you open, with money to pay the bill, and I'm obliged."

Rudy gave a courtesy nod. "See you then."

Chapter Fourteen

The sudden pounding on the cabin door alarmed Laura. Startled, she stared at her daughter before she recovered to fetch the pistol Konn had given her.

"Anyone home?" came the sound of a man's desperate plea. "Can you please let me in?"

Laura moved over to the door, removed the bar, and opened it a crack. She peered out to get a look at the man. He was soaked from the wet snow, a once-expensive hat drenched and drooping, and his jacket was soiled and clung to his upper body like a dirty wet rag. His costly trousers and boots were soiled and smeared with mud.

"What do you want?" she asked.

"L-lost my horse . . . supplies . . . everything!" he cried. "I spent last night buried under pine needles to keep from freezing. H-haven't e-eaten for two days." He clasped his hands together as if praying. "Please, madam! Take pity on a lost soul who desperately needs your help."

Laura was moved to sympathy, but she was also fearful of allowing a stranger to enter the cabin while Konn was away.

"I-I can't go on any longer," the man gasped, noting her hesitation. "I'm nearly frozen and about starved. My strength is gone. If I don't find food and shelter I'll die."

Laura tucked the pistol into the fold of her skirt, stepped back, and allowed the man to enter. He practically fell inside, then rushed over to the fire and squatted before the burning embers, stretching out his hands to absorb the heat.

"I'll get you a blanket," she said. "You can remove your jacket and boots. We can set them aside to dry while you warm yourself by the fire."

"I shall proclaim your mercy to the heavens, madam."

Laura subtly slipped the pistol under a cloth near the table, out of sight yet within easy reach, and picked up the extra blanket Konn used at night. Thinking of his strength and confidence when dealing with almost any situation, she realized how much she had come to rely upon him. He would have let the man in, taken charge of the situation, and she and Abby would have hardly been inconvenienced. But now a stranger was inside the cabin with them, and they were alone and unprotected.

Laura immediately dismissed her fears. Yes, he was a stranger, but he hardly looked like a hired killer sent to be rid of her. He had an odd sort of accent, as if he had not been out west long enough to pick up the jargon. She could not remember the last time she had been addressed as "madam," as opposed to "miss" or the slang term "ma'am."

Rather than prepare a fresh meal for the man, Laura cut a large portion of day-old bread and added a full tin of beans. If the man was suffering famine as he claimed, he would be thankful for even a cold meal.

Some thirty minutes later it was full dark outside, and the newcomer had recovered from the cold. He'd eaten the meal and now sipped at the last of his second cup of coffee. He introduced himself as JW Fentworthy and explained how he had come to lose his pack animal, his mount, and all of his supplies. He then added how he had been attempting to reach the stream so he could follow it to Lonesome Creek. Once dry, warm, and fed, he displayed his first bit of curiosity.

"I smelled the smoke from your chimney for what seemed like miles," he said, searching the room with his eyes. He took notice of the bed against one wall, the addition of another small room, and undoubtedly recognized a child's hammock. He didn't make a point of saying it, but his curiosity was apparent with his next sentence.

"When I saw the corral was empty, I didn't know what to expect."

"Yes, well my . . . brother"—she decided to be evasive—"is out doing some hunting. He most likely took shelter from the storm, but he could also return at any moment. He knows these mountains as well as any Indian."

A dark light of suspicion danced in the man's eyes. "You live way out here with your brother?"

Abby had raised her brows at Laura's lie, but she gave her daughter a quick look to transmit her intention. "My husband was killed a short time back," she clarified. "We had no place else to go until spring." She hesitated briefly, suddenly at a loss to think of Konniger's first name. Everyone referred to him as Konn or Konniger . . . what the devil was . . . "Keith," she continued once more, relieved she had remembered his name, "works for the railroad and often sells meat to the nearby mining towns or even the forts. He is very well known in this part of the country."

"An' he's the best shot in the whole world," Abby bragged. "He can shoot horseflies!"

JW smiled at her. "That's some shooting!"

"He drove off a whole bunch of Indians who attacked us one time!" she exclaimed. "Saved us from a bear too!"

"Sounds like quite a man."

"Yes," Laura said with a smile, "Keith Konniger is something of a hero in our family."

"I surmise, as you are widowed, you don't go by Mrs. Konniger?"

"No, I use my married name . . . Darla Conrad," she said, borrowing the name of the wife of a banker acquaintance. "This is my daughter, Abigail."

"Keith Konniger, huh?" he repeated the name. "I've not heard of him, but I am not familiar with this part of the country. I've been following opportunities westward, you see—travel the country, seek your fortune, that sort of thing. I left my uncle and a good job on a bit of a whim, intent upon doing some prospecting." He uttered an embarrassed chortle. "You can see where my wild seed has brought me."

"Traipsing around the mountains for days, sleeping on the

ground, eating from a can, and washing in cold mountain streams," she smiled. "Seems a lot of work to find a little gold dust."

"Right you are, good lady," he replied cheerfully. "I have learned my lesson and will be returning to civilization at my first convenience."

Laura's mind kept working, turning over possibilities. The house had been more than adequate for the three of them, but with a stranger in the house, it would be stifling and terribly crowded.

"Your brother sleeps on the floor, does he?" JW asked, as if he had been thinking along the very same line.

"He will put another bed in the new addition once he returns from this hunting trip. We joined him rather unexpectedly, and he hasn't had time to finish all the necessary work."

"Then he does sleep on the floor."

"Yes, Keith is not accustomed to comfort. The blanket I gave you is all he needs. Everything else, he carries on his horse."

"Not to worry," JW said, displaying an amiable grin. "I shall not be needing anything more than a single blanket either. I can stoke the fire during the night so the house doesn't get too cold."

Laura allowed herself an uneasy smile of agreement, but having a strange man in the house seemed a severe intrusion. She couldn't put the man out in the storm; it would be un-Christian and might mean his death. But the idea of having a man sharing their small cabin, other than Konn, did cause a foreboding.

Konn kept watch from a dark corner of the saloon. He had a beer on the table in front of him, but he had taken only a sip or two. He suffered melancholy, the worst he had known since his father died. It took little brain work to understand his current state of brooding was due to the letter in his pocket. What kind of man would sit back and let his woman fight her own battles? If the guy loved her, he should have rushed to her side at the first word of the Indian attack. If he was unable to come join her, he should have demanded she return to him!

Konn grunted to himself and wondered, *What kind of sniveling milksop have you chosen as your fiancée, Laura?*

He lifted the glass but set it back down. Blast it all, he wasn't thirsty and he wasn't a drinking man! To his way of thinking, booze only made people act stupid, and there was already an abundance of stupid without any outside help!

Trying without success to put Laura and Abby out of his head, he glared about the room. Let the troublesome brothers come. His foul mood twisted his insides into a knot and the blood smoldered like molten lava in his veins. If he didn't vent a little steam, he was going to explode. Dwelling over the damnable letter in his pocket, which relentlessly burned a hole through his heart, he welcomed the chance to mix it up!

The place soon filled with miners and a few cowboys and businessmen. The saloon owner and Flynn were running the floor and setting up drinks. The two girls—aged doves named Alice and Molly—floated from table to table, seeking a free drink or a gratuitous chip from a lucky winner at one of the gambling tables. Everything was running smoothly and under control, until the three men entered together. They all bore the same prominent nose and shaggy, clay mud–colored hair.

An immediate hush fell over the crowd. A few revelers cast nervous or wary glances at the three men. Many of them appeared anxious they might be the target of the Jacobs brothers' fun for the evening.

Before the trio had gone ten feet, one of them gave a miner a shove.

"Outta the way, you Dutch goat," one snarled after the man. The pusher was the largest of the trio and looked to be the oldest brother.

The miner whirled about, but held his tongue. Rather than start something, he grumbled under his breath and moved away.

Men parted to make a path as the brothers approached the bar. The counter had been shoulder to shoulder, but suddenly there was ample room for the three of them.

"Set us up with three whiskeys, Flynn!" the elder one spoke loudly. "And don't try and shovel any of that rot-gut poison our way."

"You tell him, Heath," the youngest-looking one spoke up. "Me and Barney want the good stuff, not no bottom of the barrel snake spit."

Konn deduced the youthful speaker was the third brother, Luke. Flexing his fingers into a fist and then relaxing, he cautioned himself to forget about the letter. If he lost his temper, he might do more damage than he intended. From his unobtrusive viewpoint, he kept an eye on the trio, waiting to see if they would get out of line and pose a problem for Flynn.

As for his friend, Flynn was abruptly alone behind the counter. The boss suddenly decided he needed to make a nature call or found another excuse to disappear. Flynn regarded the three with a steely expression but wordlessly poured them each a glass of whiskey.

The three men were loud and boisterous, continuing to drink for a time while often belittling a number of nearby miners with words or slurs. It was pretty harmless until one of the two working girls got too close.

Heath shot out his hand and grabbed the woman by the wrist. "Hey, Alice," he sneered, yanking her around and shoving his face to within a few inches of her own. "How come you and Molly don't never come over and drink with us?"

Luke chimed in at once. "Yeah, ain't our money no good?"

Before the woman could reply, Barney sidled up next to her. "Easy, guys," he jeered, "don't you know who this is?" He did a mock bow. "Why, hell sakes, boys, this is Alice Nobody." He scoffed. "They call her that cause she don't never get friendly with *nobody*!"

All three erupted in raucous laughter.

"Would one of you boys like to dance?" Alice asked eagerly, trying to break the chorus of taunts. Showing an experienced bravado, she displayed a fixed smile, though her eyes shone brightly with her suppressed fear. "I'd be happy to dance with one of you."

Heath bore into her with a cruel stare. "Run away from your husband, so I hear," he slurred the words. "What, wasn't he good enough for you?"

"Yeah, bet that's it," Luke added. "Bet Alice here thinks she deserves a rich, handsome prince or something!"

"Or the guy wanted a real woman and not some prissy little witch for a wife!" Barney tossed in his own heckling.

"Please, guys," Alice said sweetly. "How about that dance? Or we can sit down for a drink if you want."

"I think I prefer a kiss," Heath grated through clenched teeth. "How about you give me a big ole kiss instead?"

Alice forced a laugh as if he were joking. "Come on, Heath," she coaxed. "You know I only drink or dance with customers. Wouldn't you rather just dance?"

Heath had made up his mind. He pulled her to his chest, pinning her there by wrenching her arm behind her back. She gasped from the sudden pain and a naked fear spread across her face.

"Please, Heath," she begged. "Don't do this."

"You've played high and mighty ever since we started coming to this two-bit watering hole." Heath scathed her with his words. "You think you're too good to give a man a little ole kiss? Well, honey, I aim to taste those lips of yours and see what's so almighty special!"

Alice began to struggle. She used her free hand to push at Heath, but he batted it aside, while keeping her other arm twisted up behind her back. When he leaned down, she could not avoid having him kiss her forcibly.

"Get her, big brother!" Luke cried.

"Yeah, save me a turn!" Barney called out. "I'm gonna kiss her next!"

Alice battled, twisting and squirming against Heath's superior size and strength. She tore the sleeve of her dress trying to get loose, but his powerful grip prevented her escape.

Konn was on his feet and moving. He shouldered his way past the onlookers and gave a slight nod of his head to Flynn. With all attention fixed on Heath and Alice, the other two brothers were not aware of Konn stepping in behind them. He reached up, using his hands to cup Luke by the right side of his head and Barney by the left. Before either had a chance to react, he rammed their heads together hard enough that everyone in the room heard the loud, sickening smack. The brutal force of banging heads sent both men to their knees howling from the sudden pain.

"What the . . . ?" Heath broke contact with Alice, shocked to discover his brothers were both on the floor.

Flynn didn't give him time to think either. He reached out, latched hold of Heath's free arm with both hands and gave a mighty tug. Heath lost his grip on Alice as he was jerked off his feet and dragged over the bar. Flynn slammed him bodily down on the floor, and before Heath knew he was in a fight, the bartender hammered him with several punishing blows.

Luke recovered enough from knocking heads to start to rise. Konn's big fist pulverized him at the base of the neck with the power of a double-jack. The young man splattered on the floor like a dropped egg.

Barney remained on his knees holding the side of his head. A lump had already formed above his ear from the contact with his brother's skull. He glanced up over his shoulder at Konn, towering over him like a two-story building, and sat right down on the floor with his back against the bar counter. He quickly raised both hands in a show of surrender.

"Hold it, fella!" he cried. "I ain't got no quarrel with you!"

Konn took hold of his collar with one hand and lifted him to his feet. He bared his teeth and drew back a fist, ready to mash the man's face into pudding.

"Wait!" the man screamed, throwing his hands over his face. "Please! I give up!"

Konn kept his fist poised, but he didn't strike the man. Instead, he shoved him back against the bar and held him there. The man finally lowered his hands and stared fearfully at Konn.

"You're going to swear an oath here and now," Konn ordered. "With every man-jack present as witnesses. You either promise Flynn that you and your brothers won't come in here and cause any more trouble, or I'll reach down your throat and pull out a handful of your innards!"

"We promise!" the man wailed. "I swear, we'll be perfect gentlemen from now on. We will!"

Konn whirled him about to face Alice. "Now apologize to the lady."

"We're sorry," he muttered. Konn gripped his neck with his free hand and squeezed. "I mean it, as God is my witness!" Barney cried, red-faced and wincing from the torturous pain. "We're damn sorry!"

"You owe her for a torn dress!" Konn hissed through his clenched teeth.

Barney dug into his pocket and pulled out some money. "Here!" Barney wailed, shoving it into her hand. "Take the money, and no hard feelings . . . okay?"

Alice was too surprised to reply. She stared at Konn in awe.

Flynn dragged Heath to his feet. He had to hold the man up bodily to keep him standing upright. Dazed and disoriented, Heath had blood running from his nose, both eyes were swollen, and he had a split lip.

"Did you hear your brother, Heath?" Flynn asked him sharply. "You got about three seconds to make the same promise or we'll step outside and finish this—just me and you!"

Heath had the stunned look of a man who had just realized his wagon didn't have but three wheels. He stared glassy-eyed at Flynn and dumbly bobbed his head up and down.

"Say it!" Flynn commanded him. "Say it, or I'll grind you into powder!"

"Yup," was the only word Heath uttered. However, he repeated it several times. It sounded like he had a case of the hiccups. "Yup . . . Yup . . . Yup."

Luke got up under his own power but he was unsteady and groaning. He had one hand on the swollen side of his head and the other holding the back of his neck and shoulder.

"Be thankful you had your back to me, sonny boy," Konn told him, reaching out to jab him in the chest with his pointed finger. "Otherwise I'd have busted your collarbone, and you wouldn't have been able to work for a month."

Luke recoiled from Konn. Stark terror flashed across his face, and he looked about one breath away from bolting for the wide open spaces. Barney met Heath at the end of the bar and helped to support him. Luke gave Konn a wide berth and hurried to join them. The three men leaned together for support. Moving as one, the trio staggered in unison as they went out the door and into the night.

Once gone, there was a round of applause from the men in the saloon. Even the owner reappeared, a wide grin showing on his face. "Well, about time we took care of those three troublemakers, eh, Flynn?"

"Yeah," Flynn replied dryly, *"we* sure did."

"Mr. Konniger!" the owner exclaimed, the smile still pasted on his face. "Anything you want to drink tonight, it's on the house."

Konn grunted. "You can give my share to Alice here." He paused to eye the cowardly man. "I'd say ten drinks ought to cover it."

The owner opened his mouth as if he might argue, but Konn put a hard look on him. "If you don't think ten is square, Flynn can set up twenty and I'll drink till they are gone!"

"No, no!" the man said quickly. "Flynn, credit Alice with ten extra drinks. It's only right she earn something for having to put up with those troublesome Jacobs boys."

Alice held the sleeve of her bodice to her shoulder with one hand and smiled her thanks at Konn. He didn't feel the need for anyone's gratitude or company. His mind was still focused on the hated letter in his pocket. During the past few weeks, he had kept hoping Laura's man would have moved on, perhaps found another girl. It had been silly to dream about his relationship with Laura growing into something more, but Konn couldn't help it. She and Abby had become important to him—they were all he wanted in life—but Laura was spoken for. He knew giving her the letter was going to change everything.

"If there's any way I can repay you, Mr. Konniger?" Alice said quietly, having moved over next to him.

Konn about cut her off abruptly, but paused as an idea popped into his head. "Maybe we could get together tomorrow? I do need a favor."

Alice's face lit up like a lamp turned to high flame. "Anything I can do, I'll be around all day." And with those words, she hurried away to change her dress.

"Konn?" Flynn asked. "You want a drink?"

"No thanks, Flynn. I 'spect I'll call it a night and head up to your room. Try not to step on me when you come to bed."

"Just don't you start snoring or I'll stick one of my socks in your mouth," Flynn teased, displaying a grin. He quickly added, "And thanks for the help."

Konn lifted a hand and went toward the back stairs. It would be hard to get any sleep until the noise died down, but at least he would be alone.

Better get used to the feeling, he cautioned himself. *When the circuit judge arrives in town, you're going to be alone again . . . probably for the rest of your life.*

Chapter Fifteen

The next morning Laura was up early and lit the kitchen lamp. She eased open the window a crack and discovered the storm had abated. The air felt crisp, but she could hear water dripping, which meant it had been a wet snow that had not gotten cold enough to freeze during the night. She hoped it meant Konn would be coming home later today, though it didn't seem very likely. He had said four days if the weather held. The storm had arrived the day after he left, so it was logical he would be at least a day late on his return trip.

Laura had provided several animal skins for the guest to use during the night. With a bed of hides and the blanket as covering, JW seemed to have slept soundly. It stood to reason, as he was exhausted. The man could not have gotten much rest buried in pine needles the previous night.

Her moving about awakened JW, and he sat up. When he noticed her looking out the window, he asked the time and about the weather.

"It's coming on to daylight and looks like the storm is over," she replied. "Konn ought to be starting for home today."

"Thought his name was Keith?"

Laura wondered at him jumping on her slip of the tongue. "Yes, well most people call him Konn. He prefers it over Keith."

"I understand." He said cordially, "I too adopted initials to shorten my name and simplify it for people to remember."

Laura closed the shutter and turned to business. "If you will draw us some water from the creek, I will start breakfast." He automatically looked at Abby. "She's awake," Laura told him. "She always pretends to be asleep in the morning so I'll let her stay in bed a while longer."

JW chuckled and put on his jacket. He had remained fully clothed during the night. The wood box had suffered from his constant vigilance, as he had used more kindling in one night than Konn did in three. As Laura presented the man with the water bucket, he stared directly into her eyes. She found his scrutiny unnerving.

"You are a fine-looking woman, Darla Conrad," he complimented her. "I'm surprised you don't have a host of suitors lined up at your door."

"Hence the necessity of living up here with my brother," she replied a bit crisply. "I am not yet prepared to encourage a new courtship."

The man took the offered bucket and pivoted for the door. "Life is short," he said, showing her a crooked grin. "One should not let the sands of time slip away without trying to reap the most from each day."

Laura laughed, as if he was making a humorous remark. "So says the man who has spent—how many weeks?—wandering the hills searching for treasure."

JW joined in the mirth as he went out the door. As soon as it was closed, Laura went over and helped Abby down from the hammock.

"Why did you tell the man the wrong name, Mommy?" Abby asked.

"We have to pretend," she explained. "We don't want anyone to know we are staying here with Mr. Konniger until spring. If someone found out, it could make it harder to win the case in court and get back our store."

"What 'bout Mr. Kon'ger? How will he know your new name?"

"That's something I'll worry about when he returns," she explained. "If JW is still here, you must remember to call him Uncle."

Abby displayed a worried frown. "I wish he was here."

Laura reached over and gave her shoulder a slight squeeze. "So do I, dear, but we can get by on our own until he returns, can't we?"

Abby's face brightened with a smile. "Yeah, we can."

JW returned a few minutes later with the water. He carefully cleaned the snow from his shoes before entering and placed the bucket next to the kitchen counter.

"You were right about the storm," he announced, removing his jacket. "Clear sky in all directions this morning."

Laura moved over to the fireplace to check the frying pan. It rested evenly on the framework of flat stones Konn had provided. She began with two diced potatoes, then added pieces of salt pork, cooking them thoroughly. Once they were ready, she used a couple of their precious store of eggs to finish off the skillet breakfast. It was more than she should have used, but JW was a guest.

Considering the man, he struck her as polite and charming, with an easy smile and the cultivated manners of an aristocrat. While eating their meal together he told them stories about crossing the ocean as a young man. He had seen whales blowing water spouts and watched show-off dolphins circling the ship. They would race alongside, breaking water with their jumps, then dash across the bow, as if taunting the slow-moving craft.

Next he recited tales of the big cities back east, of his travels through New York, Philadelphia, and Chicago. A literate man, he described mental pictures of the street cabs, buses, and some new train cars, which were as plush as the finest mansions in the country. It seemed he had been everywhere.

Once Laura finished washing the dishes, she suggested he cut some wood for the fire. JW was agreeable at once but wondered how they would ever burn such wet wood.

"Konn keeps dry wood under the lean-to around the back," Laura explained. "You cut wood from that pile and replace it with some of the damp tender he stacked next to the house. Hopefully, by the time it's needed, the wet wood will have dried."

"A thoughtful planner, your brother," JW said. "How about the three of us do something outside afterward? I would venture a game of Run Sheep, Run would be good exercise for Abigail."

"We'll see," Laura replied carefully. "I wouldn't want her to get wet and cold and maybe catch a chill."

"It sounds fun!" Abby piped up. "Mister . . . um, Uncle Kon'ger said we would play some games when the snow came, but it melted too fast the last time it snowed."

If JW noticed her mistake in calling Konn "mister," it didn't show on his face. He shrugged into his coat and went out the door. Within a few minutes he could be heard chopping away at a piece of wood.

"I messed up," Abby apologized. "I forgot to call Mr. Kon'ger "uncle' for a minute."

"That's all right."

"Can we play some games outside like the man said?" she asked eagerly. "I'm tired of reading and sitting inside this dark old house."

"I believe we can go outside for a little while," Laura gave in, "unless a cold wind starts to blow."

"Is Mr. Kon'ger going to get back today?"

"No, I'm afraid the storm will have forced him to wait a day or so. I'm not sure when he will get back."

"I kinda miss him, don't you?"

"Yes," she replied, then mentally added, *especially with us entertaining a house guest!*

Skinny Bob raised up from his bunk as Crow entered the tent. "Don't leave that flap open," he complained at once. "It's as cold as an ice house in here already!"

"Why isn't there fire in the stove?" Crow wanted to know. "I rode all night to get here!"

"Spanish lost his money gambling the other night. I already paid my share, so I'm not going to buy any more coal. They want two bits a sack, and a sack only holds about twenty pounds. It don't last but one day and night."

Crow pulled the flap closed and glared at Bob. "I bought the stove so I didn't have to pay rent, yet I'm supposed to freeze my tail off because you guys won't pull your own weight!"

"I told you, Spanish is broke and I ain't got but a couple dollars to keep us from starving. We ain't had a lick of work since the snow began to fly!"

"I'll buy some coal, but I'm going to start keeping track of how much you two beggars owe me."

"What're we gonna do, Crow?" Skinny whined. "They 'bout stopped working at the mine lately 'cause of the snow and mud. Not much freight going out, so we only get a load once in a while. And as for Copton, he only needs a wagon load of supplies once a month. We're going to starve!"

Before Crow could reply, Spanish opened the tent flap. He had a sack of coal in either hand.

"Thought you were broke?" Crow challenged, dismissing any other greeting.

"I collected on a bet."

Skinny frowned. "What bet?"

Spanish chuckled. "I seen that big trapper, you know, the one who killed Two Bears?" Crow piped up with "Konniger," and Spanish nodded and continued. "Anyhow, I seen him sitting down with Flynn over at the hash house, them two being all friendly-like. Well, Pudge Gomez and I got to talking later and Pudge says how Flynn was worried about the Jacobs boys visiting the saloon and tearing up the place. You guys remember how Flynn took down Heath a couple weeks back, and everyone expected payback from him and his brothers." A grin spread across his face. "I told Pudge how Flynn ain't running scared and he would figure a way to handle them three troublemakers. We argued back and forth, and I finally bet him ten bucks that the Jacobs boys would end up getting tossed out on their ears."

Crow was paying attention now. "Konn is back in town?"

Skinny nodded affirmatively, but Spanish raised his hand to keep either of them from ruining his story. "Sure enough," he continued, "Heath and his two brothers showed up at the saloon, walking tall and primed for a fight. Before the three of them knew what was happening, Konn clubbed two of them down on the floor, and Flynn is beating the hell out of Heath!" He laughed again. "The Jacobs brothers were forced to apologize to the whole world and left the saloon dazed, bloody, and with their tails tucked between their legs. I collected on the bet this morning and picked up some instant heat for the stove!"

"Way to go!" Skinny shouted happily. "I just been telling Crow here how you had lost all your money!"

Crow narrowed his gaze. "Supposing Konn hadn't stepped up?" he wanted to know. "How would you have paid your debt?"

"Got me," Spanish said, grinning crookedly. "Guess I'd have had to sell my horse."

Crow remained thoughtful. "I wonder what Konn is doing back in town."

"He had to order more supplies," Skinny said. "I seen him packing some goods from Brown's place, and then he went over to Copton's store. He left Rudy a list to fill."

"Teach him to let a woman do his shopping," Spanish snorted. "What would Mrs. Morrison know about buying supplies for an entire winter?"

"Speaking of the woman," Skinny said, looking at Crow, "did you find out where the lady and her kid went?"

"Denver is the most likely place, but there's no need to make the trip until spring. When the time is right, we'll approach Rudy with our demands. He can either pay up or risk losing the store and going to jail for fraud."

"How much we going to ask for?"

Crow shrugged. "I figure it ought to be worth the five or six hundred dollars we need to start up our own freight outfit."

"Dang, that sounds good!" Spanish declared. "I can hardly wait."

"We have to survive the winter first," Skinny reminded him. "If we don't get a few more freight jobs, we're going to starve."

"Something will come up," Crow told them. "You two keep mingling and try to earn a few dollars. This winter may be tough, but we're going to make enough to start our own outfit in a few more months."

"I'll drink to that!" Spanish said. Then he added with a shrug, "Well, I would drink to it, if we had anything to drink!"

Crow uttered a sigh. "There's a half bottle of scorpion juice in my saddlebags. Help yourselves."

Konn had risen early and left quietly so as not to wake Flynn, who had worked until the wee hours of the morning. He walked to the livery and checked his animals, then stopped for a cup of coffee and some toast for breakfast. He returned to the saloon and stood on the walk looking over the clear sky. If not for being Sunday, he could have started for home.

"Face it, Konn," he muttered under his breath, "you're stuck here till tomorrow."

"I wondered who a man like you talked to, spending so much time alone," said a female voice, breaking the morning silence.

Konn whirled about and discovered Alice had come out onto the porch.

"I wouldn't have expected you to be an early riser, ma'am."

She smiled. A woman beyond her childbearing years, with the haunted eyes of a person who had known a hard life, Alice was still on the handsome side. She folded her arms for warmth and stepped over next to him. He noticed she was not wearing the usual rouge or powder on her face. The more natural look suited her.

"I didn't know how long you would be in town, Mr. Konniger," she said. "After you rescued me last night, I didn't want you to have to come looking for me."

He accepted her explanation without discussion. "The favor I need has got to be kept a secret."

She displayed a serious expression. "You can trust me. I'm not a gossip, and I never drink too much and say things I shouldn't."

Her comment caused him to grin. "I 'spect you have had enough practice to know how to hold your liquor."

Alice laughed. "Molly and I drink a little beer but very little whiskey, Mr. Konniger. When a drink is sent over for one of us it's usually a ginger ale. We earn the fee of a drink that way, but it costs the house less than half the price. It's how we make our money."

"I see. And you keep your senses about you and don't end up passing out or getting silly from too much drink."

"So what's the favor?" she asked.

He reached into his pocket and pulled out a double-eagle and a small piece of paper. "Here's twenty dollars," he said. "I'd like for you to visit Brown's store and buy the two things on this list . . . without anyone knowing you are buying them for me."

Alice took the coin and looked at the items. When she looked up at him, Konn knew she had guessed the reason for the favor. Instead of saying anything about it, she appeared thoughtful. "I know exactly how to handle this. You can trust me. I'll manage it without any questions being asked."

"If it's not too much trouble, I'd appreciate it if you could wrap up the stuff and place it next to Flynn's door. Just write my name on the outside, and I'll pick it up sometime today."

"It will be my pleasure."

"I did the sums in my head, so there will be enough money for everything. You keep whatever is left."

"That isn't necessary," Alice protested. "After what you did for—"

But he put on a stern look, and it caused her to stop in mid-sentence. She sighed her acceptance. "I'll see that everything is properly wrapped for travel and leave it outside Flynn's door."

"Thanks, Alice, I appreciate it."

She reached out with her free hand and touched him gently on the shoulder. "I hope everything works out for you, Konn. I really do."

He didn't speak again as she turned and hurried inside. There was no reason for him to think she would do anything other than what he had asked. For a moment he wondered how much anyone really knew about Alice. Someone said she had arrived in town with a number of bruises, the victim of abuse by a worthless husband. Flynn had mentioned one time that she never got too familiar with the customers. She would drink with them at their table, laugh and socialize, and she did like to dance, but it never went any further.

He decided her life was out of his hands. Whether she still held true to her wedding vows so as to not commit adultery or if she simply held herself to her own moral standards, he didn't know. Were he a dozen years older and had the time, he might have tried to find out.

On a whim, Konn left the saloon porch and wandered a short way up the street to the little hut between Dodd's place and Brown's Pharmaceutical. It was the Chinese laundry and bath house. He had never paid for a bath, but Laura and Abby would certainly appreciate him getting cleaned up. Of course, he would have a twenty-hour ride on his return, but it ought to be better than the washing of his hands and face—all he usually bothered with.

Surprisingly, the Chinese were already up and working. He knew they were an industrious lot, having been around some of them at the labor camps when hunting for the railroad. From the stories he had heard and what he had seen for himself, there were no harder workers in the country than the Chinese.

A man working at the front desk noticed him outside the door and beckoned him inside. He decided to take a chance and entered the small office-like room.

"You wish some help, Sir?" he asked in pretty good English. "I am Mock Doy and we do laundry, make hot bath, do shave or cut hair. Anything you need, we can help."

He smiled at the man's enthusiasm. "Name's Konniger. Konn to most folks." He tipped his head to indicate the rear of the building. "I see a couple women working in the back," he commented. "Don't hardly ever see a female around one of your places."

"Very hard to bring Cantonese women here to America," Doy said. "Work permits only allow for men. The two in back dressed as men to make journey. They are my wife and sister."

"Nice-looking ladies," Konn told him.

"They work hard," Doy said. Then with what resembled a grin, "Make sure Mock Doy work hard too."

Konn chuckled. "I reckon women are pretty much the same, no matter where they come from."

Doy gave a bob of his head. "We are in agreement, Mr. Konn."

"I was thinking about doing it all . . . bath, haircut . . ." He grinned and ran a hand over his beard. "And if you have some sheep sheers, a shave too."

The man smiled, humor glinting in his eyes. "You offer challenge, Mr. Konn, but I believe we have a blade sharp enough to cut the beard from your face."

"Worries me some," Konn replied. "I've had the beard ever since my first whiskers began to grow. I might not even recognize myself when you're done."

"Should you forget," Doy said with a smile of his own, "I will remind you."

"I'll slip up the street and get my spare clothes."

"We will start water to heat. Do you wish a bath with tub or to stand and wash?"

"Uh, tub I think. I don't relish the idea of having someone stand over me and dump water on my head."

"Very good, Mr. Konn. We will have the bath ready."

Some fifteen minutes later Konn had settled his big frame into a tub of rose-scented water. The soap had a sweet smell as well, and he wondered if Hammerhead would allow him to get close enough to saddle up. However, the water was hot and soothing, relaxing in a way no bathing in a stream or lake could match. The steam rose up and produced beads of moisture on his brow.

He rested his eyes and allowed his mind to wander. The first images to enter his brain were Laura and Abby. He should have shaken them from his head, but he enjoyed the vision. It caused an odd mixture of lightness in his chest and a heaviness in his heart. They were so special, more valuable than anything he had ever imagined. He would do anything to make them his permanent family, yet he knew it wasn't to be. There was another man in their lives, a man whose letter was in his coat pocket. He hated the tiny piece of paper that had the power to remove Laura and Abby from his very life.

"You're a hopeless sap, Konn," he groaned aloud. "It's like tossing a rope at the moon. There ain't a lasso in the entire world long enough to reach it."

Chapter Sixteen

Flynn sat up in bed and drew his gun. "Hold it there, stranger!" he growled the words. "Those things belong to a friend of mine. You keep your big paws off!"

Konn glowered at him. "Very funny, Flynn. You and Alice ought to start a little theater act. She could sing and dance, and you could tell jokes."

Flynn's belly shook with his laughter. "It's just that I'm used to seeing a big, burly-looking brute when I look at you. Hell, you're no uglier than me without hair down to your shoulders and a bushel of whiskers on your puss."

"Tell you the truth, I feel about half naked."

"Did you save the hair?" Flynn asked, swinging his feet over the side of the bed. "You could stuff a fair-sized mattress with what they took from your head and face."

"Like I said, you should be telling jokes for a living."

"Alice come by a short while ago with a package for you," Flynn said, growing serious. "I put it there with your other things."

"Thanks."

"So, now that you've been back to living alone for a few weeks, tell me how it felt to be a family man for few days. Do you miss Mrs. Morrison and her little girl?"

Konn paused to rub the smoothness of his jaw line, a sensation he could not recall from his youth. "I have to admit, Flynn, they weren't near the trouble I might have expected. I was almost sorry to see them board the stage."

"You ever learn anything about that man the lady mentioned, her beau from back in Kansas?"

"She never mentioned him to me at all."

"That strikes me odd, Konn. If the guy was supposed to be part of her future plans, I wonder why she didn't talk about it? And why didn't he come here to be with her . . . or take her back home with him?"

"I've asked myself the same questions," Konn admitted.

"But you're certain the guy really existed?"

Konn felt the weight of the letter in his pocket. "Yeah, I'm sure."

"Ever wonder what it would be like if you and the lady had hit it off? Be a sight different up at the cabin with you and them . . . you know, as your wife and daughter."

The man's words stabbed him in the heart, but Konn shrugged. "I'm a loner, Flynn. I wouldn't have any idea of how to take care of a woman like Mrs. Morrison."

The statement caused Flynn to laugh. "You should have been here when Alice brought your package by." At Konn's curious frown, he went on. "She stood right at the door and told me she wished she had married someone like you."

He was incredulous. "She what?"

"I don't think it was only your stepping up for her last night, because she knows I twisted your arm for some help with the Jacobs brothers."

"If not the rescue, then why?"

"She said it was because of the list you gave her." He watched Konn and waited for him to respond. When he said nothing, he sighed. "You touched her heart with something you are doing." Flynn shrugged his shoulders. "I don't know what was on the list, but her comment did cause me to take a better look at Alice."

"She looks a sight better without all the stuff on her face, don't she?"

"I had her pegged to be several years older, you know, because of the way she hid behind the powder and rouge she puts on her face. In truth, she's not any older than me and not a bad-looking woman either."

"Maybe you ought to talk to her some, get to know her, Flynn," Konn suggested, glad to have turned the conversation away from himself. "You could do with a woman to take care of you."

Flynn rubbed his jaw thoughtfully. "I have nothing to offer a woman. This job pays room and board, and there isn't enough marshalling to make much money that way. I'm about past my prime for much else."

"Ain't you the one who was just telling me how I ought to have tried to win over Mrs. Morrison? Both of us are on a path to grow up alone." He expelled a breath. "And I can tell you, it's weighing heavy on my mind right now, the being alone part."

"I'll give it some thought," Flynn replied. He added with a grin, "If you will do the same."

Konn uttered a sigh of surrender. "You about ready to get out of bed? I had some coffee and toast a while ago but it wouldn't count as a meal."

Flynn began to pull on his boots. "Now that you mention it, I'm about as hollow inside as a badger's living room. The Chinese make a potluck Sunday dinner. Four bits and you can eat all you want. They serve rice, egg muffins, noodles, and a host of things I don't even know what they're called. But you sure don't go away hungry."

"I seen the women working in the back, but I figured it was laundry stuff."

"With the saloon closed on Sunday, it's the only place that serves a meal, other than the eating emporium where we ate at yesterday. Mostly they dish out chili on Sunday or the leftovers from the same stew we had for dinner."

"Their stew makes a man realize why you hardly ever see a stray dog or cat around town."

Flynn chuckled. "That's all too true, my friend."

"I 'spect the Chinese food sounds better, though I've seen the dried fish and rice those Cantonese railroad workers used to live off of. Don't know where they got the strength to do such hard work on such poor rations."

"This meal is a whole lot better than that. And you can bet there will be a chow line by noon, so we best not dally."

"Chow line? That a Chinese name for an eating place?"

Flynn grinned at the question. "Actually, Lo Chow *is* the name of one of the cooks, along with the two women, but no. That there's a slang term for mess or a dinner call," Flynn explained. "First I heard the term was during the war. Don't know where it came from."

"Well, I don't care what it's called, so long as it means I get to eat."

Flynn had his boots on and picked his coat off the wall. "How's the weather?"

"Sun's shining, but it's not melting the snow very fast yet."

"Let's get going," he said, anxious now. "They set up a few benches, but not enough if all the miners show up at once."

"You lead the way, Flynn. I'll be right behind you . . . along with my appetite."

Crow filled his plate with some stringy noodles and sprouts, a pile of fried rice, and a couple of dishes he hadn't tried before. They served a tea for those wanting something to drink, but he didn't care for it—tasted like hot water and seaweed or some such thing to him. However, he did like most everything else they offered. He paused to look around for a place to sit when he spied Flynn and Konn in line—at least the man resembled Konniger. He was too big to not be the hunter, but he looked almost normal. No shaggy hair, no wild unkempt beard. It was the first time Crow had ever seen the man's face.

"Yonder is a good spot in the sun," Skinny Bob said from behind him. "Let's sit over there."

Crow walked over to the bench and took a seat. Holding the plate up, he used a fork to shovel in a mouthful of rice.

"What you looking at?" Spanish asked, sitting on the opposite side of Skinny.

"Konniger," Crow said, tipping his head toward the line of men waiting to reach the serving area. "Never saw the man without a beard before."

Spanish picked him out. "Kind of takes the scare out of his size, don't it? I mean, he looks pretty much like an ordinary guy."

"Except for his size," Skinny joined in on the conversation. "He's still about the biggest guy in town."

Crow took another bite. He liked the food much more when it was still warm, so he didn't put off eating the meal. On the trail he often got by with a can of beans or some dry hard chunks of bread. He'd even made do with Indian rations: seed cakes, dried fish, or wild berries. It was the distinction between eating for the taste and enjoyment or eating for necessity. Today was enjoyment.

"Why do you think he got himself a shave and haircut?" Spanish asked.

"Didn't you say he stuck up for Alice last night?" Skinny asked Spanish. "Maybe he is putting on his best face for her."

"That's possible. I seen her talking to him this morning," Spanish informed his two companions. "They were both out on the porch of the saloon."

"What were you doing up so early?" Crow wanted to know.

"I drank too much before going to bed. I didn't get up by choice."

"And he and Alice were having a conversation on the porch of the saloon?" Crow queried. "After she was up most of the night working?"

"Don't know why she was up so early, but she kind of touched him on the arm before they split up, you know, friendly like."

Crow didn't ask how he could determine her touch had been "friendly like," but it was still curious. Alice was not over the hill, but she certainly had reached the mountain crest. Konn was still fairly young, probably in his mid-twenties. That didn't sound like the proper age alignment for a romance.

"Something isn't right," he muttered to himself.

"What did you say?" Skinny wanted to know.

Crow swallowed the mouthful of rice. "Makes no sense, a hunter shaving off his beard at the beginning of winter."

"Spanish could be right," Skinny said. "Maybe he is trying to make a little hay with Alice."

"She's gotta be ten years older than him, maybe more."

"Could be he don't care!" Skinny argued. "How many hunters and trappers have you run across with Indian wives over the years? It's not the same for their sorts as most other men. They often take the gals who have no choice."

"It's true," Spanish joined in on the subject. "I have known more than one mountain man who married a saloon gal or Indian outcast, because they couldn't find any other woman who would accept such a life."

"You guys are probably right," Crow admitted, so as to stop the debate. "I guess I'm barking at the wrong cat."

"Tell you one thing," Skinny observed, "Konn don't look near so tough without all that hair. He looked like a wild man before, but more of a regular type guy now."

Spanish laughed. "Yeah, a regular guy I still wouldn't want to tangle with."

Crow joined in with the jollity, but he still mentally questioned Konn's motive. As if to confirm the suspicions of his two pals, Alice and Molly arrived. The men in line stopped their forward progress, and the two women were allowed to move ahead of all of them. In a mining town men were particular about being gentlemen, considering they usually outnumbered the women folk by fifty to one.

Konn and Flynn had reached the front of the line, so they were the last two to step back and allow the two women to be served next. Alice smiled and said something to the pair but it was Flynn who spoke in return. Whatever he said, Alice laughed politely and gave him a bright smile.

However, once the two gals had filled their plates, they moved off to a solitary spot and sat down together. Konn and Flynn went in a totally different direction. If Konn had shaved for Alice, they were definitely playing the game of romance close to the vest.

Spanish spoke up after a moment. "Only trouble I've found with this food is how a plate of it can fill you up until you can't take another bite, then an hour later you're hungry again."

"I think it's good for keeping a man's innards in order," Skinny said. "You never hear of a Chinese with a stomach problem."

"Surely not indigestion," Crow mused. "The food they serve is mostly stringy noodles and sprouts or rice, so it hardly needs chewing."

"If I was to lose too many teeth, I reckon this is what I'd eat," Skinny said, flashing a grin. "Like Crow says, it's like eating already chewed food."

"That's a fine thing to say when we're having our meal," Spanish complained.

"I gotta go along with Spanish," Crow said. "One more remark like that and we'll put it to the test about you eating only Chinese food because you have no teeth left!"

As darkness covered the hills, Laura went out into the chill of the evening to look down the trail. With the trees and brush, she could only see a short way, but she hoped against reason to hear or see Konn and his horses. The stillness was broken only by the rustle of a few dead leaves being stirred by the breeze.

A chill caused her to hug herself for warmth. There was little chance he would arrive late. He had obviously had to wait out the storm and been delayed by a day or two.

"What are you doing out here in the cold?" JW's question startled her.

"I wanted to take a last look for my brother. I hoped he would be back before now."

"Travel within these hills, with the snow melting out of the trees, he would very probably catch his death if he attempted such a ride."

"Yes, I'm sure you're right."

"A woman such as yourself," he began, stepping up to stand right behind her, "should not be tucked away in this mountainous terrain, hidden from the world." Laura felt his breath on the back of her neck. "You deserve a real house, with a water pump and glass windows. Abigail should be attending school, wearing a pretty dress to Sunday meetings and learning to understand this wide wonderful world we live in."

Subtly, Laura stepped to the side and turned for the door. "I better see if the stew is ready. It will keep, should Konn arrive later tonight."

"You don't have to be afraid of me, Mrs. Conrad," JW said, flashing a smile. "I would never think of pursuing a woman who found the notion repulsive." His gaze was more intense. "If, however, you should find me less than objectionable, I should enjoy a . . . closer relationship with you than hostess and guest."

There it was—she had suspected as much. The man had developed a measure of infatuation with her. With the words out in the open, it made the situation much worse. Now she had to deal with it.

"I appreciate your concern," she said quietly, "but you should set aside any notion of furthering a relationship with me. Although it is none of your business, I will tell you that I already have another man in my life."

JW took a step backward, as if her words had struck him with some force. "I thought you told me . . ."

"I am telling you now," she cut him short, "so there will be no misunderstanding."

"Yes, yes, of course." He was verbally backpedaling. "I was only trying to . . ."

"Perhaps you would cut some more wood tomorrow?" she suggested. "My brother will be tired when he returns. I don't want him to feel he must attend to all the chores right away."

"I'll start work straightaway in the morning," JW promised.

Laura waited until he had gone inside before she let out the breath she had been holding. For the briefest moment she wondered why she had told JW such a thing. He seemed a very proper gentleman. Why the need to dissuade him from pursuing her?

She thought of Konn, but he had been careful to keep her safely at arm's distance. Even when she had made a slight overture, he had not reciprocated. There was no reason to safeguard her emotions on his account. He seemed content with his life and would likely be happy to be rid of her and Abby.

She gave her head a toss. It made no difference what Konn thought about her, she would not—could not—consider romance until she had her store back. Rudy and Elva had robbed her—possibly had a hand in killing Ben too—and she would not rest or allow herself to be interested in another man until that score was settled!

Chapter Seventeen

Konn had his horses outside the general store by the time they opened the doors. True to his word, Rudy had the order ready to go. Skipping the small talk, Konn thanked him, paid the bill, and had the supplies packed on the horse within a matter of minutes. He had said his farewell to Flynn the night before—a passing good-bye to Alice also—and was headed home before the sun peeked over the eastern mountains.

Konn kept a quick pace, although slowed by snow drifts in many places. He made fairly good time early, but once the snow began to melt, the trail became more slippery underfoot for his animals.

With the steady climb and unsure footing, fatigue soon set in for Hammerhead and the two pack animals. He was forced to rest each hour and let them recoup their strength. By the time the sun went down, he was still hours away.

Konn kept moving until dark, but then he dared not try and keep going once he could no longer see the trail clearly. It wouldn't do to injure one of his animals with haste, as he could not reach the cabin before morning anyway. Although eager to reach home and make sure Laura and Abby were all right, he had to be patient.

Finding a small enclosure in the trees, Konn tended to the animals and then kicked most of the snow aside to allow him a place to spread his poncho and ground blanket for a bed. It was going to be a cold night, but he had his buffalo robe to ward off the chill. After eating some hardtack and a thick piece of venison jerky, Konn settled down with the coat up around his ears.

He tugged his hat lower, feeling the chill of not having the shag of hair covering his neck. His face was exposed and susceptible to the elements, and he mentally cursed his impulsive behavior. It was a dumb idea trying to impress Laura. Why cut his hair and shave for a woman he could never have?

Konn felt a rush of ire at carrying the letter which would remove any possibility of him ever sharing more than a passing friendship with her. The only thing cutting his hair and shaving off his beard proved was that he was a complete fool!

"Good thinking, dummy!" he muttered. "Sure gonna help you go to sleep with that thought bouncing around in your empty head!"

Laura waited until the sun was up before getting out of bed. She paused to open the window enough to peek out the crack, expecting to see Konn come up the trail at any moment. He had said four days, yet it was already five.

"What are you looking for?" JW complained, rising up from his bed on the floor. "With so much snow still on the ground a man couldn't travel at night."

She shut the window and wordlessly began to mix up the meal for pone. Some called the concoction johnnycakes, a mix of cornmeal, sugar, and a little water. Frying up the pone and a couple thick strips of salt pork would take care of breakfast.

JW folded up his blanket and came over to stand at the table. He watched her, as if waiting for her to speak. When she offered not so much as a "good morning," he grew impatient.

"Keeping an eye on the weather again?"

"It looks as if it will be clear today. Hopefully, that will melt some of the snow. We still have some work to do before the worst of winter snows us in."

"Is it time to get up?" Abby asked from her hammock.

JW walked over and helped her down. "You hungry yet?" he asked.

"Not so much," she replied. "I wish it was summer again. I like it better when I can go outside and play."

"Tough life, being a kid," JW teased.

Breakfast was a quiet affair, yet there was an underlying current of apprehension. JW was not his usual jovial self. He appeared in deep thought and was unresponsive to Abby's chatter.

Once the cleanup was finished, Abby put on her coat and went out to visit the little house in back. That's when Laura found herself confronted by JW.

"When do we stop playing games, Mrs. Conrad?"

She paused from wiping the table to look at him. "What are you talking about?"

"I don't think you have a brother out hunting," he stated. "I might not be as experienced as most men about such things, but I can't believe anyone would go off to hunt in the middle of a snowstorm and not return for nearly a week."

Laura frowned at him for a moment, but he did not back down. She sighed and put her back to him again. "If you must know the truth of it, Konn left for Lonesome Creek before you arrived. We needed more supplies to get through the winter, and having you as a guest hasn't helped with our rations."

The mention of him sharing their food put a twist into his verbal straight-line attack. He floundered for a moment before speaking again.

"Why the subterfuge? Why not tell me the truth?"

"I don't invite strange men into our house, Mr. Fentworthy. You were stranded and would have died without food and shelter. As such, I was compelled to take you in, but I didn't know if you could be trusted."

JW pulled a face. "Yes, but you must have come to know I'm not a stranded highwayman or a malicious killer. Why continue with the ruse?"

"Konn was due back yesterday. I can only think the storm caused him to delay his return."

The man continued to scrutinize her. "There are no horses in the corral, so I assume you are telling me the truth . . . unless your animals got away or were stolen."

"Of course I'm telling you the truth!"

"Makes a person wonder about the rest of your story. Is this Konn character really your brother?"

Laura glared at him with fire in her eyes. "How dare you!" she hissed the words, trying to keep her voice low enough that it wouldn't carry from the house to Abby. "Just what are you insinuating, Mr. Fentworthy?"

He held his ground. "I'm not concerned about the *why,* Darla. I am merely searching for a sign of ownership. You claim you have a beau, but what manner of man would allow his woman to spend the winter up here isolated, vulnerable, with a guardian who has yet to put in an appearance since I arrived!"

"You forget you are a guest in this house!" she fumed. "What did you say, 'I needn't worry about you'? Are these the kinds of questions a man asks when he claims to be trustworthy and a gentleman?"

JW moved a step closer and took hold of Laura's upper arms, pinning her against the counter. "They are the questions a man asks when he is more than interested in a woman—romantically inclined would be a better term."

"Get your hands off me!" Laura said, her voice rising an octave.

"And if I don't?" JW jeered.

"I'll rip them off at your shoulders and beat you to death with the bloody stumps!" boomed the answer from the doorway.

JW let go as if Laura's body had turned white-hot. He backpedaled so quickly he tripped and fell over one of the stools. Before he could regain his feet, a huge hand wrapped about the back of his neck, and he was physically dragged from the house.

"Wait, Konn!" Laura cried. "He didn't do anything!"

But Konn towed the lamely kicking and struggling man to the door and, with a mighty heave, tossed him ten feet out into the snow. JW sprawled face first and rolled over, sputtering from a mouthful of slush.

Konn took a step toward him, but Laura caught hold of his arm.

"Konn, please!" she cried, clinging to him. "He didn't mean any harm."

JW wiped the snow from his face and eyes, rolled over, and sat up. He flashed a terrified look, seeing an irate giant ready to pummel him to within an inch of his life.

However, Konn glimpsed the concern on Laura's face and Abby came hurrying from around the house, having obviously heard the fuss. He held himself in check, suppressing the urge to dismantle the man like a wooden toy.

Searching for answers, he looked down at Laura. She appeared flustered and a little out of breath, but he read no shame in her expression. He felt certain the man hadn't hurt or done anything to her. Konn realized his ire was primarily because another man had dared put his hands on her.

"All right, I'm listening," he said.

"Mr. Kon'ger!" Abby cried, running over to throw her tiny arms around his waist. "You're back!"

He patted her on the head and tussled her hair. "Yeah, I'm back, little muffin. Sorry it took so long."

She stepped back and squinted up at him, the morning sun causing her to blink at the brightness of the snow. "You don't got no whiskers!" she declared.

Konn momentarily forgot about the man sitting in the wet snow a few feet away. "Well," he winked at her, "you promised you would kiss me goodnight if it wasn't for all the hair on my face. Isn't that what you said?"

"You bet!" she said happily, showing her toothy grin.

"Konn," Laura was speaking again, looking him directly in the eye, "if you'll give me a chance, I'll explain about Mr. Fentworthy."

Konn did listen, keeping a tight rein on his temper. When she finished, he offloaded the nearest pack horse and stacked the supplies next to the house. While JW stood awkwardly by, uncertain of what to say or do, Konn retrieved the man's jacket from the house. He grabbed up a sack of hard rolls from the supplies and shoved the coat and rolls into the man's arms.

"There's enough food in the bag to hold you until you reach Lonesome Creek. The snow and the nearby creek will provide water, and you can wrap yourself in the horse blanket tonight." He gave JW an opening to speak, but the man did not offer a word. "Follow the trail I left, and you'll reach town by early tomorrow morning."

"I'm in your debt, sir," JW said quietly.

"Just leave the horse at the livery and tell the hostler I'll be around to pick him up come spring."

"You can rely on me to do exactly that," JW said. When Konn gave him a nod, he climbed aboard the horse and looked over at Laura.

"I apologize for grabbing you by the arms, Mrs. Conrad. I . . . it's just that you are a most delightful and desirable woman. I fear I allowed my heart to overrule my head."

"I accept your apology," Laura replied. "Good luck to you, Mr. Fentworthy."

"Bye!" Abby called to him.

JW turned the horse and began the long trek toward Lonesome Creek.

"You didn't have to run him off like a wayward Indian," Laura said as the man disappeared beyond the trees.

"I figure he wore out his welcome," Konn replied. "He's durn lucky I let him leave with all his limbs attached."

She laughed. When he looked down at her, the laughter became an enticing smile. Without warning, she reached up and stroked his cheek.

"I wondered what you looked like under all that hair."

"About froze my face last night," he complained.

Her fingers played softly against the skin, and Konn felt a host of goosebumps race up and down his spine. Even his heart changed speeds.

"You shaved this morning too," she said. "Must have been quite a chore doing it in the dark and this cold."

"Lucky I didn't cut my throat and bleed to death."

She put on a serious expression. "I'm glad you're back, Konn. I was becoming worried."

"The snowstorm and it being Sunday cost me the extra day." He paused to rub his chin. "I used the time to get spruced up like a New York dandy. Even had the laundry clean my buffalo robe—wore out three Chinese laundry workers in the process."

There was something very pleasing about the way Laura was looking at him. If he didn't know she loved another man, he might have . . . The letter! It swiftly blocked any ridiculous notions.

He reached into his pocket and removed the dreaded envelope. "This came for you," he said. As soon as the vile document reached her fingers, he whirled about and headed for the two remaining horses. "I'd better get the animals taken care of," he said tightly, not looking back at her. "They've had a hard trip."

If Laura said anything in reply, he didn't hear it. He put his attention on the horses, unpacked the remainder of the supplies, and moved the bundle of straw next to the house. He would make an actual bed for Laura and could use the excess of hides to provide him a little more insulation from the ground. When it became colder, the frozen earth from the outside would creep under the walls.

Once the horses were in the corral, both fed and watered, he put the supplies away, except for the special package. He put that atop the cupboard where it was pretty much out of sight.

"What on earth are you sticking up there?" Laura asked.

"Spare ammunition and a couple new traps," he lied convincingly.

"I've fixed you some breakfast," she offered, moving the heavy skillet to the table.

"How come the stranger called you Mrs. Conrad?"

"I didn't want him to know our real names. He might let it slip when he passes through Lonesome Creek."

Konn sat down on a stool and pondered the notion for a moment. "You did say the feller was headed for Denver?"

"Yes, but he might talk to someone in town. After all, he has to find passage to Dover Flats."

"Never thought about that," Konn admitted, starting to eat. "Guess I'm not much good at this game of hide and seek."

"On the positive side, he will be eager to beat the next storm. I do believe he has had enough of the wilderness to last him a lifetime."

Konn worried if he talked to the wrong people, it could mean trouble. Rudy may not have had anything to do with Two Bears and his warriors being at Dry Basin. It was possible the raiding party was in the wrong place for Laura's family. But Konn had seen the new rifles the Cheyenne were carrying. And the one brave had definitely tried to kill Laura when Two Bears attacked them outside of Lonesome Creek. It could have all been a coincidence, but it was plenty troublesome.

As he ate, he decided on a course of action. He would set up an early warning system of some kind. He had some twine, and a couple of cans with a rock or two in them made a lot of noise. Plus he had a number of traps at his disposal and other snares he could set out.

"Did ya get everything on the list, Mr. Kon'ger?" Abby wanted to know, when he had finished his meal.

"I think so, muffin." He felt a lightness in his chest looking at her bright eyes and quick smile. "But I made a mistake and ended up with something I didn't plan on."

"You did?" Her eyes widened in wonder.

He reached over to his coat where it was hanging on the wall and dug out a small sack. "Somehow these got mixed in with my order. I 'spect your ma will know what to do with them."

He passed the sack to Laura. She opened the top, smiled at the contents, and remarked, "Hmm, this looks like a bribe of some kind."

"What is it, Mama?" Abby said, craning her neck and trying to see. "What's in the bag?"

"Ten . . . no, twelve sugar sticks."

"Candy?" Abby's eyes grew big. "Mr. Kon'ger brought us some candy?"

"Yes, but you can't have it all at once. It's a long winter, so you need to make it last."

Konn threw on his coat. "I've some catching up to do before the next storm hits." He hesitated, but the question burned in his brain like a hot poker. He had to ask.

"Was the letter good news?"

"The best I could have hoped for," Laura said, practically beaming. "I knew I could count on Dexter. When the circuit judge arrives in the spring, we are going to win the case!"

Konn wondered if the man was a lawyer or some such thing,

but it didn't matter. The letter had given her the best news she could have hoped for. *What else needed to be said?*

Crow about walked past the man, thinking him another out-of-work drifter. He would have, had he not recognized the fashionable, though weathered, Western-style hat with a shiny silver band.

"JW?" he called, stopping the man in his tracks.

The gent turned around and looked at him. His eyes were bloodshot, he hadn't shaved in a day or two, and his clothes were close to being rags. His face lit up with his greeting.

"Crow!" he exclaimed. "Well, I say! It's good to see you again."

"Man, you look like you were dragged through a briar patch, and then buried alive for about a week."

JW explained how he had ended up afoot and eventually made his way to a trapper's cabin. He skipped the several-days stay until Konn's arrival.

"Man threw me out . . . literally!" He shook his head. "Lucky the snow was deep enough to keep me from breaking my neck."

Crow laughed. "Konn is a tall tree in the forest, no doubt about that."

"He gave me some hard rolls—more like rock biscuits—and sent me packing. I about froze last night, bundled up in a horse blanket. The hair caused me to itch all morning. I just left his pack animal at the livery. I'm headed for a store to buy some new clothes, then get a bath and shave. If there's a bed available, I'm also going to get about twenty hours of sleep!"

"You do look a might rough around the edges," Crow said with a grin. "Are you headed back home then?"

"Soon as I can make my way to Denver," he replied. "My prospecting days are over and done."

"Didn't find a single grain of gold, huh?"

"Not one decent sample, even before I turned loose the pack horse and my riding mare ran off. I'm definitely not cut out to be a gold miner."

"I must say I'm a little surprised at Konn. The man usually opens his camp to a straggler. He shared his food with me one time when I met up with him out in the middle of nowhere."

"Yes, well it's unlikely he walked in to find you with your hands on his sister. I made the mistake of trying to have a serious talk with her."

Crow's smile vanished. "Konn has a sister?"

"A Darla Conrad," JW answered. "She lost her husband some time back and is staying with him."

Crow was stunned but hid the sudden rush of emotion. "Handsome woman is she?"

"A jewel among the stones," JW told him. "She is most fortunate to not look even a tiny bit like her brother."

"She didn't have a little girl with her, a cute kid of seven or eight?"

"Abigail," Crow said.

More supplies, Crow thought, and a shave and haircut! *Konn had taken the Morrison woman and her child to live with him!*

"What's the best and quickest way I can get back to Denver?" JW showed a meek smile. "Without having to do it on horseback, that is."

"Do you have enough money to pay your way?"

"Thankfully, I was carrying my money belt on me."

"The fellows I room with are taking a load of ore down the hill in the morning. You can catch a ride with them and take the stage from Dover Flats as far as the railroad. You ought to be in Denver in a couple days."

"How much for the ride to Dover Flats?"

Crow shrugged. "Offer the pair a couple dollars for the courtesy, and you'll have friends for life!"

JW smiled. "Things are looking brighter." He stuck out his hand. "And again I have you to thank for helping me."

Crow took his hand, but grew serious. "A word of caution," he spoke softly, as if to keep his voice from carrying, "I wouldn't say anything about your run-in with Konn." He gave him a stern look. "He has a lot of friends here in town. If someone thought you had actually touched his sister or insulted him in any way, you might get chewed up more than a tough steak."

"Really?"

"He tamed three of the toughest hombres in town when he was

here this past Saturday. About killed one of them with his bare hands."

"He certainly appeared to have the size and temper to do just that."

"Like I said, keep quiet about him and his sister. No need taking any chances."

"Thanks to your information and comrades, I shall not be around long enough to invite curiosity."

"I'll let the boys know you need a ride. Their job is guarding an ore wagon. Slow way to travel, but you'll get there in one piece. You be at the livery at sunup, and I'll introduce you around."

"I will and, again, I owe you a debt of thanks."

"Not at all. We fellows with long, complicated names have to stick together."

"Hear, hear."

Crow pointed JW toward the store and the Chinaman's place. Once the dude had wandered off down the street, Crow settled down to thinking how best to use the information handed to him.

Chapter Eighteen

After thorough consideration, Konn decided on the most likely ways anyone would approach the cabin. He spent a full day setting alarms and placing several traps and snares. Satisfied he had done all he could for protection, over the next few days he began to hunt and trap in earnest. He knew they wouldn't have long before the heavy snows came. Most of the game had moved to the lower hills or were in hibernation, but he managed to get enough meat to last them through the winter. And he could always catch a few fish out of one of the beaver ponds or the stream. The natives were small but edible.

Less than a week after his return the snow came. It dumped two feet of snow in two days and showed little sign of letting up. Konn did the chores and kept rotating his wood, replacing each load for the firebox with fresh tender so it could dry out under the protective lean-to.

Occasionally, Abby and Laura would come out to help when he was clearing paths to the corral or around the door or to the little house out back. The three of them would often get into a game of tossing snowballs or playing other games. Konn constructed a homemade sleigh out of a framework of poles and two beaver pelts. Using a rope, he pulled Abby around by hand and even behind Hammerhead a couple of times.

The storm moved on but Konn knew there would soon be others. To prevent trapping something and having it suffer because he could not reach the traps, he removed all but the few that were closest to the cabin.

In the evenings, Laura and Abby would sit by the fire and play

games or read together. Konn seldom took part, satisfied to sit
back and watch and listen. It occurred to him that he had never
been so comfortable with life. If not for the letter and Laura's
continued confidence about the coming spring and her hearing,
he might have believed they were an actual family.

Time passed rapidly, but Konn kept track of the days. One
morning, he told Laura and Abby he was off to check on his traps.
When he returned several hours later he was pulling a small
spruce.

"Hey! In the house!" he called out. "Brung you something!"

Abby heard him and quickly opened the door. She stared at
the tree and then at him. "What's that for, Mr. Kon'ger?"

"Tomorrow is Christmas," he told her, lifting the shapely spruce
to shake off the excess snow. "I thought we would put up a tree."

She uttered a cry of delight, a squeal that brought Laura rush-
ing over to see what was going on.

"A tree for Christmas?" she marveled. "But we have nothing
to decorate the tree!"

"I figure Abby can color us some pictures of bows or bells. And
we've got plenty of thread for sewing buckskin and the like. Plus,"
he dug into his coat pocket, "I picked up several pine cones."

Abby was dancing about and singing the only Christmas song
she knew, while Laura held the door so Konn could bring in the
tree. He quickly fashioned a stand and stood it up. As Laura began
to tie the individual cones so they could be hung on the branches,
he went to the cupboard, reached up, and took down the package
from above the shelf.

"I thought this might be a good idea," he said, removing a
small bag. "I picked up five pounds of popping corn. Figure we
could string some and eat some too."

"That's wonderful!" Laura exclaimed. "We haven't had any
popped corn since the country fair last year."

"I love popped corn!" Abby shouted. "Can I eat as much as I
want?"

"It appears Konn has brought enough for several servings. I'll
get a pan and a bit of lard for the oil. Good thing I have a lid."

Konn felt good inside, as good as he had ever felt. For the next two days he was not going to think of the letter, of Laura's beau, of the lonely existence he would have once they were out of his life. He was going to make this a Christmas to remember.

Rudy's complexion blanched at the news. He sat down on the edge of a pickle barrel and shook his head. Elva was more animated, storming about the room, waving her hands, and using some very unladylike words.

"I didn't bother telling you before because Spanish and Skinny Bob took that job down at Dover Flats. They just got back this morning."

"Yes, wait until the eve of Christmas to tell us!" Elva snapped.

"It doesn't matter," Crow said. "Soon as we get another hard snow, it will be too deep to go prowling up the mountain anyway. Unless we have an unusually warm winter, Konn won't be able to come to town until the spring thaw."

"This is terrible," Rudy whined. "How can we stop her from coming to file her claim against us when she has Konniger on her side?"

"We've still got the contract!" Elva declared hotly. "There's no way that little witch can expect to win against us when everything is written down in black and white."

"She must have a plan," Crow pointed out. "Why else would she consent to spend the winter confined in a rundown old shack with a mangy hunter like Konniger?"

"Maybe they got married secretly or something?" Rudy asked.

Crow grunted his doubt. "The fellow who stayed at the cabin said she claimed Konn was her brother. If they had been going to get married, she could have said they were already husband and wife. As a stranger, she could have claimed the little girl belonged to her and Konn. Besides, only Dodd could have married them, and he would have told us about it. No, the only reason to lie is to hide her real purpose in staying close to Lonesome Creek."

"What are we going to do?" Rudy asked the question as if he didn't have a clue in the world.

"We've got to get rid of those meddling troublemakers once and for all!" Elva snapped. "I'm not about to give up all we've worked for these past months. This is our store, our future we're talking about. I don't care what it takes, Rudy, the time has come to be rid of them all!"

Crow backed up from her fury. "Hey, I've done some bad things in my life, but I've never killed a woman or child!"

"Elva, honey," Rudy whimpered, "are you sure that's necessary?"

"I want that woman gone!" She fired the words at Crow this time. "I want an end to our ever having to worry about her again!"

"Konn won't make that easy," Crow said.

Elva was thinking now, her usually pretty face contorted and twisted into an evil sneer. "It's simple enough for a six-year-old," she replied, pinning Crow with burning, rapier-like eyes. "You bar the door and set fire to the cabin. No one comes out!"

Crow flinched. He considered himself to be tough and cold-blooded at times. He had killed a number of men, even a kid of about sixteen during a shootout once, but this? Damn, when it came to ruthless, he was a babe in the woods next to Elva!

"You're talking a triple murder, Mrs. Copton," he told her.

"We'll pay you and the others well. It's a straightforward job, and no one will ever know it wasn't an accident. There are fires all the time. All it takes is one spark, one unguarded moment at night when everyone is asleep. Whole families die sometimes. It won't be any different for them."

Rudy looked from Elva to Crow and back, as if he was watching a bizarre play of some kind. There was a vacant look in the storekeeper's eyes, as if his brain had excused itself and left the room.

"Six hundred dollars," Crow told Elva. "Three men doing the job at two hundred each."

Elva uttered a shrill laugh. "You must be out of your mind. I was thinking more like two hundred for just you."

Crow remained steadfast. "I'm not going after Konniger alone, no matter what the plan. You have my offer. If you want the job done, you'll pay the price."

"We'll pay three hundred—a hundred for each man—not a penny more!"

But Crow had figured out how much they would need to start

up their own freighting outfit. And there would be living expenses until they found the right place. He was not prepared to haggle. He turned and walked for the door.

"Four hundred!" Elva shouted.

Crow didn't even slow down. When his hand reached the door, she nearly shrieked the words. "All right! We'll pay your price!"

He stopped, hiding the smile which threatened to come to his lips. Even before he could turn around, Elva was there, breathing down the back of his neck.

"We'll pay your exorbitant price, but only if you do the job right away. And I don't care how deep the snow gets! I don't want this to happen in the spring, when it could appear to have anything to do with the store." She bore into him with a murderous lust. "You do it late at night when they're all asleep. Simply bar the door and douse the place with coal oil. I don't want a single stick standing when you're finished. Do we understand one another?"

Crow had never taken bullying from any man. He had fought gunmen, Indian warriors, marshals, and hard case men from every walk of life. No one had ever caused Crow to take a single backward step. But facing Elva's hateful stare, he felt a queasy sensation inside, as if his icy fortitude had turned to warm water. This was not a woman he would ever want to cross.

"Six hundred in cash money or gold before we leave to do the job," he said, using every ounce of strength he could muster to meet her molten gaze on an even plane. "Once it's done, we will be heading for open country and not coming back here. We don't intend to be within a hundred miles when the bodies are found."

"Good." She was agreeable. "It's better if we never see you again." Then with an icy stare she added, "Just make sure you do the job."

"I'm a man of my word," Crow replied. "I've never taken a dime for a job I didn't do."

"Then we have an agreement. Give us an hour to get the money together."

Crow gave a bob of his head and went out the door. He felt compelled to hurry his step, eager to tell Skinny and Spanish. Their dream was about to come true. They would soon have their

own freight outfit. All that stood in their way was a single dastardly chore—the death of a woman, a child, and a very dangerous man named Konniger.

The tree was decorated with two strands of popcorn, several
sticks of sugar candy, a couple dozen cutouts of snowflakes and
paper bells, along with the pine cones—all hung with short pieces
of thread. Konn used his knife to fashion a piece of tin into the
shape of a star for the top, and their Christmas tree was complete.

"It would be a perfect tree," Abby said wistfully, "if only
there was som'tin under it." She expelled a deep sigh. "You know,
like presents?"

"We are lucky to be alive," Laura told her. "We have so many
things to be thankful for."

"Yeah, I guess so," Abby agreed reluctantly.

Konn pulled down the package from above the cupboard again.
This time he unrolled the outside paper. Alice had indeed wrapped
the items for him, each with a colored length of ribbon. He knelt
down at the tree and slipped the two packages under the tree.

"Does that look any better?" he asked.

"Presents!" she cried. "You brought us presents?"

"Only one for each of you," he told her. "I didn't have a lot of
money to spend."

"You shouldn't have!" Laura protested. "After everything
you've done for us and the way . . ."

Konn held up his hand to stop her. "I know, I know," he said.
"But it's the first real Christmas I've had since I was knee-high to
a toad stool. And the muffin's right, it won't seem like Christmas
without a couple presents under the tree for morning."

Rather than debate the issue further, Laura put her attention on
Abby. "It's getting late, dear. We better make our trip out back
and get to bed."

"Okay, but I ain't gonna be able to sleep."

"Don't use the word *ain't*, dear."

"Yes, Mommy."

"Get your coat on, and we'll visit the little house."

As the two went out into the darkness, Konn went over and

knelt down at the fireplace. He added a couple of larger pieces of firewood so as to bank the fire for the night. By positioning them carefully, the logs would burn slowly and last for several hours. He next chose a couple for early morning and placed them nearby so he could practically add them in his sleep.

It was a definite pain shaving each morning, but when the two gals returned, Abby trotted over and made it worthwhile. She threw her small arms around his neck, hugged him tightly, and then kissed him on the cheek.

"It's like having a real daddy again," she whispered next to his ear. "I love you, Mr. Kon'ger."

Konn had to swallow a lump of emotion before he was able to look at her. Then, taking her into his arms, he lifted her up, carried her over to the hammock, and took a moment to see she was tucked in for the night. "See you in the morning," he said huskily.

Abby giggled. "Bet'cha I'm awake before you are."

"I won't bet with you on that. Not tonight."

Konn stepped back and marveled at the way such a small child could make a man feel ten feet tall.

"This was all very thoughtful, Konn," Laura murmured, having come over to stand very close to him. He looked at her and felt weak in the knees. She had the warmest expression he had ever seen on her face, as if she was thinking of something wonderful.

"Been a hard year on you two," he said, keeping his gravelly voice lowered. "And it's a long winter up here. Didn't figure it would do any harm."

"You planned this from the day you left for town, didn't you?"

"More like it came to me when I was buying supplies."

"I . . ." Her voice seemed to crack, and she took a step back. He watched as she whirled about, moved over to put out the lamp, and went to her bed. When she sat down, she had gathered her poise and regained her speech. "I never thanked you for the bed. It's much more comfortable with the straw filler than it was with the mat of hides."

"A lady deserves a little comfort," he said simply.

"You're a very special man, Keith Konniger."

He stared in her direction, able to see her outline because of the firelight, and watched her climb into bed. She and Abby each wore a nightdress to bed, both for modesty and warmth. Laura had been frugal with their money, saving as much as she could for when they returned to claim their store. She said she wanted to buy new clothes for the hearing and pay for anything else they needed at that time. In case it took two or three days to get a hearing, she would need money for meals and a room. Hence, she had not spent more than a small portion of the money Rudy had given her.

Konn stretched out on his pad of hides, using the single blanket to stave off the morning chill. He knew that a man too snug under the covers would often not wake up until the fire had died. He didn't intend to let that happen. Of course the worry was less this night. He was excited about Christmas—not like a child who expected a present, but as a parent who dearly loved to see the excitement of his own child. If only . . .

Yeah, if I had a dollar for every "if only" in my life, I could buy the store from Rudy and hand it over to Laura!

Laura lay quietly listening to Abby squirm in the hammock above, too keyed up to sleep. She smiled and wondered what Konn had bought for Abby. She had a bit of curiosity about her own present too. Abby's package was about the size of a breadbox, while the other was no larger than a pound of butter. It really didn't matter because, for a solitary man like Konn, it was the thought that counted. She would be outwardly thrilled with whatever he had bought for her.

Considering the big taciturn man for a moment, she wondered how he truly felt about her. She had seen the obvious yearning in his eyes, but he had been a complete gentleman, more honorable than any man she had ever met. As for his feelings for her, the man had shaved and cut his hair, something he hadn't done in years—if ever. He claimed it was to please Abby, but she doubted he would have gone to so much trouble for a simple peck on the cheek at nights.

His feelings were a puzzle. The coveting glances, the fact he went out of his way to please her, the hunger she visualized whenever they were standing very close, it all indicated he wanted more than friendship. And there was the way he went after JW. His anger was more than protective. Jealousy perhaps? Yet he had not made a single amorous advance. He might be holding back, afraid of how awkward the situation would be if she refused him. Strange that a man of such courage would be afraid to speak his mind, but it was the only scenario which made sense.

She tried to blank all thoughts from her mind so she could get to sleep, but too many emotions were floating about in her head. At the root of her insomnia were her own feelings for Konn. He had rescued her several times over and offered them sanctuary for the winter. He was the strength and resolve to aid in her own purpose, plus something more. It was the *more* part that toyed with her inner emotions. She could not deny a yearning of her own, the need to be more than friends, the desire to be held close, to feel the reassurance of his arms around her.

Laura moaned inwardly, battling the demons that were at war inside her. She knew if she encouraged a romance, it would change everything. It was the same fear she assumed prevented Konn from making any overtures toward her. What would become of them if they were not compatible?

He's a hunter, a loner, a man who lives a solitary existence, she thought, *while I want to own and operate my own store. I will need help, but could I take him away from his home, his zone of comfort, his very life?*

An hour before daylight, Konn leaned over to put a little wood on the fire. He had not yet laid back down when a tiny voice whispered, "Is it Christmas yet? Can I open my present?"

He might have shushed Abby, but Laura raised herself to a sitting position. "No one is asleep, Konn. We might as well get up."

Konn got to his feet, lit the lamp, and turned up the wick to give off as much light as possible. Before he had finished, Abby had climbed down from the hammock on her own—no easy chore—and hurried over to squat next to the tree, waiting impatiently. Konn moved next to the tree and also hunkered down. Then he looked to see if Laura was ready.

"Go ahead," Laura told him, "before she crawls over your back to get to her present."

Konn removed the larger package and handed it to Abby. He would have enjoyed dragging out the gift giving, but she tore the paper off with frantic hands, pulling and tugging and ripping until she could see what it was.

"It's a baby!" she cried with delight. "Mommy! It's a dolly!" Abby pulled the doll free and jumped to her feet, cradling it in her arms as she whirled about.

Laura gasped as well. "A Basque doll? Wherever did you find one of those way out here?"

"Brown said some French prospector traded it to him for supplies. It was either buy her that or one of those corn husk and cloth dolls. I figured the muffin deserved the best."

"I'll bet it was expensive," Laura declared. "You shouldn't keep spending your money on us."

Konn didn't reply, but looked at Abby and smiled.

"A baby!" she continued, both happy and giddy. "I've got a baby! I'm not alone anymore!"

"I've been whittling some sticks and setting them aside," Konn told her. "We can put together a cradle for the doll today, after it gets light."

"Really?" Abby said, her eyes more dazzling than the crackling fire. "Did you hear, Mommy? Mr. Kon'ger is gonna make a bed for my baby!"

Taking note the doll was attired in a white, very plain nightdress, she suggested, "We can make her a dress and moccasin shoes from small pieces of buckskin too."

"This is the most wonderful Christmas ever!" Abby said gleefully.

Konn removed the other package and passed it to Laura. "I never tried to shop for a woman before."

Laura could not suppress her own tingle of excitement. She did manage a degree of composure, opening the package more carefully than Abby. She discovered a tiny box inside the wrapper and when she opened it, she gasped in surprise.

"A cameo necklace!" She removed the chain and examined the

piece of jewelry more closely. "It's beautiful, Konn," she murmured. "It really is."

"Like I said, I never tried to buy anything for a woman before. When I saw this in Brown's glass display case it seemed to call out to me. I 'spect you think it's wasteful, but a woman ought to have at least one piece of jewelry."

Laura didn't say a word. She moved over to Konn and, before he realized what she had in mind, she kissed him! Not a peck this time, but an on-the-mouth, world-shattering, toe-curling, hotter-than-a-baker's-oven sort of kiss!

She pulled back before Konn had time to think about what he should do, and he was shocked to see tears in her eyes.

"I didn't . . ." he began.

Laura placed two fingers on his lips to keep him from speaking. Then she hugged him tightly and laid her head against his shoulder. It was the most wonderful sensation Konn had ever felt, holding her in his arms. He had never had anyone in his life before. Now he knew the full extent of how much he had been missing.

Chapter Nineteen

Crow stopped the other two and lifted his head. It was the dead of night, and traveling the last mile had been slow and tedious. There had been a storm since JW had ridden the path from Konniger's cabin, but the couple inches of snow had not concealed the trail. He smelled the smoke and knew the clearing was only a short way.

"We're getting close," he told them in a hushed voice. "We'll move in on foot."

"I'm numb from the cold," Skinny complained. "Riding all day and half the night—we'll catch our death out here."

"If Konn hears us, we'll be dead much quicker," Spanish remarked softly.

"Tie off your horses and bring the other can of oil," Crow ordered. "I'll take this one."

"I've got it," Spanish said.

"Skinny, you move over to the right and I'll move to the left. Spanish can keep following the trail. Everyone keep your guns handy."

After the horses were secured, they spread out and began to move toward the smell of smoke. Crow remembered the hunter's shack from a ride through these hills a season or two past. His stomach churned with anticipation and, despite the freezing temperature, he was sweating. He anchored his jaw and firmed his resolve. He had never killed like this before—a sneak in the night, barbecuing people alive. In the past, he had heard death wails, the weeping of women or children who had lost a loved one. He feared the sights, smells, and sounds of this night would haunt him forever.

They were three shadows, moving through the trees, the crunch of snow under their feet the only muffled sounds. With a full moon and clear night sky, the cabin slowly came into view. Crow spied a tendril of smoke rising from the chimney; it looked completely peaceful.

"Seems more of a sin to kill someone on Christmas night," Spanish whispered from the main trail.

"It's after midnight," Crow replied, already on edge. "That makes it the day after Christmas. All right?"

"Yeah, I didn't think about it like that."

Spanish took another step and there came a clinking sound as rocks were rattled in cans above their heads. He cursed and called softly, "I tripped on some blasted string, right on the main trail!"

Before Crow could reply to him, there was a sudden noise off to the right, a muffled *clank*, and Skinny gasped in pain. "Great God Almighty!" the thin man hissed through his teeth so as not to scream. "I just stepped on . . . It's a bear trap!"

Crow realized the approach to the cabin had a ring of protective devices. "Watch out! Konn must have this whole area rigged with traps and alarms."

"What'll we do?" Spanish wanted to know.

"Help me get this trap off my leg!" Skinny cried, beginning to panic. "It went right through my boot and pants! I think I'm bleeding, and it hurts like hell!"

The sound of the cabin door being pushed open sent shivers down Crow's spine. He dropped the can of coal oil he'd been carrying and drew his gun. When Skinny began to whine, he snarled at him.

"Quiet, you stupid fool! Konn is outside. He's coming for us!"

Spanish did an about turn. "I'll see you boys later. I'm not taking that man on face to face."

"You run, and I'll kill you!" Crow warned him, pointing his pistol at his back. "Help Skinny get out of that trap, and we'll all backtrack together."

"Little late for running, boys," Konn's voice cut through the still night.

Skinny and Spanish both opened fire. Something flashed in the dim moonlight, hurtling through the air.

Skinny groaned and went down.

Spanish cast a hasty look. "He got Skinny with a knife in the throat!" he called to Crow. Then he shouted, "Damn you, Konniger!" And he began to fire wildly.

A blast from Konn's rifle put a quick end to his shooting.

Crow instantly fired at the muzzle flash from Konn's gun—three rounds—one at the flash itself and another a foot or two to either side. Then he ducked behind a tree and waited.

"I'm hit hard," Spanish moaned. "Got me . . . in . . . the . . ." And his voice died out.

"Spanish?" Crow whispered. "You hear me?"

Only silence.

Mortal terror tied a knot in Crow's stomach, and he gasped for air. This is exactly what he hadn't wanted. In a stand up gunfight, he could have probably put Konn down. It might have taken three or four shots to do it, but he was confident he could have killed him. But this—wandering around in two feet of snow, with traps and twine running to alarms all around—Konn held all the cards!

Several tense minutes passed. Crow shivered from the cold, while he listened so intently his head began to ache. There was not a single whisper of sound. Finally, he could stand it no longer. He cleared his throat and spoke up in a normal voice.

"I don't want to die, Konn. If you're hit, I'll help get you into the house. This was a really stupid idea, and I no longer want any part of it."

Something cold touched the base of his neck and he froze.

"Little late to try and talk your way out of this, Crow. I pull the trigger, and you are food for the wolves."

Crow dropped his gun in the snow. "I should have known this was a fool's mission. We should have never agreed to this job."

"Rudy send you?"

"His wife does most of the talking for him," Crow replied.

"That is one coldhearted, evil woman, Konn. She ordered us to fire the cabin with the three of you inside."

"Hands behind your back, Crow."

Crow did as ordered and a strip of buckskin was snuggled around one wrist and then the other. There was no chance to fight back, and he was too cold to even think of trying.

"We were going to start our own freight outfit," Crow explained to Konn, as they began to walk toward the cabin. "Man lets his ambition drive him sometimes and it gets him into trouble."

"You were dealing with Two Bears too," Konn said confidently. "New rifles in exchange for killing the Morrison family."

"It was only a business deal from my end, Konn. I've never hurt or killed a woman or child."

"Roasting us all like Thanksgiving turkeys would not have been doing Mrs. Morrison or her little girl any favors."

Crow sighed. "Like I said, a fool's mission."

"It's been almost a week. We should have had them report back to us!" Elva sounded off at Rudy for about the hundredth time. "What do you think happened? What if they left the country without doing the job?"

"Crow prides himself on being a man of his word, Elva, dear," Rudy replied. "With the deep snow it might be spring before anyone finds the bodies."

The front door opened, and Dodd hurried through. He marched over and put a hard look on them both.

"Tell me you didn't do something foolish!" he snapped. "Something is going on, and I want to know what it is!"

"What are you talking about?" Rudy asked.

"I just heard that Flynn has taken possession of three bodies today. Seems they were found up at Konniger's cabin."

"Three bodies?" Elva displayed complete innocence. "Was someone staying with Mr. Konniger?"

Dodd shook his head and paced nervously around the room. "Flynn sent off a telegraph message for a deputy U.S. marshal and the circuit judge. They will be here tomorrow for an inquiry."

"Why should any of this interest us?" Elva was carefully objective. "We don't know anything about Mr. Konniger or any bodies."

"You don't think Mrs. Morrison and her child went to stay with Konn for the winter? If they died of the cold or something, I would feel responsible," he lamented. "I backed you up on the store. I sent her packing."

"You really ought to get together a search party and look for your backbone, Dodd." Elva sneered at him. "If, by some misfortunate happenstance, the woman and her child end up dead, the matter of the store is settled permanently. No one is going to point a finger at you."

"It's just that . . . well, I'm not comfortable with the idea of a lawman coming here with a judge. If it's only an investigation, why have the judge come too?"

"It seems simple enough to me," Elva said. "The deputy has to ride up to Konniger's cabin and have a look around. Once he determines that it was an accident or whatever, the judge will rule the case is closed."

Dodd remained apprehensive. "I suppose there is some logic in what you're saying, but . . ."

"We have nothing to worry about," Elva stated firmly, putting an icy stare on Dodd. "Not unless you go and do something stupid. We are totally in the clear on this. There's no reason why anyone would even think the store is connected to any tragedy up at that hunter's cabin. After all, we have a contract giving us title to the store, so any claim by that silly Morrison woman would have been dismissed outright. You are working yourself into a hissy fit for nothing."

"All right," Dodd said, attempting to recover his decorum. "I only wanted to make certain we had no reason to worry."

"None whatsoever," Elva assured him.

Dodd bid them good day and left the store. Rudy ducked his head once the door had closed and fought back tears.

"They really did it," he said. "Killed them all."

"It took every cent we had to pay those clowns, but it will be worth it. No one is taking what belongs to us, Rudy," Elva vowed. "This is our store, our future. It belongs to us and no one else!"

"Soon as the railroad starts in this direction and the town begins to boom, I want to sell out."

Elva frowned at the weak little man. "Just so long as we get enough money for the store so we never have to work again."

"Yes, dear, I know."

Elva put her hand on Rudy's neck and playfully tickled his ear. "Everything is going to be as we planned. Once we are living in a fine house, with money, prestige, and status, we'll be able to enjoy life."

Rudy did not respond in his usual giddy way. He remained solemn and didn't say a word. Elva wondered how long she would have to put up with his brooding. Once the store was sold and she had the money, she might unburden herself of Rudy. He was not really the sort of man she envisioned spending the rest of her life with.

The court convened with Judge Bannister presiding. He was provided with a desk in a corner of the saloon, with a witness chair placed a few feet away. Rudy, Elva, and Dodd were summoned to attend. When they entered the court, the deputy marshal and Flynn placed the three of them under arrest.

Rudy and Elva began to protest, but Dodd bid them to let him handle the situation. Even as the Coptons were led to their chairs, the lawyer approached the judge's desk.

"Your Honor, I don't fully understand this," Dodd announced. "Why have we been arrested? What are the charges against me and my clients?"

"You will sit down and be quiet until I allow you can speak," Judge Bannister informed him curtly. "I will outline the indictment in due time."

Dodd remained as blustery as a whirlwind, but took a chair next to the Coptons.

"First order of business is a case of fraud," the judge announced. "Mr. Flynn, would you bring in the client."

Konn entered with Abby and Laura. Konn saw Rudy and Dodd's jaws drop, and Elva suddenly looked ready to chew railroad spikes. He ignored them and led Abby aside to sit down,

while Laura went up to take a seat in the chair next to the judge's desk.

"As we don't have an actual prosecutor for this hearing, I will be asking the questions," Judge Bannister said. He paused to look over at Dodd. "The defense may cross-examine the witness when I'm finished."

Konn hid a smile of satisfaction as Elva and Rudy whispered frantically back and forth. They could hide neither their fear nor their guilt.

"You state in your complaint that half of Copton Mercantile belongs to you, Mrs. Morrison," the judge began. "Please tell the court the reasoning behind your claim."

Laura explained about the deal made with Rudy, how her father-in-law and she had sold everything they owned to finance the store. She narrated ahead and told of the Indian attack, the subsequent rescue by Konn and what happened when they arrived in town. Finally, she removed a letter from her dress pocket and handed it to the judge.

"This is a deposition from the bank in Garden City, Kansas, Your Honor. The bank manager is Dexter Conrad, who handled our banking and also the sale of our property. Dexter knew both Ben Morrison and my husband, Steve, for a number of years."

The judge examined the letter. "It states here that Ben could neither read nor write," he said.

"The contract the Coptons showed me had the signature of Ben Morrison," Laura explained, "but Ben never learned to write his name. Rudy Copton told me Ben and he had a contract written up before he left Kansas to come here and start building. The only man in town who wrote such contracts was the banker, Dexter Conrad, and he would have personally witnessed the signing of any agreement. As for my father-in-law, whenever Ben had to sign anything, he would make an X an someone would witness it for him. The signature on the document is proof the contract is a forgery."

The judge put a scowl on Dodd. "The deposition from Dexter Conrad, unless it can be disputed, is substantiation that the con-

tract you and the Coptons have is counterfeit. Would you care to explain that?"

"I know nothing about it!" Dodd declared, jumping to his feet. "The document was shown to me, and I concluded it was legal."

"If I could make a point here, Your Honor," Flynn spoke up. "The contract is not only a forgery, it points a finger at those involved in murder and attempted murder."

"Now wait a minute!" Dodd cried. "I don't know where this is going, but that's a complete falsehood!"

Flynn continued. "I believe if you compare Mr. Dodd's writing to the contract, it will show he is the one who wrote it up."

Dodd was sweating, his eyes wide with fear. "All right, all right! I was only doing Rudy a favor. I had no idea anyone had been killed."

Elva jumped to her feet and screeched, "Dodd, you idiotic, lying skunk!"

Bannister pounded his gavel on the desk for quiet.

"We've a witness who can clear up most of the details, Judge," Flynn said, once Elva sat back down. "He is willing to tell the truth providing the only charge brought against him is attempted murder."

The judge looked at the deputy marshal. "Have you been apprised of the facts in this case, Deputy Siever?"

The deputy gave an affirmative nod.

"And are you agreeable to this?"

"Seems the best way to shorten this hearing and get to the truth, Your Honor," he answered. "We would likely end up in the same place after a day or two of argument and testimony."

"I don't intend to be stuck up here for the duration of the winter. We could get another major storm at any time." Bannister tapped his gavel on the desk top. "Bring in the next witness and let's hear what he has to say."

Flynn opened the door to the back room, and Crow entered. He had shackles about his wrists and did not look very happy. Even so, he walked straight to the judge's desk. Laura vacated the chair as he came to a stop.

"You're going to tell the truth and nothing else, swear before God."

"I'll tell you straight, Judge," Crow avowed.

"Sit down and let's hear what you have to say."

Crow didn't mince words. "Soon as that woman, Elva," he pointed, having to use both hands because of the chains, "showed up here, she talked Rudy into trying to steal the store." He turned his head to look at the judge as he spoke. "Rudy sent a letter with a map for Ben Morrison to follow. Meanwhile, he had me ride out and contact Two Bears. We agreed on a price, and I gave him payment to do the ambush at Dry Basin."

The judge scowled, and Crow hurried on with his testimony. "The job was working out fine, but Konniger managed to rescue the woman and her child. Soon as I found out what had happened, I hurried back to tell Rudy and Elva. That's when they came up with the plan of a phony contract to steal the store legally. By the time Mrs. Morrison arrived, them two and Dodd had fixed up the fake document. With no way to dispute the ownership until spring, everyone figured the lady had gone to Denver or back to Kansas.

"Some time later a prospector arrived in town riding one of Konniger's extra mounts. He told me the woman and child were staying the winter with him." He shrugged his shoulders. "I reckon the Coptons must have been worried that Mrs. Morrison had a plan for getting her store back because they paid me, Spanish, and Skinny Bob six hundred dollars to kill them."

Bannister frowned at the marshal. "I begin to think an attempted murder charge is not sufficient for this man."

"The thing is," Crow went on, eager to finish his story and get the judge to thinking about other guilty parties, "Konn had set out traps and run trip wires tied to tin cans to alert him of anyone's approach. Skinny stepped into a bear trap, Spanish jingled one of the alarms, and the next thing I knew, Konn had a gun in my ear and my two partners were both dead."

"I knew nothing about the murder attempts!" Dodd cried. "I only helped write a contract for Rudy and Elva. It was my only involvement!"

"You sniveling sap!" Elva barked at him. "You couldn't wait to take our money!"

"Actually," Rudy spoke up, "I never wanted any of this. I only wanted to make Elva happy!"

"And you shut your mouth, you lily-livered dimwit!" she shrieked. "Don't you have an ounce of guts?"

Rudy spun on Elva, his face burning red. "Guts!" he yelled. "You're the one who ordered the deaths of Mrs. Morrison and her daughter. I'm sorry I ever met you! The real crime here is that I've never been a man and stood up to you!"

"He's lying his head off!" Elva snarled at the judge. "It was all his idea! He promised me a fine house, money, and clothes . . . the world!" She glared at him with open disgust. "And I got nothing but a whimpering, snotty-nosed mouse for a husband!"

Judge Bannister banged the gavel to quiet the two. After a moment, he looked about the room until he spied Konniger.

"Your name has come up repeatedly, Mr. Konniger," he said. "Do you have anything to add to the testimony before I pronounce sentencing?"

Konn self-consciously cleared his throat. "I only got one thing to add, Judge," he replied, standing tall enough to peruse every person in the courtroom. "Mrs. Morrison has always been a proper lady throughout this here ordeal. If any man should suggest otherwise—regardless of who it is—I'll rip him apart like so much paper and feed him to the vultures." He softened his tone at once. "As for the lady and her child, my only notion was to protect them both from any harm."

The judge smiled at his caring statement. "As for myself, I certainly entertain no doubt concerning your honorable relationship with the lady, Mr. Konniger." Then, turning serious, "What about the deaths of the two men with Mr. Crow?"

"They come to do us mortal harm," he answered. "If I hadn't put up some warning traps, they would have burned my place to the ground with the three of us inside. I didn't figure I had a lot of choice when it came to killing them."

"Is that the truth, Mr. Crow?"

Crow bobbed his head. "We were carrying the cans of coal oil when Konn heard us coming, Your Honor."

He looked over to Laura. "Anything you would like to add before I pass judgment, Mrs. Morrison?"

"Only that Mr. Konniger saved us from certain death on more than one occasion. We owe him our lives."

"Sounds like a man you trust," the judge remarked.

Laura put a serious look on her face. "He is the most decent man I've ever known in my life, Your Honor."

"What about you, Mr. Dodd? Any last words?"

He lowered his head. "My only part in this was to write up the phony contract. I knew nothing about the murder attempts."

The judge nodded. "I won't ask you, Mr. Copton," he moved to the other accused, "as we know your wife does the talking for you." There was a round of laughter from the crowd. When it quieted down, he bore into Elva with an icy stare. "And I believe you have made your position clear, Mrs. Copton, so I am ready to rule on the charges before this court."

Judge Bannister took a moment to let the room grow quiet. "Having listened to the testimony, and considering the gravity of the crimes perpetrated, these are the court's decisions." He pointed the gavel at Dodd.

"For using a government office to commit forgery, I sentence you to two years behind bars and revoke your status as an attorney." Next eyeing Crow, "As for you, I can see you are guilty of far more than attempted murder, but I will abide by the terms set forth by the marshal and sentence you to five years behind bars." Then, pointing at Elva and Rudy, "And I find the two of you guilty of fraud, plus the murder of Ben Morrison and the attempted murder of Laura and Abby Morrison, as well as Mr. Konniger. You will each serve twenty years at the state prison."

Finally, he looked at Laura. "Considering the outcome of these proceedings, I find that the store and all of its worth belong to you, Mrs. Morrison. I also offer you my condolences for the losses and hardships you have suffered."

He banged the gavel again. "Deputy Marshal Siever, you will

take charge of the four prisoners and see to their transport. This court is dismissed."

Konn was the lucky recipient of Laura's jubilation. She ran across the room and nearly leapt into his arms. She kissed him and hugged him tightly, before turning her attention to Abby.

"You see, dear," she said happily. "We have our store."

Abby did not look as cheery. "What about Mr. Kon'ger?"

Laura looked directly at him. "Yes, what about you, Mr. Konniger?"

"I don't know," he mumbled uncertainly. "What about your beau in Kansas?"

She laughed. "Dexter is not my beau. He is nearly sixty and has a wife and four grown children. He's the only man I had waiting for me in Kansas."

"But you told Flynn . . ."

"I didn't want a bunch of suitors chasing after me, Konn." With a sly sort of simper playing on her lips, she added, "I was pretty sure I'd already found a man I wanted to share my life with."

"Don't know how handy I would be in a store," he admitted.

"The way you build furniture? You'll be fabulous."

He laughed. "Never been called that before."

Laura grew serious. "But it's up to you, Konn. I know you've always been alone and had your freedom. It would mean giving that up."

Konn reached down and lifted Abby up in one arm. He put his other arm around Laura's shoulders. "If you two would have me, I'll sure give it my all to be the best husband and father I can be."

"You'll be great!" Laura said merrily. "We'll be one happy family!"

"Yippee!" said Abby. "I'm gonna have me a daddy!"

Konn, never one for a lot of words, could think of nothing to say. He hugged both of them to him and knew he was the luckiest man alive!